EMBARKING ON MURDER

A BEANIE AND CRUISER MYSTERY

EMBARKING ON MURDER

SUE OWENS WRIGHT

FIVE STAR

A part of Gale, Cengage Learning

Detroit • New York • San Francisco • New Haven, Conn • Waterville, Maine • London

GALE
CENGAGE Learning™

LIBRARY OF CONGRESS CATALOGING-IN-PUBLICATION DATA

Wright, Sue Owens.
    Embarking on murder : a Beanie and Cruiser mystery / by Sue Owens Wright. — 1st ed.
        p. cm.
    ISBN-13: 978-1-59414-780-7 (hardcover : alk. paper)
    ISBN-10: 1-59414-780-9 (hardcover : alk. paper)
    1. Women private investigators—Fiction. 2. Cruise ships—Fiction. 3. Murder—Investigation—Fiction. 4. Tahoe, Lake (Calif. and Nev.)—Fiction. 5. Mystery fiction. gsafd I. Title.
PS3623.R565E63 2009
813'.6—dc22   2009001219

First Edition. First Printing: May 2009.
Published in 2009 in conjunction with Tekno Books and Ed Gorman.

Printed in the United States of America
1 2 3 4 5 6 7 13 12 11 10 09

7628

For Dad, with eternal love and gratitude

ACKNOWLEDGMENTS

Heartfelt thanks to those who have supported and encouraged me since I first embarked on this long literary voyage. I won't list names. You already know who you are.

CHAPTER ONE

The setting sun gilded the lapis waters of Lake Tahoe as the *Dixie Queen* embarked on her July 4th dinner cruise to Emerald Bay. Red, white and blue banners trimming her railings ruffled in the alpine breeze. My daughter, Nona, had flown up from San Francisco to join Sheriff Skip Cassidy and me aboard the paddle wheeler for my Big 5-0 birthday celebration. It almost turned out to be my last.

In case you don't remember me, I'm Elsie MacBean, better known as Beanie to my friends. I've earned a reputation as Tahoe's resident Native American sleuth ever since my basset hound, Cruiser, and I sniffed out the Tahoe Terror one winter. Cruiser did most of the sniffing.

The year I turned fifty, weather conditions went from snowboards to snow cones in the span of only a month. By April Fool's Day, we were wearing shorts and sandals instead of parkas and ski boots. With the arrival of summer, the inevitable caravan of tourists snaked bumper-to-bumper over Echo Summit into the Tahoe basin to get away from it all by homesteading tent-to-tent in overcrowded campgrounds.

A shroud of smog obscured the majestic Sierras, guardians of the Washoes' native land they inhabited for thousands of years before Kit Carson set eyes on this hidden wonder in the sky. Noisy jet skis spun donuts on the lake's mirrored surface. Motorboats churned the big water of Da-aw like giant eggbeaters. Legions of oily sunbathers clogged and fouled her once pristine shores. Everything seemed pretty normal for summertime on Lake Tahoe . . . or so we thought.

A jet ski rider waved at the passengers aboard the *Queen* as he buzzed past her bow. Several people waved back, including me.

"Fine night for a cruise, Skip," I said. "I'm glad you could get the night off."

"Me, too. I would've hated to miss your birthday celebration."

"And the Fourth of July fireworks," Nona said.

"Since I have to turn fifty, I might as well do it with a big bang."

"Oh, Mom," Nona said. "You're the youngest fifty-year-old I know."

"It sounds so much older when you say it, dear."

"At least it's better than the alternative, Beanie."

"Ahoy there, Skipper, you're right behind me. Let me know how it feels when you get here." I flopped down on one of the deck benches. Skip and Nona flanked me like bookends.

I surveyed the assortment of white-haired retirees paired up on the top deck. Another decade and I'd be sixty and fit right in with these Sierra seniors. Suddenly, I wanted to jump ship right there in the middle of the lake. Skip picked just the right moment to present me with an oblong, gift-wrapped box. It looked like jewelry might be inside, but I knew old penny-pincher Skip better than that.

"What's this? I thought we agreed no gifts."

"We did, but I saw these and knew you had to have them," Skip said, presenting me with a second gift.

"You got me more than one present?" I was stunned. Skip was even thriftier than my Scottish husband, Tom, had been. Getting two gifts at once from Skip was like finding two oases in the Sahara.

"Well, what are you waiting for?" Skip said. "Open them."

"Hurry up, Mom!"

"Okay, okay, I'm opening." I tore off the wrapping and opened the box. I was right. It wasn't jewelry. Not even close. It was something no old Girl Scout should ever be without, especially if she lives alone in a rustic mountain cabin—a Swiss army knife. It was one of those fancy ones with every utensil you can imagine, and even some you can't. I extended each one—knife blades, corkscrew, can opener, eating utensils, screwdriver, toothpick—then held the whole ensemble up in front of me, batting my eyes and fanning myself like Madame Butterfly. Leave it to Skip to give me something every woman has never wanted. At least it wasn't a toaster or a vacuum. Men!

"There she is, folks. Elsie the Tool-Mom MacBean," Nona said.

"You know what all those gadgets are for?" I knew Skip was dying to demonstrate how every single one worked.

"I'm sure I'll figure it out. Thanks. I expect it will come in very handy. Sometime." Next time I wanted to waive the corking fee at a fancy restaurant or extract my own teeth. I folded up the collection of utensils and dropped the apparatus into my purse.

"Now, this one's for you and Cruiser." Skip handed me a larger box, gift-wrapped in paper printed with basset hounds.

"Nice paper. Where did you find it?"

"Petropolis. That fancy pet store over in Crystal Bay. You and Cruiser should check it out."

"We definitely will."

I untied the bow, tore off the paper and looked inside the box. Wrapped in some tissue was a fifties steering wheel knuckle-buster engraved with dice along with a slogan, Born to Cruise.

"It's for your new PT Cruiser," Skip said. "There's something else in there, too."

I kept digging through wads of tissue paper until I found a sun visor for me and a smaller doggie-designed one for Cruiser, which was printed with the same slogan as the knuckle-buster. There was also a pair of dog goggles. I laughed. "I can just see Cruiser in this getup."

"Yeah, he'll be the coolest hound in town," Nona said.

"Thanks, Skip. You really went overboard. This is the niftiest birthday I've ever had."

"Nifty for fifty, Beanie."

"Don't you mean 'bitchin', Mom?"

"Smarty." I gave Nona a noogie. "Totally cool. This really rocks. There. Is that better?" She laughed.

"You're welcome," Skip said. "Say, speaking of rocks, I heard you're covering some geographical studies about Lake Tahoe for the paper."

"You heard right. I'll be interviewing the guy who's heading the project."

"What's he studying?" Skip asked.

"The lake's bottom."

"Why, Mom?"

"It has something to do with increased seismic activity in the area."

"Yeah, that shaker last month in Markleeville was really something," Skip said. "They even felt it down in Sacramento."

"I know," I said. "There's been some real rocking and rolling around this lake lately."

"I've always heard Lake Tahoe is bottomless," Nona said. "How can they study the bottom of the lake if there is no bottom?"

"Oh, I don't think it's really bottomless, although it may be deeper than previously believed. That's just a rumor that got started because when people drown in the lake, they're rarely found."

"Your mom's right," Skip said. "The lake never gives up her dead."

"Why is that?" Nona asked.

"No one really knows," I said. "Probably because it's so cold. I'm sure I'll be learning much more about it in my interview with Crispin Blayne."

"Crispin?" Skip said. "Sounds like breakfast cereal. What kind of a name is that, anyway?"

"English, I think. Say, you two, enough shoptalk. Let's party already! I think I'll go below and have a drink before we reach Emerald Bay. Care to join me?"

"Let's go, birthday girl," Skip said. "My treat."

Those were words I didn't hear from Skip very often. "You're on, Mr. Trump."

Skip followed me downstairs to the bar.

"Hey, wait for me!" Nona said.

The spray from the churning paddle wheel against the steamer's rear viewing window reminded me of a car wash. Cruiser loves a good summertime cruise through the car wash and likes going out on the lake with Skip and me on Skip's boat, the *Trout Scout*. But that's about as close as he ever gets to coming in contact with water on purpose other than at bath time, which he detests.

Cruiser's pendulous ears may look like oar paddles, but basset hounds were bred for tracking game, not treading water. My best buddy and fellow news hound had stayed ashore for my birthday, mostly because they don't allow dogs aboard the *Dixie Queen*. He wouldn't have liked the noisy fireworks, anyway. My fur friend and I would celebrate later over biscuits and warm milk; biscuits for him, warm milk for me. I hadn't been sleeping very well lately.

"What'll you have, Beanie?" Skip asked.

"A strawberry margarita, frozen, no salt."

"Got it. How about you, Nona?"

"Sex on the beach."

"Excuse me?" Skip's ears pinked.

"Relax, Skip," I said. "It's a cocktail."

Skip cleared his throat. "Oh."

While Skip fell in line to order the drinks, I couldn't help overhearing the conversation between the couple seated at a nearby table. Amid their discourse I distinctly heard a dog whining. Apparently the No Dogs Allowed policy on the boat didn't extend to every dog. Of course, a bichon frise is a little easier to smuggle on board than a basset hound. No one seemed to pay any attention to the fluffy white stowaway in our midst, except its owner, who fed it tidbits from her plate.

"Does Bitsy want a treat?" the lady crooned to the little dog. She winced when the dog got a little more ladyfinger than she intended. Then she petted the dog as though apologizing to it for being so careless as to not retract her hand fast enough to avoid its teeth. The attractive woman with the pampered pet on her lap appeared to be much younger than her middle-age husband—funny how all of a sudden I referred to anyone over the age of fifty as middle age; when I was Nona's age, I'd have just called him old.

Judging from the tiered cake with white icing and the stack of gifts wrapped in paper printed with bells and doves, it had to be either a wedding or an anniversary party. The answer to that matter was quickly spelled out by the lettering on the cake— Happy First Anniversary. I stood close enough to hear the couple as they chatted alone at the table.

"Dixieland jazz? Frank Diggs! You know how I hate bleedin' banjo music," the petite redhead said to her partner, circling a perfectly manicured finger on the rim of her glass until it sang.

A string of pearls matching those around her neck rose to the top of the champagne glass.

She wore a red-and-white-striped silk scarf draped like one of the *Dixie Queen*'s all-American banners over a navy blue designer suit that clashed with her sea green eyes. A star-shaped diamond pin and earrings completed her Independence Day ensemble. Oddly patriotic attire, since I judged from her accent she was as British as the Queen's corgis and clearly abhorred something as uniquely Yankee as Dixieland jazz.

"What kind of music did you expect to hear on a paddle wheeler called the *Dixie Queen*, Ivy?"

"I don't know why we had to drag everyone out on this tub, anyway."

"But you said you wanted to go on a cruise for your anniversary."

"To the Caribbean, Frank. The Caribbean!"

I was starting to get the feeling that Bitsy wasn't the only pampered pet at this table.

"Perhaps next year, dear. You know my health hasn't been good."

"Top me up." Ivy held out her glass for another refill.

"Maybe you'd better not."

"Just pour the bubbly."

Frank ran a hand through his thinning hair, then poured his wife and then himself another glass of Dom Perignon.

Suddenly aware that I was eavesdropping, Ivy shot me a look that said "MYOB." I took the hint and sidled over to the glass-bottomed viewing area. I looked down at the blue-green water flowing beneath the *Dixie Queen*, feigning interest in the rocks and plankton below. As I stood watching the water but still trying to grasp snippets of dialog for a future novel, a large shadow passed beneath the steamer's hull. At first I thought it was another boulder.

"See anything interesting down there?" Nona said, nudging my elbow.

"Funny you should ask. I thought I saw something a moment ago."

"What?"

"I don't know, but it was big!"

"Maybe it's the wreckage of Captain Dick's boat," Nona said.

"The hermit of Emerald Bay? No, he was shipwrecked off Rubicon Point."

"Well, isn't this where they scuttled the old steamer, *Tahoe*?"

"No, that's at Dead Man's Point near Glenbrook. They sank the old *Meteor* somewhere around there, too. It's a veritable steamboat graveyard."

"So, like, what's your point, Mom?"

I tugged one of Nona's curls and laughed. She rearranged her pretty chestnut hair, just in case there were any eligible bachelors on board. It was probably wasted effort, since there weren't many men here under the age of sixty.

"Hey, I know! Maybe it was Tessie." I tried not to crack a smile when I said it.

"Who?"

"Didn't you know that Lake Tahoe has its own prehistoric sea monster, like Loch Ness in Scotland has Nessie?"

"Oh, you mean like how the lake is bottomless?"

"Surely you've heard the local tales about a creature that lives in the lake?"

"I don't subscribe to the *National Enquirer*, Mother."

"If you subscribe to the *Tahoe Tattler*, you're not far off."

"Why did they decide to change the name of the *Tahoe Times*?" Nona said.

"You'd have to ask Carla Meeks that question. She used to work for the *Enquirer* before she took over as managing editor of our paper." I was concerned about stylistic changes that had accompanied the new moniker, a resurrection of the very first newspaper in the Tahoe area, which was called the *Tahoe Tattler*. In Carla's view it was sensationalism, not good writing, that sold papers. "She tells me there have been some recent sightings of something in the lake."

"Have the two-headed, pygmy aliens from Planet Velcro landed, too?" Nona quipped.

"Smarty pants." We both laughed. We became aware of someone else's laughter intermingling with ours. A young man had suddenly appeared at our side holding a bottle of Bud Light. Well tanned with sun-bleached hair, he looked like one of the Malibu Ken dolls Nona used to play with as a child. Things hadn't changed much with my daughter, as I would soon discover.

"Actually, the idea of dinosaurs around Lake Tahoe isn't that far-fetched." I noticed his speech seemed a bit slurred, but Nona paid it no mind. He was a hottie, as she referred to good-looking young men, and that's all that mattered to her. The man magnet edged coyly along the brass rail closer to where he stood and gave her opulent mane a come-hither flip.

"Really? Why is that?"

"Fragments of a three-million-year-old mastodon were found over in Gardnerville."

"Oh, yes. I read about that," Nona said.

Sure you have, Nona. My daughter is such a shameless flirt.

"I'm taking classes in paleontology over at the college," the young man said.

"Oh, you dig dinosaurs, huh?" Nona said, unaware of her double entendre. Maybe it was only a double entendre to someone my age. Today's youth don't say they "dig" something if they like it.

"You could say that, I guess," he said, and then laughed.

"Can I buy you a drink?"

"Thanks, but I think I have one coming right now. Maybe later, okay?"

"Here you go, girls," Skip interrupted, balancing three drinks on a tray as he walked toward us. He blew a wisp of straw-colored hair from his eyes.

"Quick, Skip!" I said. "I think I need that drink."

Just as Skip handed me my drink, the *Dixie Queen* pitched violently. The tray and drinks were instantly airborne, and strawberry margarita splashed on my white slacks. Nona and I grabbed the brass rail surrounding the viewing area before we both went flying, too. Some passengers screamed, several swore, and the few who didn't grab onto something toppled from their chairs onto the floor. An elderly woman's walker cartwheeled across the deck, barely missing Nona. Skip and I collided, and I hooked his elbow in the nick of time to keep him from falling.

"I didn't want the drink that quick," I said, dabbing the pink stains on my slacks with a cocktail napkin.

"What the heck happened?" Skip said.

"Did we run aground?" Nona said.

The first mate was on the lower deck in a flash. Other staff helped passengers to their feet, making sure no one was injured. The captain ordered everyone to vacate the lower deck while the crew checked for any damage. We left our drinks where they lay and filed up the stairs to the upper deck. I was happy to oblige. If we were about to experience a sequel of *Titanic,* I wanted to be prepared to abandon ship. As it would happen, the *Dixie Queen* wasn't the only thing to end up dead in the water.

Standing with the crowd on the upper deck, I spotted the same jet skier we'd seen before. As others were distracted by the confusion on the paddle wheeler, I watched the skier speed off toward Rubicon Point. A moment later, I saw a spray of water in the distance. At first, I thought he had wiped out and watched for him to resurface and reboard his small craft. He didn't. The skier had vanished. It was as though the lake had swallowed him up, jet ski and all.

CHAPTER TWO

The sun dipped below majestic Mount Tallac as the paddle wheeler's crew finished checking for any damage or injuries.

"We apologize for that little jolt, folks," the Captain said over the intercom.

"Little jolt?" I muttered.

"Apparently, we struck some debris. My mate informs me that everything is in perfect order. We will now proceed with our dinner cruise. Again, our apologies for the disruption. Please resume your evening's entertainment aboard the *Dixie Queen*." The cheery sounds of slide trombones and thrumming banjos resumed. Once more we descended to the lower level and Skip ordered us fresh drinks to replace the ones that had spilled. Several passengers coupled up on the dance floor, happy that the emergency had passed and the evening's fun could continue.

"What do you suppose we hit back there?" Skip said.

"Maybe something hit us," I said.

"Could have been that guy on the jet ski I saw buzzing around earlier," Nona said.

"I doubt it."

"He probably already headed back for the dock. It's too dark now for skiers," Skip said.

"I saw him and he was headed for Rubicon Point, but I don't think he made it."

"What makes you think so?" Skip said.

"Because he disappeared, that's why."

"Disappeared? What do you mean?"

"I mean he disappeared. One minute he was there, and the next he wasn't."

"You were staring into the sunset, Beanie. It was probably just the light playing tricks on your eyes. The lake does that sometimes, and when it's hazy like it is now, it's worse."

"I know what I saw, Skip. My eyes weren't playing tricks on me and I didn't imagine it, so don't make me out to be Looney Tunes."

"Hey, Mom. Our drinks are up."

Nona knew a frozen strawberry margarita would sweeten me up and cool things down. She'd grown used to my menopausal mood swings, but this was no mood swing, and my peepers were just fine, thank you very much.

Meanwhile, another angry exchange was erupting between Ivy and her husband at a nearby table, and this time I wasn't the only one aware of it.

Ivy's voice grew as shrill as a bobby's whistle. "Really, Frank. If you'd quit giving handouts to those bleedin' leeches you call your family, maybe we could be in the Caribbean right now."

From where I stood, it looked like Bitsy was the one getting all the handouts. The little dog licked Ivy's hand. Whether it was to beg another treat or calm her mistress was hard to tell.

"Mummy's not mad at Bitsycums." Ivy slipped another sample of food from her plate to the dog and cooed to it like a child, something that wasn't too much of a stretch for me to understand. I had been accused more than once of outrageously spoiling Cruiser.

"I'm only trying to use some of my money to help Ted with the business," Frank said. "You can't expect me to turn my back on my family entirely, Ivy. I've practically cut them off as is."

"What do you mean *your* money? It's my money too, Buster

Blue Eyes. This is California, and I'm entitled to half of everything you own."

"But I've already given you everything I own. What else do you want from me?"

Ivy's face turned so red it nearly matched her hair. She was ready to blow like a volcano, and she did.

"I'm sick of you and your whole family. I'll tell you what I want. I want a divorce."

Frank adjusted his tie, which appeared to be suddenly too tight. "Please, honey. Let's not fight. It's our anniversary."

"Our first and our last. I'm leaving you, Frank, and I'll take your last penny in the bargain." A heavy silence settled on Frank and Ivy when a server appeared with a tray and began serving the meals. Frank dissected his sirloin with a steak knife. He gripped the handle so tight his knuckles turned whiter than the tablecloth.

"You don't mean that," he said to her when the server left.

"I most certainly do." I saw Bitsy's ears perk up when Ivy hissed at him like a cat.

Frank's jaw muscles twitched like he had a mouthful of Mexican jumping beans. For a moment, I thought he might lunge across the table and strangle the little woman and her little dog, too. It was clear by now this wasn't a *Love Boat* cruise we were on.

The music stopped and the rest of the anniversary party joined the couple, not a moment too soon from the looks of it.

"Is everything all right here?" A stocky blond woman was first on the scene. She appeared considerably older than her stepmother. "Your color looks a bit hectic, Dad." She took his wrist in her hand to take his pulse.

He snatched his wrist away. "Stop fussing over me, Dora. I'm fine."

"You sure you're okay, Father? You don't look well," said the handsome fortyish man in a Tommy Hilfiger shirt and Cole Haan loafers.

"No need to call the paramedics, Ted. You can't get rid of me that easily."

"What do you mean by that?" Ted said, knitting pale blond brows over intense cobalt blue eyes.

"I'm just kidding, Teddy. Can't anyone in this family take a joke?"

"Don't call me Teddy. You know I hate that."

Frank sighed.

"Shall I get your pills?" Dora persisted, fluttering around him like a mother hen.

"No," he said, waving her aside. "I told you I'm fine. Let's just eat, okay? Where's Bobby, anyway?"

"I don't know. I saw him flirting with some girl," Ted said.

"That's the Bobby dazzler for you," Ivy cracked.

"I hope you're having a good time tonight, Dad," Dora said. "I went to a lot of trouble to plan your anniversary party." Dora cast a glance first at her father then in Ivy's direction, waiting for a thank you that never came.

"Does he look like he's having a good time, Dora?" Ted snapped at his sister.

"Would you mind putting the dog in her carrier while we eat?" Dora snapped in turn to Ivy.

The two women exchanged chilly glances. "Very well. If you insist," Ivy conceded, apologizing to Bitsy as she placed her in a tote with screens on each end. A portable kennel; so that's how she'd smuggled the dog aboard. Too bad that wouldn't have worked for Cruiser.

Skip handed me my drink. "Here you go, Beanie. Blended, no salt, just the way you like it."

"Thanks, Skip."

"When do the fireworks start?" Nona asked, excitement lighting her ginger spice eyes with their own fireworks.

"Should be pretty soon, honey. The sun has set, but the collision has delayed the celebration, I guess."

No sooner had I spoken than the first rocket shot high over the lake and illuminated the water in a kaleidoscope of sparkling color. For the second time that evening, everyone below filed up the stairs to the top deck. I hadn't had this much exercise on a Stairmaster at the gym.

Over the confusion I heard Ivy's now familiar Cockney. "Happy bleedin' anniversary!" She spat the words at Frank like sour cherries. Her chair shot backward as she bolted up and flung what champagne hadn't already sloshed onto her designer ensemble in her husband's face. She stormed up the stairs, pushing her way through the throng to the main deck. The other passengers' mouths dropped open so wide they looked like a school of beached trout.

Frank picked up his napkin, wiped his face and jacket calmly, and followed his wife topside. To make peace with her, or so I thought until I saw the wrath sizzling like a Fourth of July sparkler in his eyes.

CHAPTER THREE

A chorus of oohs and aahs filled the night air as all eyes gazed skyward. Several minutes later the show was interrupted by a commotion at the stern of the boat.

We turned away from the fireworks to join the crowd gathering. The big wheel stopped turning, and we felt the craft shudder, then slow to a stop.

"What now?" I said. "Have we hit something else?"

"My wife is missing!" a man cried out. It was Frank Diggs, the same man I had observed earlier being doused with Dom below deck.

The second mate ran over to where he was standing. "Are you sure, mister? Maybe she's on one of the other decks."

"I'm positive. I already looked everywhere. She's gone, I tell you."

"Passenger overboard!" the mate yelled. A crewman sounded the alert while another on the lower deck hurled a life preserver off the starboard side.

"I can't see anyone down there, sir," said the crewman, peering into the indigo waters.

"Someone help her!" Frank wrung his hands. Dora and Ted tried unsuccessfully to calm him down. Soon everyone was peering over the railing trying to spot Ivy.

Skip kicked off his shoes and, before I could say jumpin' Geronimo, he leapt over the top railing and into the lake. I'd told him to go jump in the lake plenty of times, but I never thought he'd really do it.

Nona and I ran down to the lower level where the crew was still searching the waters for Ivy. We watched as Skip dove underwater several times, surfacing intermittently for air before diving again. Then nothing. Just like the guy on the jet ski, Skip had vanished before my eyes, but this time there was no question about what I was seeing.

"Skip! *Skip!*" I called again and again, scanning the water for some sign of him. I was hanging so far over the railing that I almost fell overboard myself. Nona snagged the hem of my jacket and pulled me back.

"Oh, Nona. Skip's gone!" I cried. "Somebody do something!"

I was about to jump in after Skip myself when he bobbed to the surface like a cork, sputtering and coughing.

"I see him. There he is!" The first mate yelled.

Skip managed to grab onto the life preserver that had been meant for Ivy, and the crew pulled him aboard. He stood on the deck dripping wet and shivering.

"Someone get a blanket," I said.

I wrapped Skip in the blanket, and we helped him into the dining room where it was warm. We seated him and called for a brandy from the bar. While he sipped, I rubbed his arms vigorously through the blanket. Soon, he stopped shaking. All of a sudden, the craft lurched again, and this time I heard something scrape along the length of the boat's hull. I braced myself and managed to catch a goblet in mid-air before it rolled off the table beside me. I realized this was the same table where Frank and Ivy had sat arguing only minutes before.

Bitsy was barking her head off in her cake-splattered pet carrier. The scene looked like the aftermath of a freshman food fight. The white tablecloths were stained and soaked with drinks. Plates full of food had been tossed everywhere and table settings lay askew. The couple's unopened gifts lay scattered on the floor along with what was left of their anniversary cake. Something broken tinkled inside a gift box when I picked it up and set it back on the table. It seemed somehow symbolic of the unhappy occasion I had earlier witnessed. Then I noticed something else—Frank's steak knife was missing.

"I couldn't find her," Skip said, shaking his head. "I tried, but she was gone."

"You did all you could, Skip."

"You really scared us," Nona said. "We thought we'd lost you."

"It's a good thing you weren't wearing that Sam Browne belt of yours," I said. "You'd have drowned for sure."

"I almost did anyway. Something had hold of me down there."

"Must have been more debris."

"No, y-you don't understand," Skip said. "I mean something *caught* me!"

I glanced at Nona, who cocked her right eyebrow in disbelief.

"Maybe that giant trout you've been trying to hook for years is finally getting even with you," I teased.

"I'm not joking," Skip said, and I could see from his face he wasn't. "I tell you I was being pulled down. Something had hold of my leg. I couldn't break free. Then it suddenly just let go."

"You probably were snagged on something. Or it could have been the current. I'm sure it felt like you were being pulled down in the water."

"Well, whatever it was almost ripped my leg off."

Skip rolled up a shredded pant leg. We stared at his bloodied ankle. It looked like a pit bull had mistaken his leg for a chew toy.

"Wow!" Nona said. "They don't have piranha in this lake, do they, Mom?"

"No, they only live in the tropics." Gators? Killer whales?

Jaws? I'd never heard of any of those living in Lake Tahoe, either.

The steamer's piercing whistle began shrieking again, and we all scrambled out to the railing, thinking the woman Skip had tried to save had been spotted. Skip limped after us. We peered into the purple evening that had started off so pleasantly. All we saw were the eerie ruins of a miniature castle, Mrs. Knight's famed "Tea House," silhouetted in the moonrise on the rocky island in the eye of Emerald Bay. I thought I heard a thin wail rise in the night air. Was it Ivy's final desperate cries for help, or was it something else?

CHAPTER FOUR

The sound of sirens broke the pall that had fallen upon our festive Emerald Bay tour. No one had expected a carefree holiday cruise to end in a drowning. A patrol boat pulled alongside the *Dixie Queen*. Several officers boarded her to investigate the situation and take a report.

"That wound looks pretty serious," one officer said to Skip.

"Oh, it's not too bad."

"You sure? I can have someone take you ashore to have it treated."

"I don't want to leave my friends stranded out here."

I thought how gallant of Skip until I realized he didn't want to miss out on any further developments. He knew they would be questioning passengers about the incident. I stood close enough to overhear the conversation with Frank, who appeared to be terribly distraught. I found that puzzling, considering the fracas that had occurred just prior to Ivy's disappearance. Dora tried to console her father as an informal inquiry proceeded.

"When did you first miss your wife?" an officer asked Frank.

"We were watching the fireworks, and I told her I was going to use the restroom. When I came back, she wasn't there," Frank continued. "I asked where Ivy had gone, and my daughter said she thought maybe she'd gone to the restroom, too."

The officer turned to Dora. "Did you see where she went?"

"Not really," Dora said. "But I'm pretty sure that's where she must have gone. We'd all had a lot to drink."

"Especially Ivy," I heard Ted mutter. The officer turned his attention to Ted, who was cooler than the lake's water under the officer's stern gaze. "She was standing right over there at the railing when I went to check on Dad. I was concerned about him when he didn't come back right away. He'd seemed upset at dinner. He has a heart condition, and I thought he might be having some difficulty. Maybe Bobby knows something." Ted turned to the younger version of himself. Bobby-come-lately, who had suddenly rejoined the party, appeared to be the youngest of the three siblings. He was the same fellow who had chatted with Nona earlier.

"Nope. Didn't see her again after we left the lower deck when the fireworks started."

I wondered which fireworks he was referring to. I was also beginning to wonder if we were talking about an invisible woman here. No one seemed to know anything about the sudden disappearance of a woman I imagined was hard to miss for very long.

"Weren't you and your wife having some sort of disagreement earlier?" I asked. The officer looked perturbed that I was butting in on their little Q&A session, but I didn't care.

"Well, yes. But how would you know that?"

"I was standing near your table. I couldn't help overhearing." In my defense, I quickly added, "Everyone knew you were arguing when they saw your wife throw her drink on you. She must have been pretty angry to do that in front of all those people."

"Of course she was angry," Frank said. "But what business is it of yours, anyway?"

"I noticed her eavesdropping on your conversation, Dad," Dora volunteered. "Some people should learn to mind their own business."

"Yes, they should," Frank said, with a look in his eyes not unlike the one I'd seen just before he followed his wife topside.

"Let's backtrack a little," Skip interjected.

"Who are you?" Frank asked.

"I'm the county sheriff, Mr. Diggs. What happened after the drink-tossing incident?"

"Nothing," Frank said. "I went after my wife to apologize, and I did. About that time the fireworks started."

"We were all distracted," Dora proclaimed in her father's defense.

So was everyone else, I thought. Perfect time to give the old, or in this case young, ball and chain the heave-ho into the deep.

CHAPTER FIVE

Finally, we heard the engines turn over, and the big wheel began to churn once more. I heard several passengers echo my sigh of relief. We would all be glad to get back safely to land. Dog paddling out in the middle of the lake in the dark with a dead body and heaven knows what else was not my idea of a perfect birthday celebration. I've never been an Olympic swimmer. Cruiser isn't a great swimmer either, but he could easily out–dog paddle his mom.

At last, the *Dixie Queen* rounded Fannette Island for the return trip to the safety of Ski Run Marina where we had boarded the paddle wheeler three hours earlier for this killer cruise. I saw the searchlights of rescue boats on the opposing side of the island skimming the waters for any sign of Ivy. A diver bobbed to the surface, and as the officer helped him aboard, I saw him shake his head. There would be no body to recover this night or in the succeeding daylight search for Ivy Diggs. The dark waters of the ancient lake had claimed one more soul to her mysterious depths.

After getting Skip's leg patched up at the emergency room, Nona and I dropped him off at his place, then headed for the old log homestead. I was still awaiting delivery of my new inferno-red PT Cruiser from the dealership in Reno, my fiftieth birthday present to myself from the jackpot I'd won at one of Tahoe's casinos. And speaking of Cruisers, my pooch pal was waiting eagerly at the door to greet me. I was glad to see a friendly face, especially after the one I'd seen earlier that evening on a man named Frank moments before his wife took an unexpected moonlight dip.

Everyone, including the police, assumed it was an accident and that Ivy had fallen overboard. Maybe it was and maybe it wasn't. I couldn't help wondering if this public dunking mightn't have been a convenient way for a man to get rid of his witch of a wife. I'd heard of plenty of marriages going to the dogs, but they didn't usually end in murder. While we were all distracted with the fireworks display, had Frank stabbed Ivy with his steak knife, then tossed her overboard? Maybe it was just my overactive imagination running away with me again. But I hadn't imagined the jolts the *Dixie Queen* took in Emerald Bay. We'd all felt those.

Nona and I sat on the sofa. I decided to try some Sleepy Time herbal tea instead of the usual warm milk. Cruiser had already polished off his nighty-night biscuit and, true to form, was begging for another.

"With all the excitement tonight, I almost forgot to give you this," Nona said, handing me a gold-wrapped box with matching gold bow. Perfect for a golden oldie, I mused. "Anyway, I wanted us to have our own private celebration here."

"With all the excitement, I almost forgot it was my birthday, honey." Cruiser nosed the gift, sniffing for the scent of biscuits. I kissed him on his pointy little head, then gently nudged his drooly muzzle aside so I could finish unwrapping my present, which I was fairly certain wouldn't be dog biscuits. Growing impatient, I finally resorted to ripping the pretty wrapping paper. "You know I didn't want you to get me any gifts. You should be saving your money."

"Don't be silly. What's the use in having a birthday without gifts?"

33

I had to admit she had me there, especially if the birthday was your fiftieth. I lifted the lid on the box. Inside was a printed card. Thank goodness it wasn't my AARP membership card. I expect that would be arriving in the mail any day now.

"What's this?" I reached for my reading glasses. I'd just graduated to bifocals several weeks before my birthday.

"It's a gift certificate for a spa day and makeover at Oh, Heavenly Lady Day Spa."

I understood now why Nona had waited to give me this gift without Skip around to razz me. "Makeover! You think I need a makeover?"

"Of course not, Mom. You look great!" Nona's brow furrowed when she realized that she might have given the wrong gift to her hypersensitive mother.

"For my age, you mean."

"For any age, silly. I've had one before. It's just a day of pampering. Look here." Nona pointed to the card and read it to me like I wasn't able to read it for myself. " 'Includes massage, body wrap, facial, manicure, pedicure, makeup, hairstyling.' See, you get the whole enchilada, Mom."

"*Yo quiero* tummy tuck."

Nona giggled, partly with relief that I could joke about the age thing at all. I started to laugh, too. What else can you do? Before long we were howling with laughter, and Cruiser joined in, which made us laugh harder.

Perhaps Nona was onto something. Maybe it was time to reinvent myself. A new look couldn't hurt. I'd kicked my chocolate chip cookie habit, ordered Richard Simmons's "Sweatin' to the Oldies" video, and over the past six months had finally managed to lose twenty of the thirty pounds I'd collected over the last decade. Perhaps I shouldn't stop there, I thought. I hadn't been very happy with the frumpy photos I'd had printed with my author bios. With my first mystery novel completed and finally represented by an agent, I might soon see my face on the dust jacket of a book. Nona was right. A make-over couldn't hurt.

"Thanks, honey. This is very thoughtful of you." I kissed her on the cheek and set the gift certificate aside on the end table.

"Wait, that's not all." Nona handed me another gift-wrapped box. This one was larger.

"More gifts? You didn't need to go overboard." We'd already had two people go overboard tonight.

Cruiser had grown tired of being ignored. Time to bring out the heavy hound dog artillery. Usually too proud to beg, when push comes to shove he is not above using his one and only trick to get what he wants. Now that his weight has also reduced, it's easier for him to do the only trick I've ever known a basset to do well—sit up and beg. When you think of what it must take for Cruiser to hoist all seventy pounds of that torpedo-shaped body into a vertical position, using his long, powerful tail as a tripod, it's quite an impressive sight. It's also a cunning canine ploy, because such grand feats are, of course, performed only for treats.

"All right, Cruiser. I give, but this is the last one." I dipped into the biscuit jar, handed Cruiser his treat and resumed my gift opening. I untied the yellow ribbon and ripped off the paper. I saw from the picture on the box that I was the proud new owner of a cell phone, whether I liked it or not. What was I going to do with this thing? I couldn't stand all those rude cell phonies blathering on their phones in grocery stores, theaters, funerals. Like it or not, it looked as though I was about to join the club. "Well, isn't this nice. But you shouldn't have, Nona. Really!"

"Time for you to join the twenty-first century, Mom."

"Well, I'm really not sure how much I'll use it."

"Trust me, you'll use it."

"If you say so." I hoped my brain wouldn't turn to Styrofoam.

"It'll give me peace of mind about you up here snooping around all the time. You'll always have immediate contact in case you get into trouble, or in case Cruiser does."

"I give Cruiser credit for being pretty smart, but I don't think I can teach him how to phone home."

"You won't have to with the rest of your gift. There's more in that box. Keep opening."

"This really is too much, honey. You shouldn't have spent so much on this . . . dog collar?" Gee, so far Cruiser was doing better with my birthday than I was. Hats, goggles and now a fancy collar. It had what looked like a transmitter attached to it. "I've never seen a collar quite like this. What is this thing on here?"

"It's a GPS navigator."

"GPS for a dog?"

"Yes, in case Cruiser ever gets lost up here, you can locate his whereabouts with this by using your cell phone."

Now that was one thing I wouldn't mind using a cell phone for. "Will you show me how it works?"

"Sure." Nona was just like Skip and his army knife gift. She couldn't wait to show me how to use all the features on the GPS collar and the tiny telephone, too. Although I was sure all this cost a bit more than Skip's presents, I credited her for not wanting to one-up Skip with her more expensive gifts. She knew Skip could be even more sensitive than her mother. She set the ringer on the phone to play "Scotland the Brave."

"Tom would have loved this." I felt a tinge of sadness that my husband couldn't be here to help me celebrate this milestone in my life. Being single at my age wasn't going to make this transition any easier. At least I wasn't entirely alone. I still had my main man, even if he had four legs and a tail.

"It even takes photos." She demonstrated by snapping a photo of Cruiser. My boy looked as handsome as ever.

"Pretty cool, huh?"

"Cool as can be. Thanks for all the nice gifts, Nonie." I gave her a hug.

"You're welcome, Mom. Happy birthday again."

"Thanks. Will you be able to stay the week?"

"I can do better than that. Mind if I stay the whole month? My next modeling shoot doesn't start until August."

"Mind? Are you kidding?" I whooped with excitement and hugged Nona again. Cruiser jumped to his feet and leapt into our collective laps, licking Nona's face, then mine.

"Down, Cruiser! Down, boy," I commanded.

"He thinks we're going for a . . ."

"Shh. Don't say the word. Don't even spell it."

"Oh, please. Are you trying to tell me this dog can spell?"

"You bet your bloomin' biscuits he can. He can tell time, too."

Nona laughed and petted Cruiser's head. "Gee, boy. Next you'll be attending Berkeley University."

"Don't you mean Barkeley U?"

"You're way funny, Mother."

"Way."

"Say, I have an idea. Why don't you and I rent a couple of ATBs while I'm up here and go for a ride?"

"ATBs? What's that stand for? You know I don't speak Acronym."

"All-terrain bikes. I'm dying to try the Flume Trail."

"Gee, I don't know. It's been years since I was on a bicycle. I might fall and break something."

"It's like sex. You never forget how to do it."

I wasn't so sure I hadn't forgotten how to do that, too.

"Besides, all you'll break is a sweat. We'll stick to the easy

37

trails. Come on. It'll be fun. You'll see."

"If you say so, dear. Maybe we can rent one of those baby trailers so Cruiser can come along."

"You're kidding me, right?"

"No, I'm not. You know the rule around here. Love me, love my dog."

"Whatever." Nona rolled her eyes. "You think Skip might want to join us?"

"Maybe. Depends on his leg. It took nearly fifty stitches to patch him up."

"He's a real trooper staying on board the *Queen* with a wound like that. What could have cut him up that bad?"

"Beats me. He could have gotten hung up in the boat's motor blades, I suppose."

"But we weren't moving."

"True. They'll do a more thorough search, I'm sure, especially after the *Dixie Queen* was nearly scuttled."

"It was kind of scary thinking we might sink."

"There were enough life vests on board if it had come to that, but the lake's pretty cold, even in mid-summer. Hypothermia can overcome you pretty quickly."

"I know. People always underestimate how chilly Tahoe is."

"Add alcohol consumption and the thinner air, and you've got a recipe for a drowning."

"You think that's what happened to that poor lady tonight?"

"From what I saw, Ivy appeared to be neither poor nor a lady, but I suppose we can assume so. I expect that the police will continue searching for her a while, but I'll be surprised if they find anything out there. Like Skip said, the lake never gives up her dead."

"What a terrible thing to happen on your birthday."

"Even worse for Ivy on her anniversary."

"How did you know it was her anniversary?"

"I saw the inscription on the cake." And the handwriting on the wall. "They didn't exactly seem like Ozzie and Harriet."

"Ozzie and Harriet?"

"Sorry, Miss Millennium. I keep forgetting you didn't grow up in the fifties."

"Oh, you mean like *Leave it to Beaver.*"

Thank heaven for syndicated reruns. "Let's just say they didn't seem like they were blissfully married. They were fighting like ferrets."

"Oh, all married couples fight."

"Your father and I didn't, did we?"

"Well, not much." Nona smiled. Her eyes twinkled with mischief. Always the tease, just like her father.

"Anyway, we were nothing like those two. It was getting pretty ugly there at the dinner table. Next thing I know, she goes over the starboard side."

"You mean you think the old guy pushed his wife overboard?"

"It's possible. And besides, he wasn't that old. He was probably in his late fifties, early sixties tops." Her mouth was open to answer. "Don't even think it, young lady!"

"Relax. I wasn't going to make a crack about your age."

"Gee, I'm sure relieved about that." I leaned forward for my teacup and sighed when I saw my reflection in the glass-topped coffee table. Too many sleepless nights had put a set of bags under my eyes that could pass for carry-on luggage. Perhaps more than a spa day was called for. Too bad Nona hadn't given me a gift certificate for blepharoplasty. With my dark complexion, I couldn't do laser or chemical processes to allay the aging process without the risk of permanent scarring. I wondered if my old tribal rival, Sonseah Littlefeather, had gone in for a few nips and tucks. She was fairer skinned and always on camera promoting Indian casinos or other Washoe interests in the Tahoe basin.

"Are you working on another mystery, Mom?"

"What makes you ask that?"

"Sounds like your imagination's working overtime again. Murder? Sea monsters? I think you'd better have that spa day soon."

"Smart aleck." I cuffed Nona on the head playfully, and she laughed. Underneath the playfulness, I was concerned. I'd heard old wives' tales about some women flying over the cuckoo's nest when they reached middle age. I was hoping that the new me wouldn't be sporting one of those white jackets with extra-long sleeves.

CHAPTER SIX

The morning of my interview with Crispin Blayne, I awoke with a splitting headache. I wanted to blame it on the birthday margarita the night before, but since most of the drink had ended up on me instead of in me I was more inclined to attribute it to my funhouse of midlife symptoms. The Estrogen Dip wasn't a carnival ride or something you serve with potato chips, but an unpleasant aspect of aging I hadn't counted on.

I brewed some decaf coffee and even popped a couple of aspirin, which I rarely ever did, hoping the headache would subside before my 10:00 a.m. appointment at the college. At least I already had my interview questions ready. I was sure glad I hadn't waited until this morning to prepare for the interview. This guy Blayne was no doubt going to be one of those "techno weenie" types who spoke fluent Jargonese. Sigh. I eagerly anticipated the day when I could quit freelancing and live off of the royalties from my mystery novels. In your dreams, Beanie.

I heard the kitchen door open, expecting to see Nona. Then I heard the leisurely click of toenails on linoleum.

"Hey, Cruiser. Decided to sleep in this morning, big fella?" Cruiser was usually my furry alarm clock. "Where's Auntie Nonie, Boy?"

Cruiser looked at me with eyes as bloodshot as mine and sauntered over to his "Top Dog" dish. I heard the crunch of kibble being chewed. Every crunch seemed magnified tenfold this morning. When he began to bark, then shuffled off to the front door, my temples throbbed with renewed pain. I shuffled off right after him when I heard the doorbell ring.

I peeked out the window. It was Skip. I unlatched the door and Cruiser's nose popped out.

"Hey there, Cruiser, old buddy." Skip patted Cruiser's head. "Morning, Beanie. Sorry to drop in unannounced."

"It's okay."

"Do I smell French Roast?" Skip gave the air a Cruiser-style sniff.

"Sure do. Come on in and have a cup."

"Don't mind if I do. I haven't had time for any yet this morning."

Skip limped behind me to the kitchen, and Cruiser followed close on his heels with a look I could only interpret as concern. He instinctively knew something was wrong with our friend. Cruiser might not be a K-9-to-5 working dog like a guide dog or therapy dog, but he possesses all the sensitivity toward humans that is inherent to his species. Besides, Skip was Cruiser's favorite fellow now that Tom was gone. I know Cruiser loves me, but I also understand that he needs a little male bonding once in a while. It's a guy thing.

"How's the leg this morning?" I asked.

"Painful."

"Go sit and prop it up. Coffee's coming right up."

About that time, I heard the sound of Nona's moccasins scuffing down the hallway. "Mmm. I smell some of Mom's wicked brew."

"I thought that would bring you to life, lazybones. Come and join Skip and me."

"We have company?" Nona quickly tidied her hair and tied the dangling sash of her robe as she entered the kitchen.

"Good morning, Nona," Skip said.

"Morning, Skip. How ya doin'?"

"Okay, thanks."

"How's the leg?"

"Mending. They stitched me up good at the hospital."

"But look, they left out some of our teddy bear's straw stuffing," Nona teased, tugging on a strand of Skip's flaxen hair as she sat down next to him at the table.

Skip laughed and blushed, enjoying Nona's attention and no doubt glad she hadn't compared him to the *Wizard of Oz* scarecrow, like some people did.

I handed her and Skip a cup of coffee, reheated my own and plopped back down in my chair.

"What brings you here so early, Skip?" I said.

"I thought you'd want to know the latest on the lady of the lake."

"Did they find her?" I asked.

"Not a trace. She's down there somewhere with the fish. Now it's just a matter of waiting for the lawsuit to surface, because it's for certain *she's* not going to."

"You think they'll sue the company?"

"She fell off the *Dixie Queen.* Her family'll probably try to claim negligence or something. People sue for a lot less than wrongful death these days."

"If it was a wrongful death."

"What do you mean?"

"I'm not so sure she fell off the *Queen.* Those railings are plenty high enough to prevent anyone from falling."

"Maybe she was leaning over too far. She'd been drinking. She could have lost her balance."

"Possibly."

"You almost fell overboard yourself, remember Mom?"

"True, true, but if you ask me, I think this woman may have had some help going over that railing."

"You think someone pushed her overboard?" Skip said.

"Could be."

"I think you're going overboard with this theory." Nona laughed.

"Don't mind her, Skip. She thinks her old mother's ready for the rocking chair Alzheimer's squad."

Skip guffawed. "Sounds like the latest rock band."

"No, Mom. I just think you're off your rocker," Nona teased.

We all laughed. Cruiser sauntered over to beg a morning biscuit, which I obediently produced from his canine cookie jar.

"What makes you think someone might have pushed the woman overboard, Beanie?"

"She and her husband were arguing below deck just before the collision with whatever the boat hit. Then she tossed her drink in his face and he followed her topside. That was the last time I saw her alive."

"But that doesn't mean he killed his wife," Skip said.

"You didn't see the look in his eyes. If looks could kill, she'd have dropped dead before she ever reached the stairs."

Skip took off his hat and scratched his head. Whenever he did that, I knew he was mulling things over. "Hmm. Sounds like this 'accident' may bear further investigation."

"Well, if you need a willing nose, Cruiser is always ready to sniff out a suspect," Nona said.

"Or suspects," I said. "I think everyone at the anniversary party should be questioned further, starting with the husband."

"Well, in that case, I need two willing noses, and I can't think of anyone nosier than you. Not even that biscuit-sniffing hound of yours. That's what makes you such a good reporter."

"Gee, I'd better shake a leg. I'm going to be late for my interview."

"What interview?"

"The one with Professor Blayne."

"Oh, yeah, him. When's that?"

"I'm due over at the college by 10:00."

"It's almost that now."

"Oh, my gosh! I didn't realize it was so late." I leapt up from my chair, and then clutched my temples. "Ohhh, my aching head."

"Better have some aspirin, Mom."

"Already had some. I'll just have to tough this one out, I guess. Help yourself to more coffee, Skip."

"Thanks, don't mind if I do." Skip stepped over to the coffeepot. "I'll fill 'er up once more with high octane before I hit the trail."

"Oh, no. I forgot to gas up the Jeep. It's nearly flat out."

"I'm headed back to the station," Skip said. "Want a lift?"

"Yeah, sure. I probably couldn't see straight to drive right now with this skull cracker I've got, anyway. I'll have Nona collect me after I'm finished."

"Go ahead and get ready. Cruiser'll keep us company for a few minutes. Right, fella?" Cruiser had just finished washing down his biscuit and sidled over to Skip, planting a sopping muzzle on his clean khakis. "Aaaaugh! Thanks a bunch, dog."

"Serves you right after dumping that margarita all over me last night."

"You can blame that on your sea monster. What did you call it? Tessie?"

"I was just pulling Nona's leg with that story. It's just a silly legend for the benefit of tourists, like the Loch Ness monster."

"I wouldn't be so sure."

I was in a hurry, but I wasn't about to let Skip's comment slip by. "What do you mean?"

"Oh, that's the other thing I meant to tell you. We've had a couple of really peculiar calls lately at the station. We would have just put them in the wacko files, except that one of the calls was from some Washington bigwig who's visiting up here."

"What kind of calls?"

"They both claimed they saw a thing in the lake."

Scenes of a 1950's sci-fi flick played in my head. "Thing? What kind of a thing?"

"One of them described it as a, well a . . ." Skip's mouth was twitching kind of funny. At first I thought it was just the new mustache he'd been trying to grow, which looked more like a fuzzy yellow caterpillar crawling on his upper lip.

"A what?"

"Sea monster."

"The correct term would be a plesiosaurus. I went to college, y'know."

Skip looked suitably impressed. Of course, what he didn't know was that science was my worst subject. Geology was the only class I'd ever flunked, which didn't bode well for my interview with the geology professor.

Nona looked skeptical about the whole thing. Cruiser just looked bored and bummed another biscuit.

CHAPTER SEVEN

Skip flicked on the siren—he just loves doing that—to clear the way and made tracks for the college. I was knocking at the professor's office door at precisely ten o'clock. If there's one thing I pride myself on, it's my punctuality. Tardiness has always been a pet peeve of mine.

"Come in."

"Hello, Professor Blayne, I'm Elsie MacBean from the *Tahoe Tattler.*" Jeez, I hated saying that. It sounded like I was a guest on the Jerry Springer Show.

"How do you do, Elsie," said Crispin Blayne, an elegant-looking man in his mid-forties. Wings of silver in his longish and slightly disheveled raven-black hair made him look even more distinguished than his posh London accent made him sound. Professor Blayne set his Elvis Costello horn-rimmed glasses on his desk and stood up to his full six foot four inches in height. I had to sit down or I probably would have fallen down. I hadn't been struck speechless in a man's presence since the night so long ago that Tom arrived at my parents' door dressed in a Scottish kilt and badger sporran for our blind date at the Tartan Ball. The professor's eyes were the same color blue as Tom's.

"I . . . Is this a good time for our interview?"

"Certainly."

"Okay, we might as well get started then. You don't mind if I tape the interview, do you?" I fumbled around in my satchel for the tape recorder and my pad and pencil. What had come over me? I wasn't usually flustered in the presence of a man, particularly while in my literary line of duty.

"No, not at all. Actually, I was just about ready to take a break. Would you care to go someplace for coffee? We could do the interview there."

"Well, uh . . ." I didn't really like doing interviews in restaurants. Clattering dishes had a tendency to drown out everything being said. Once, early in my freelance career, I conducted an interview at a fast food joint. All I heard that night as I transcribed the tape was an assortment of screaming kids. On the other hand, I didn't mind the idea of going someplace a little cozier with this interviewee.

"Where shall we go?" Blayne asked.

"There's a coffee house over on Highway 89 I think will do, only I didn't bring my car."

"How did you get here, then?"

"A friend dropped me off."

"Not to worry. I'll drive."

I followed him to his car. I didn't expect Austin Powers' Shaguar, but his convertible MGTC wasn't a far cry off. He opened the passenger door for me. That was something I hadn't enjoyed in a while, either—being treated like a lady.

"Thank you, Professor Blayne." I dropped into the bucket seat. I hadn't smelled that much leather since I used to horseback ride with my grandfather as a child. The seat leather creaked like my pony's saddle as he slid behind the steering wheel.

"Please call me Cris."

"All right. Cris." I smiled. He smelled even better than the upholstery. Like a mountain meadow after a summer rain.

"May I call you Elsie?"

"Sure." Call me anything you want to, but just call me.

"So, where are we going, then?"

"You know where Café Tyrolia is?" I said.

"Not exactly."

"I'll direct you."

The wind felt great blowing through my hair as the sports car sped down the road. I must have been grinning like an idiot, because he looked over at me and smiled. I thought I would melt to the floorboard in a puddle. What was coming over me? Suddenly, I felt like I was sixteen again. Now I understood why men bought sports cars when they hit middle age.

I was glad to see that the parking lot at the café wasn't too full. At least it would be quiet, except for the occasional hiss of the espresso machine. Only an older couple and two women were having coffee this morning. My favorite spot by the window was vacant, so I led Crispin over. A gentle pine-scented breeze wafted through the open window, rustling the white eyelet curtains. A vase of purple lupine and Coulter daisies accented the table. I was about to ask him what he wanted to order. I like to pay if I'm doing the interviewing, but he beat me to the punch.

"What would you like, Elsie?"

"The house decaf will be fine."

"Nothing to eat?"

"No, thanks." I never could eat and conduct an interview, especially when it seemed more like a date, as this was starting to. I should have insisted we do the interview at the office. I liked to keep things on a professional level.

"Right. I'll be back in a moment."

"Fine, I'll just get things set up here for the interview."

I scooted onto the peeled cedar bench and pulled out my mini tape and notepad. I noticed the two women seated at the table across from us watching Crispin as he stepped up to the counter to place our order. No doubt about it, he was definitely a bobby dazzler. The only women I knew of who wouldn't do a double take of this English crumpet were the two lesbians with the five pugs who moved into my neighborhood last month. Or Ivy Diggs, because she was dead. At least that was the consensus so far. One thing was certain, this guy surely had a string of admirers all the way from Tahoe to the Thames.

No point in getting your last hormone in an uproar, Beanie. Just do the interview, call Nona to come and pick you up, and call it another day in the life of an aging pen pusher.

"Here you are," Crispin said as he handed me my cup and sat down across from me. I could see those two women seated behind him sizing us up. They leaned in closer and one put her hand up to shield her face as she whispered to the other. Then they both giggled. I knew what they were probably saying. "What's she doing with an English stud muffin like him?" I wanted to go over and tell them, "I'm an almost-famous writer, you witches, and I'm interviewing Remington Steele, in case you didn't notice. Now, run along home and watch your soaps." But suddenly I felt frumpy and just plain old, even though Crispin couldn't have been more than a couple of years younger than I. I wanted to flee for the nearest plastic surgeon's office, but instead I opened my notebook, flicked on my tape recorder and started the interview.

"I'd like to begin by asking you about your studies of Lake Tahoe. Exactly what are you studying on the lake?"

"Actually, it's what I'm studying *in* the lake. I came here to explore the lake's depth and study the plankton levels for ecological purposes, but this project has taken on an entirely different aspect since it began last month."

"How so?"

"While conducting studies of the *bathymetry*, or relief, of the lake bottom, I've discovered a fissure."

Well, Nona, the bottomless lake debate has been answered.

"A fissure? How large a fissure?" I asked.

"Approximately a kilometer in width and close to ten kilometers in length."

"A kilometer. Let's see. That's about two-thirds of a mile, isn't it? That would mean the fissure covers over a quarter of the lake's length."

"Correct." When Crispin poured milk in his tea, I noticed he wore no wedding ring, although the ring finger was narrowed slightly as though he might have worn one fairly recently. Divorced? Widowed? I wondered which.

"You think that's the cause of the earthquakes we've been having?"

"Possibly, although there is an entire network of fault lines in this area."

"Doesn't surprise me," I said. "We've had some pretty good shakers around here lately."

"As you probably know, Lake Tahoe was formed millions of years ago by violent shifts in the earth's crust."

"Most people around here believe that Tahoe was once a volcano."

"That's a common misconception. In fact, it was formed by lava flows from volcanoes located near what is now the North Shore, but seismic activity from the shifting of those faults is still occurring and could be just as catastrophic to the area as a volcano. That's what I'm here to study, among other things."

"Other things?"

"In addition to being a professor of geology and paleontology—"

"Rocks *and* dinosaurs?" I interrupted.

"Yes, to put it simply," Crispin said.

"I see. I heard that a mastodon was discovered around here recently."

"Yes, that's correct. However, you didn't let me finish."

"Sorry, go on."

"I'm also a cryptozoologist."

"What's a cryptozoologist?"

"Someone who studies ancient lore of legendary animals to evaluate the likelihood of their existence."

"You mean like sea monsters and mermaids?"

"Yes, those would be typical study subjects for a cryptozoologist. We also investigate terrestrial creatures like Sasquatch, vampires, and werewolves."

"I see." It's a good thing I was getting this on tape because no one would believe it. I only hoped that none of the patrons of Café Tyrolia was eavesdropping on our conversation; they'd call the nice, young men in clean white coats to cart us both away to the nearest basket-weaving seminar.

"As a matter of fact," Crispin continued, "I'm currently investigating reports of a prehistoric creature that is purported to inhabit this lake."

"Oh, you mean Tessie?" I laughed, recalling my discussion with Skip.

"Yes, I believe that's what the locals call it. I've conducted studies of Nessie in Loch Ness as well."

"Is there really a Nessie?"

"It's entirely possible that there is. There have been far too many sightings there to pass off as drunken hallucinations or overactive imaginations."

"But there have been so-called Nessie sightings since the 1930s, haven't there?"

"True, but recent technology is shedding new light on the indisputable existence of such a creature."

"But can't new technology also create better hoaxes?"

"Point taken, Elsie, and we certainly have our share of doubters and detractors, but the sightings are increasing in frequency and the people making these reports aren't daft crackpots.

They're scientists like me and reporters like you. For instance, a recent report in the *Dundee Courier* stated that strange grunting sounds were heard coming from deep in the Loch."

"Couldn't those have come from whales or dolphins?"

"No, the sound was unlike either of those species. It wasn't the chattering of dolphins, nor was it the long, high-pitched song of a whale."

"So you think Nessie has a sister?" I said. "Most people say that Tessie is really just an oversized sturgeon."

"Well, I'm going to be exploring the lake bottom and collecting water and mineral samples here at Tahoe for the next month, so I hope to find out whether or not that's the case. Fortunately, the clarity of Lake Tahoe far surpasses that of Loch Ness. The plankton levels there made for murky viewing at best."

"The plankton levels in Tahoe are increasing, too, though. Our blue jewel may soon turn green."

"Yes, algae is growing at an alarming rate due to global warming, but it's still nothing like the plankton levels in the Loch. Visibility was near zero, hence the need for a better method of taking readings. Plankton makes for good dinosaur dining, though. That's what they live on."

"You really think you'll find a dinosaur living in Lake Tahoe?"

"If there's anything down there to find, we'll find it."

"But the lake is nearly seventeen hundred feet deep and thirty-nine degrees Fahrenheit. Divers can't go that deep, can they?"

"No, they can't. I wouldn't be either, if it weren't for DART."

"What's that?"

"It's a new technology, similar to sonar but far more sensitive."

"I mean, what does DART stand for?" Acronyms! . . .

"It stands for Digital Audio Reverberant Topography."

"Can you explain how it works?"

"Not in the time we have, but to put it in layman's terms, it works a bit like the radar of a bat. Only with DART, digital sound waves bounce off of objects, and then an extremely accurate topographical map is generated by a computer."

"Is it as accurate as sonar?"

"Far more accurate. To a hundredth of a millimeter."

"That's pretty accurate, all right. Can you demonstrate how it works for me?"

"Certainly. Do you suffer from claustrophobia?"

"No, why?"

"You'll see." He laughed, and I felt a little shiver run up my spine. I hadn't felt that in years, either. I saw the two women's heads snap around at the sound of his sexy, resonant laugh. This time I didn't mind them gawking because they also noticed my writer's paraphernalia spread out over the table and seemed assured this was strictly business. If only I were as certain.

"What say you come along with me for a demonstration later this week, Elsie? I'll be conducting some more tests then."

"Sure."

He smiled at me. Suddenly, I noticed my headache had vanished.

CHAPTER EIGHT

"How'd the interview go?" Nona asked as I climbed into her new Miata convertible, a step up from her old Volkswagen. Modeling had paid off nicely for my beautiful daughter with her Anglo/Native American good looks, even if I didn't always approve of what she was modeling.

"Oh, fine. Just fine." My mind was still on the interview, and Crispin.

"What's the matter with you?"

"Nothing's the matter with me. Let's get going, huh?"

"Yes, ma'am." Nona saluted and then hit the gas.

My head bounced against the headrest. "Ouch! Take it easy, Ace."

"Sorry. This thing's a little zippier than the old Volksy I had. I'm still not used to it."

"It's supersonic compared to the one I had when I was your age. Any phone calls while I was gone?"

"Yes, several, but you'd already know that if you had your cellular. *Hel-lo!* When are you going to give in and use that cell phone I gave you?"

"And get brain cancer?"

"There's no proof cell phones give you brain cancer."

"Yeah, well, they used to think cigarettes weren't harmful, either."

"Oh, mother, you're so not with it."

"Never mind. Who called?"

55

"Carla Meeks from the *Tattler*. Oh, and Skip called."

"I just saw him this morning. Did he say what he wanted?"

"Something about a murder investigation."

"Did he say whose?"

"No, but it's probably that woman you think was pushed off the *Dixie Queen*."

"Well, it looks like now I'm not the only one who thinks so."

I'd seen murder in Frank's eyes just before his wife took a moonlight dip in Emerald Bay, but so far that was all I had to go on. Had Skip discovered some new evidence? Only one way to find out. Business before bodies, though. I'd have to call Carla first.

When we pulled into the driveway, I saw my doggie in the window drooling on the curtains in his eagerness to see me. Good thing my name isn't Martha. I'll bet those Chows of hers never set a paw in that perfect New England TV stage she called home before she checked in at Camp Cupcake. Dog hair in the soufflé is *not* a good thing. Knowing Martha Stewart, she'd probably knit the dog hair into a nice Afghan—an Afghan hound, that is.

"Auntie Nona, will you take Cruiser out for a little jaunt while I change clothes and make some calls?"

"Yeah, sure. With the cell phone, you could walk and talk at the same time."

"Okay, okay, I get the point. Now scram, you two."

"C'mon, Cruiser. Walkies."

No sooner had Nona said the magic word than Cruiser was at the front door waiting for the door to open. And they say bassets aren't smart.

I slipped into my literary leisure suit, baggy blue jeans and a tattered "I love Tahoe" sweatshirt. Now I was ready to get down to writing business.

"Hello, Carla? Elsie here. My daughter said you called. You

have another assignment for me?"

"Yes, if you'd like to take it on. I thought since you're already doing the piece on the lake studies that you'd be interested in this one, too, even if it's a little different from usual."

She'd said the magic word. Right now, the one thing I needed lately in my life was different. "Sure, what have you got?"

"Well, we've had some odd reports around Tahoe lately, as you already know."

"You mean about a creature living in the lake?"

"Yes. I warn you, this is a little weird, but with the recent trouble on the *Dixie Queen* and a drowning, it all kind of meshes for our cover story."

"Should make for some interesting copy, anyway. You have anyone in mind for me to interview?" I already had a cryptozo-ologist on the line, but it never hurt to ask for contacts.

"Yes, several, including some old recluse who lives over on Rubicon Point. That's where most of these sightings have taken place. I'll e-mail the details to you. I'd like you to get as much information about this as you can. We want to do a series of articles on Tessie and other lake legends. I figured with your Washoe heritage, you'd be the perfect one for the job."

"A series, huh? I think my price just went up."

"That's okay. Just let me know what works for you and give us a good article on time."

"Don't I always?"

"Yep. That's why I called you first. Let me know if you have any questions." The second I hung up the phone, it rang again. This time it was Skip.

"How'd the interview with the professor go?"

"It went fine. Nona said you called earlier. Whassup?"

"We've got another floater."

"Yeah? Who?"

"Some guy in a speedboat. A tourist, probably. They get up

here and think they're experts at handling watercraft."

"How'd he drown?"

"The usual way. You know, lungs fill up with water, body sinks like a sandbag."

"C'mon, Skip. I'm serious." I knew his usual black humor was kicking in. How else could a person handle the experience of collecting cadavers and keep his sanity for long? Tahoe seemed to have had more than its fair share of corpses lately.

Skip shut off the funny business and got down to police business. "According to our one witness, the boat suddenly capsized. He wasn't wearing a life vest, even though there was one on board."

"That's odd, though not uncommon. They're cumbersome. People always are reluctant to wear them, kind of like seatbelts in cars. Thank goodness they've passed a law so children have to wear flotation devices now. I hope dogs are next."

"I'm surprised the company doesn't insist everyone wear them. Leaves them wide open for lawsuits."

"Which company?"

"Diggs Dive and Expedition."

"Oh, yeah. I've heard of them."

"Some old hermit who lives over at Rubicon Point saw the whole thing. He says he tried to save the guy, but he was too far out in the water for him to get to. At least that's his story. Boney Crider's his name. He smokes a little recreational grass, I hear, so I don't know if he's going to be a very reliable witness."

"I'll bet it's the same guy I'm supposed to be interviewing for the *Tattler*."

"I was going to go question him about the accident, for what it's worth, but since you're talking to him anyway, let me know what you find out, okay? We need to rule out foul play."

"Does this mean I'm on the Bod Squad again?"

"Yep. Want me to get you a Junior G-Man badge?"

"Make that G-Woman, and only if Cruiser gets one, too."

As if on cue, the door opened and in walked Nona and His Slobberness. Cruiser made a bee-line for my new white summer purse and nudged around inside for biscuits, leaving the stains from whatever he'd just sniffed out in the forest all over it. I nabbed the purse away from him before he could do any further damage or discover the Snickers bar buried at the bottom. Okay, so I hadn't totally kicked my chocolate habit. When I reached into the purse to retrieve the chocolate bar, my hand hit something metallic. It was the Swiss army knife Skip had given me for my birthday. I pulled it out of the purse and slipped it into the pocket of my jeans, which would please Skip. Maybe I'd find some use for it around the house, if I kept it handy.

"I know, I know," Skip laughed. "You're a package deal."

"Yeah, so deal with it already. Anyway, Cruiser's the one with the real nose for detective work."

"And candy," Nona added, laughing.

"You could probably use his two scents' worth on this case, Skip."

"Speaking of candy, when will you be getting that new candy apple red car you ordered, Mom? I'm dying to take a spin."

"Should be any day now. I need to call and check."

"I'll bet Cruiser just can't wait to ride in your Cruiser, Beanie."

Cruiser's ears perked up when he heard his name twice in the same sentence. He knew something exciting was afoot, although neither of us knew just how much excitement we were in for. Soon enough we'd be back on the crime trail together. I wondered if my new car would come equipped with a doggie safety belt in the co-pilot's seat for my sleuthhound sidekick. Plastic seat covers would be nice, too.

CHAPTER NINE

"Wow, when you said this thing was red, you really meant it, didn't you." Skip gave my new PT Cruiser the once-over. I half-expected him to kick the tires.

"It's called Inferno Red. I've always wanted a red car. All we ever had were white cars. Tom said white won't fade like red does, but the color bores me silly."

"Well, you could have gotten a white one and had flames custom painted on it." Nona giggled.

"I entertained the thought, but I didn't want to draw too much attention."

"Yeah, like that'll never happen with this car," Skip said.

He was right. The car was already drawing the wrong kind of attention. Cruiser sidled up to the wheel and started sniffing, preparing to christen my new wheels.

"Don't you *dare,* young man!" I said pulling him away in the nick of time.

"How about taking us for a spin?" Skip said.

"Sure, why not? Everyone climb in. We'll go to McDonald's for supper." I knew that would suit Skip's budget.

What about me? Cruiser seemed to say.

"Come on, boy. You can ride in the back with Auntie Nona."

"Thanks a lot, Mom!"

I hefted Cruiser into the rear seat and we headed out for some serious land cruising. He didn't even seem to mind wearing his new cruisewear that Skip had given him.

The neon lights of the casinos at Stateline flashed brightly in the oncoming dusk. I steered the car along Lake Tahoe Boulevard using the fifties' cruising knuckle-buster Skip had given me for my birthday. Traffic on the boulevard was heavy this time of year, so I had no choice but to cruise all the way down to the drive-thru. Heads spun and folks pointed as we passed the crowded sidewalks.

"You're attracting some stares with your new car, Beanie."

"So I noticed. I feel like I'm in the Macy's Thanksgiving Day parade."

"Say, maybe you should go to the Hot August Nights cruising event in Reno next month," Skip said.

"Yeah, Mom. That would be a blast from the past."

"Maybe I'll have to look into that custom paint job after all so I'll fit in with all the vintage hot rods."

I glanced in the mirror and grinned at Nona in the back seat. She was all smiles, appearing to be enjoying all the attention we were getting. Cruiser was eating it up, too. He hung his head out the rear window, ears flapping in the evening breeze. If dogs laugh, and I'm certain they do, that was what Cruiser was doing. It hadn't yet occurred to anyone that the stares we were attracting might have more to do with the silly-looking dog in the "Born to Cruise" hat and goggles than my flashy car or my pretty daughter.

The traffic light at Stateline turned red. I slid down into the seat when people began pointing and laughing at Cruiser hanging out the window, panting, drool dripping down the side of the car. I could see my new car wouldn't be new for long, but I prefer a happy dog to a pristine car any day.

The light turned green and the traffic began to move again. We had just started to roll forward when I thought I spotted a familiar face among the crowd on the sidewalk. A brunette wearing sunglasses glanced at me momentarily, then slipped into the door of Harrah's Casino.

CHAPTER TEN

Emerald Bay was breathtaking from atop Eagle Rock. Like Cave Rock and other volcanic plugs formed eons ago, Eagle Rock has never failed to inspire those who visit this landmark. I enjoyed this view of the lake from my car far more than I had on a stranded steamboat the other night. My hound buddy, Cruiser, was also enjoying the scenery from his co-pilot's window. Nearly every inch of the car was already drool spattered. That wonderful new car smell was already fading to Eau de Basset.

Rubicon Point was just a few miles up the hairpin curves of Highway 89. I had ridden my bicycle around the lake once in my younger, more reckless summers, and it was an experience I never cared to repeat. Oversized motor homes navigating the precarious twists and turns made the going treacherous for bicyclists, particularly along this stretch of asphalt. I was glad to be surrounded with heavy metal, which was the kind of music I heard drifting out the humble digs of Boney Crider. I hadn't heard Iron Butterfly since I was living in San Francisco in the sixties. I liked it then, but now it assaulted my ears and shattered the surrounding silence of the forest.

Tucked in the woods of Lonely Glen, about a half-mile from the lake stood the Crider abode. Formerly a forest service cabin, long abandoned among the pines, the tiny three-room bungalow looked like it was hiding from the world, just like Boney.

I knocked on his door, but I'm sure he didn't hear me knock over the din. Only the warning bark of his dog alerted him to the fact that he had a visitor. I almost put Cruiser back in the car, in case Crider had a pit bull protecting his stash of pot. It didn't sound like a pit bull, though. I guess you might say I speak Dog, because I can tell a lot from a dog's bark, including what breed it is. I determined that this was the benign voice of a golden retriever. The music volume went down and the door opened as far as the chain on the door would allow. Cruiser and the retriever touched noses. The retriever stopped barking and his whole body began to wiggle with excitement. Then a pair of bloodshot eyes peered out at me. Crider might be more of a challenge to win over.

"Mr. Crider?"

"Yeah. Who are you?"

"Elsie MacBean. I'm a reporter with the *Tahoe Tattler*. I'd like to talk to you if that's okay."

"About what?"

"The boating accident you witnessed."

The door slammed shut. Oh, great, there goes my story, and my paycheck. I started to knock on the door again, when I heard the chain rattle. The door opened wide. Boney Crider must have been close to 300 pounds. He wore his long, graying blond hair in a ponytail. His threadbare blue jeans and Hawaiian surfer shirt were relics of the sixties, just like Boney. One leg of his jeans was slit up the side to accommodate a leg brace that squeaked loudly whenever he moved. I couldn't help thinking of the tin man in the *Wizard of Oz*. This guy was definitely over the rainbow.

"Come on in," Crider said.

"Thanks. Mind if my dog comes in, too?"

"No. Buster could use some company."

I stepped inside. The place was dark and kind of dingy and smelled strong of recently smoked weed. I could have gotten a buzz from just breathing the air. Cruiser and Buster were already engaged in the butt-sniff boogie.

"Does it matter where I sit?" I asked, noticing that there was no chair without a stack of newspapers or books on it. Boney Crider must have spent a good deal of his time reading, judging from the collection of printed matter. Isaac Azimov and Amazing Stories, mostly, but he was also obviously a Trekkie, judging from his collection of *Star Trek* comics and memorabilia. I had no doubt that this was going to be some amazing interview. Judging from the reels, rods and nets that made up the rest of the paraphernalia littering his place, Boney spent the rest of his time fishing. There was also a metal detector leaning in the corner with the fishing tackle.

"Oh, sorry. Let me clear a space for you."

"I see you like reading science fiction."

"Oh, yeah. I'm into pyramids, too. Did you know I can transport myself to other galaxies?"

"Is that so? Do you use a bubbler or a bong for that?"

"There are thousands of alien civilizations out there that look nothing like you or me. Some aliens are ten feet tall. Others are like dwarves."

I didn't know if there was much point in interviewing this crackpot, but editor's orders prevailed.

"Well, why don't you tell me about what you saw out there in the lake."

An odd expression came over his face that I couldn't quite read. He cleared off another chair for himself, and we settled in for the interview. His brace squeaked like a trapped mouse as he sat.

"Mr. Crider, why don't we start by getting a little background information about you? Mind if I tape?" I wished I'd started taping sooner.

"Okay by me. And it's Boney. Everyone calls me Boney." He pulled a cigar box out from a drawer in the end table nearest him and opened it. "Want a smoke?" he asked, lighting up a joint.

"No, thanks. Never touch the stuff." I wanted to stay on Planet Earth for this interview.

"I take it for this," he said, slapping the leg with the brace. "And the arthritis, too. Gets bad living on the lake, especially in the winter."

Ordinarily, I would have objected to anyone smoking anything in my presence, but I couldn't deny the guy his medicine. I watched as Boney lit a joint. Smoke curled upward in a thin, gray thread, like the threads dangling from his ripped pants leg.

"How did you hurt your leg, Boney?" I saw the scars and had to ask.

"Same way most of the guys my age did—the ones that survived. 'Nam. I traded a good leg for that." He pointed to the wall, where a Purple Heart was displayed in a frame.

"Boney, that's an unusual name. It's not your real name, is it?"

"No, just a nickname that stuck. I used to be skinny."

"How long have you lived here?"

"Long time. Near twenty years."

"Any family?"

"Buster is my family, and he's all the family I want." Buster came to his master's side at the mention of his name. "It's him that alerted me to the trouble out on the lake."

"Why don't you tell me about it."

When Boney took another drag of his arthritis cure, I began to wonder why I'd even bothered coming here. It was probably a huge waste of time, but I was here now, so I'd see it through.

"It was a couple of nights ago, around sunset. I was eating supper when I heard Buster barking his head off down by the lake. I figured something was up, so I went to see what was the matter. I thought it was probably just the coyotes. They wander past here every evening at sundown."

"I know. I see them at my place, too. What happened then?"

"Well, I saw this guy in a motorboat a ways out in the water. I was just about to holler at him when his boat flipped right over like a toy in a bathtub. He was yelling and screaming for help. Buster jumped in and swam straight for him. I tried, too, but I don't swim so good with this leg of mine. He'd already gone under by the time Buster got to him."

"Was the wind up that night?" I asked.

"No."

"Did you see any other boats in the area that could have caused a wake?"

"No other boats, and the water was as calm as could be. All except for the boiling."

"Boiling?"

"It looked like the water was boiling or like a school of fish was feeding near the surface. It happened once before when I was out fishing, just before I got yanked overboard when something took my bait and wouldn't let go."

"Caught yourself a big one, huh?" I'd have to tell Skip about this. He was an avid fisherman who was forever angling for the King Trout that lived somewhere in Tahoe.

"Guess you could say that," Boney said. "It was Tahoe Tessie." I would have laughed except for the fact that he was dead serious when he said it. I'd always heard marijuana has just the opposite effect. Of course, I hadn't forgotten to whom I was talking, either.

"How do you know that?" I asked, tongue-in-cheek.

"Why, I saw the thing with my own eyes."

CHAPTER ELEVEN

I was still thinking about my weird conversation with Boney Crider as I drove from Rubicon back toward South Shore. I would never have believed what the pothead war hero had told me if he hadn't been as convincing as he was. That plus the fact that I half-believed in Tahoe's supposed resident sea monster myself. Being part Washoe means I believe in a lot of things, like water babies and other so-called mythical creatures that inhabit the Lake of the Sky. All the strange goings-on at Tahoe of late led me to believe that the spirits of my ancestors were not pleased. I still remember how my great-grandmother cried whenever we drove through the tunnel at Cave Rock on the way from Carson City. The whites had blasted clean through *De ek wa dop push,* the sacred tor of the Washoe, to make way for progress and ultimately the demise of our civilization.

I could already hear Skip hee-haw when I told him what Boney said. At least the story would make for attention-grabbing headlines in the *Tattler,* which would no doubt please Carla. Stories of the lake monster had floated around Tahoe for years, but they were always considered folklore. The people who claimed to have seen the creature were categorized as either New Age ninnies or completely cracked. Boney Crider would surely fall into the latter category. Still, his dog had seen something out there, too. I trust dogs more than I trust most people. Unfortunately, I couldn't interview Buster. He wasn't talking.

My own dog was having the time of his life hanging out the passenger window taking in the smell-a-rama of scents in the air. I could see blue skies through the open sunroof. I figured this was as close to heaven as I'd ever get. We were just rounding the hairpin at Eagle Rock when I noticed a car coming up fast behind me. Doggone tourists! Always in such a dang hurry. If you're not going to take a little time to appreciate one of the most scenic spots on earth, why come to Tahoe and spoil it for everyone else?

I pedaled the gas. This was as good a time as any to give my new wheels a spin. I sped up. So did the black Mercedes Benz behind me until it was tailgating again. I depressed the gas pedal, but still it was too slow for the jerk hugging my bumper. This wasn't a good stretch of road on which to play jackrabbit. There was more than one dead man's curve on this highway if you weren't careful. Cruiser didn't seem to be enjoying our wild ride any more than I was. I was glad I'd installed a seat restraint for him. It was time to pull over and let this speed demon pass us.

I steered toward the shoulder and motioned for my bumper hugger to pass, but he wouldn't. He stayed glued to me. When his bumper tapped ours, I knew this wasn't just some antsy tourist. This guy meant business. The hood ornament looked like the crosshairs of a rifle in my rearview mirror. I couldn't tell much about the driver's identity through the smoked glass of his windshield, and the reflection of the sun didn't help. Right now I was more intent on avoiding being a D.O.A than getting an I.D. If Cruiser and I weren't going to end up taking a shortcut off the cliff, I'd have to take quick action. I saw my chance up ahead at the turnoff for Cascade Lake.

"Hang on, Cruiser! We're taking a detour." As we entered the next curve, I veered to the right. We shot into the turnoff in a cloud of dust, nearly colliding with a forest ranger's Jeep. I slammed on the brakes and skidded to a safe stop. I heaved a sigh of relief as the Mercedes kept going. I managed to catch a glimpse of the vanity license plate, DIGG IT, as the Benz sped on around the bend.

"You okay, fella?" My co-pilot seemed no worse for wear after our harrowing roller coaster ride. I couldn't say the same for myself.

The ranger backed up his truck and rolled down his window. "You okay, ma'am?"

"Yes, I'm fine, thanks."

"That guy was in one heck of a hurry, huh?"

"You can say that again." I was thankful that the chase was over and I was still alive to tell about it.

"Tourists. Won't we be glad when September comes and they all go home?"

I nodded. Cruiser licked my right hand, which I interpreted as agreement.

CHAPTER TWELVE

After our nearly disastrous drive from Boney Crider's hideaway, my old log homestead looked especially welcoming. Nona met us at the door, and Cruiser made tracks for his hairy pillow. He'd had enough adventure for the morning. So had I.

"Well, how was your maiden cruise with your Cruisers?"

"Not so great."

"What's wrong, Mom? You look flustered. Did you have car trouble?"

"You could say that."

"What happened? Get a flat tire or something?"

"No, the car was fine."

"What's wrong, then?"

"Someone tried to run us off the road."

"I guess Tahoe isn't immune to road rage." Nona gloated because I always complained about traffic and rude drivers in the city.

"I guess not, if that's what it was."

"What do you mean?" Nona's pretty brow furrowed as her condescension became concern.

"I got an uncomfortable feeling that the guy was trying to take us out."

"Well, that's what road rage is all about, Mom," Nona said. "Heck, people shoot at each other these days for not getting out of the way fast enough."

"At least he didn't have a gun, or I hope he didn't."

"Well, I hope you got his license number."

"Yes, I did get a fleeting glimpse."

"You can report it to Skip, and he'll track the jerk down before he really hurts someone."

"I will."

Nona shifted gears again, as befits her youth. Perhaps she intended to take my mind off the unpleasant incident near Eagle Rock. "Say, when are we going to take that bike ride together?"

"I don't know, dear."

"How about this afternoon?"

"This afternoon? Well . . . I have an interview to transcribe, and . . ."

"Oh, come on. It'll do you good to get some fresh air and exercise. You work too hard." Nona had a Cruiser-begging-for-biscuits look in her eyes, and it was always hard to say no to that. I figured the tape with Boney Crider's purple haze blather on it could easily wait. Still, I sensed there was a dash of truth in the tale he'd cooked up for this *Tahoe Tattler* reporter.

"Okay," I said. "Only you'd better check with the house hound about this plan. He looks pretty pooped to me."

Cruiser didn't need much convincing. As soon as Nona uttered the G-word, "Go," he was at the front door. I hadn't named him Cruiser for nothing.

Nona wanted to rent mountain bikes, but I insisted on a more sedate surrey with the fringe on top. The gaily-striped cover would shade us and Cruiser, who sat between us on the bench seat as we pedaled. We stopped at the Camp Richardson Resort store and bought some sandwiches and drinks. We'd stop to eat our lunch when we reached Tallac Historic Site.

"Oh, Mom. Why did we have to ride on one of these silly-looking things? Everyone's laughing at us."

"Don't look now, but I think they're really laughing at our

silly-looking cycling buddy here."

Cruiser was much more relaxed on this ride than the one we'd taken together that morning. So was I. Nona was right. It was good to get out in the fresh air and appreciate the scenery from a little safer location than at the edge of a cliff. Mount Tallac was as splendid in summer as in winter, although only a dab of snow topped her peaks in July. The sky was sapphire, a perfect reflection of the Jewel of the Sierra.

Tallac Historic Site was an ideal place for a summer picnic. Fortunately, not many people seemed to flock to this spot. The beaches at Pope and Richardson drew the largest crowds, mainly because of the campgrounds there. We found an empty table and ate our lunch while Cruiser sniffed the trees and bushes for interesting messages—postcards from the hedge. It was the only time Cruiser was keen for anything besides food.

"I forgot to ask," Nona said. "How did your interview with the old hermit go this morning?"

"Okay, I guess. Different."

"What did he say?"

"You wouldn't believe me if I told you."

"C'mon, Mom. You've piqued my curiosity. You'll have to tell me now."

"Okay, but don't laugh. He told me he saw Tessie."

"Tessie?" Nona chortled.

"You promised you wouldn't laugh, now."

"I can't help it. You mean that stupid sea monster you were joking about?"

"Yes, only it would be a lake monster in this case, and I'm not entirely sure it's a joke. There have been several sightings of late. This was just one."

"Yeah, but what were the people under the influence of when they saw it?"

"Well, this particular witness was smoking grass."

"I rest my case," Nona said.

"Call me crazy, but I'm convinced there's something to it."

"Okay, you're crazy."

"Not all the sightings have been from screwballs like Boney Crider. One of them is even a senator from Washington."

"You mean to tell me there are no screwballs in Washington?"

"Point taken. At any rate, I'm not writing this off as total hogwash. You haven't forgotten what happened aboard the *Dixie Queen* on July 4th."

"No, I haven't forgotten." Nona began nibbling on the last half of her sandwich.

"We were nearly scuttled by something, and it was something *big*."

"Couldn't have been as big as this sandwich. I'm stuffed. Where's Cruiser, anyway? I'll bet he'd like the rest of this."

"Good question. Where *is* he?" We'd been so busy gabbing that I'd lost track of him again, a constant hazard with a breed that has a nose equipped with millions of scent cells. Just then I thought I heard a familiar bark down by the water's edge. I took off down the path to round him up, and Nona followed.

"Cruiser, oh Cruuuuiiiiser!"

"Didn't you put his new GPS transmitter on his collar? You'd find him right away with that."

"No, I forgot." I wished that I had. I was wasting my time calling him, and I knew it. I'd never met a basset hound yet that would answer the call of his master while out in the field, at least not until he was good and ready, or there was reason to be disobedient. No wonder they created GPS for dogs. The inventor must have had a basset. I began to run toward the sound of Cruiser's barking, which seemed frenzied.

When Nona and I reached him, Cruiser stood at the water's edge still barking his head off at something. There was nobody around. No dogs. No squirrels. Nothing that would elicit such a response in my normally sedate dog.

"What's gotten into that nutty dog of yours?"

"Beats me. Maybe he saw some geese or something." At least that's what I thought until I saw the deep, sweeping groove dug into the sand along the beach. It looked as though something heavy had been dragged for a distance along the shore. We followed the strange tracks in the sand to the spot where they disappeared into the lake. I noticed air bubbles fizzing on the water's surface. Nona and I heard a series of odd grunts, then silence.

"What do you think that was, Mom?"

"I don't know, honey. I just don't know."

CHAPTER THIRTEEN

At day's end, I was worn out. It was good to be home relaxing with my hound dog, or trying to. After my surreal chat with Boney Crider, a harrowing brush with death on a Highway 89 hairpin, and heaven knows what on the beach at Tallac, I was ready for some down time on the couch with Cruiser. Nona was out with her friends, so I had the place to myself for a little while. Not that I mind my daughter staying with me, but I guess I've grown accustomed to living alone. At this stage of life, I seem to have a greater need for solitude. I also dwell on the obituary page in the newspaper more than I used to, and it isn't because I keep getting involved in murder investigations. I think it's more to confirm that none of my contemporaries is listed there. However, this night as I perused the obits, I spotted a familiar name.

"Ivy Diggs, 23 years of age, drowned July 4 in a boating accident," it read. "She is survived by her husband, Frank, two stepsons and a stepdaughter. A memorial will be held for her at Happy Homestead Cemetery on July 9 at 11 a.m." It had been years since I'd attended a funeral, and that was the way I had wanted to keep it. Until now.

I had an idea, but I knew Nona would disapprove. She doesn't like my getting mixed up in Skip's business, but after what I could only conclude was an attempt on my life, I felt Ivy's memorial was my business. I'd just have to keep this plan under my beanie. I wouldn't tell her that I was going to go to the memorial. What she didn't know wouldn't hurt her.

They say the criminal always returns to the scene of the crime. It would be a long time before I embarked on another lake cruise, but I figured that observing who showed up at the victim's memorial, or who didn't, might shed some light on this case. I'd have to go incognito, though, which meant Cruiser would have to stay at home this time. Almost everyone in Tahoe knew whose dog he was and would soon come to recognize the red PT Cruiser with the ears flapping in the breeze. That new car of mine was anything but low key. Good thing I hadn't traded in the old 4 × 4 in the deal. No one ever noticed a beat-up Jeep in Tahoe.

Cruiser and I had just nodded off together on the couch when we heard keys jingling in the door lock. Cruiser abandoned his hairy pillow and waddled to the front door.

"Hey, Cruiser. I thought you and Mom would be snoring away by now," Nona said, entering the door and hanging her jacket on the hall tree.

"We were. Did you have a good time?"

"Sure did. We went to that new English pub, The Cock and Bull. You'll have to try it, Mom. It's awesome. We even played darts like you and Dad used to."

"Your dad taught me how to play. I even won a competition once. They awarded me with a basket of scented soaps."

"Cool." Whenever my daughter said "cool" I knew she was thoroughly unimpressed. Nona slipped out of her heels and into her moccasins and collapsed into Tom's old easy chair. It was the same chair where as a little girl she had sat in her father's lap as he read to her. I know that sitting in it whenever she visits me is a comfort to Nona.

"Meet anyone interesting at the pub, honey? Any hotties hanging out there tonight?"

"Oh, one or two."

"Is that all?" Nona is usually close-mouthed about her male friends for fear I will disapprove of her choices. She mentioned the one now only because she was (1) getting a month-long vacation at one of the most beautiful spots in the world and free room and board to boot, and (2) certain that what she had to tell me might be of interest to me. She was so right.

"As a matter of fact, I ran into that guy from the *Dixie Queen*."

"Which guy is that?"

"The good-looking one who started talking to us when we were at the viewing area on the lower deck."

"Oh, yeah. And?"

"We had a couple of drinks and got to chatting." I noted the somewhat disturbing fact that he'd been drinking both times Nona had been with him.

"What did you talk about?"

"His stepmother mostly. He told me the memorial for her is tomorrow. He said he doesn't want to go."

"Why not?"

"Said his heart wouldn't be in it. He said Ivy just married his father for the money."

"I gathered that might have been the case. He looked quite a bit older than she did."

"Old enough to be her father. Can you imagine?"

"How much Viagra do you suppose that guy went through in a month?"

Nona laughed. "His dad is the founder of Diggs Dive and Expedition. Bob and his brother Ted work in the company, too."

"A real family affair, huh?"

"Apparently so. He gives diving lessons. He offered to teach me for free!"

"Well, that's nice, I guess, but I didn't know you were interested in diving." Great, Nona's taking up skin diving.

Something else for me to worry about. I envisioned her getting gobbled up whole by Jaws . . . or worse.

"I wasn't until now." Nona winked at me and smiled. I smiled back, but it was only on the outside. Inside, I was concerned not only about her becoming shark bait but about her getting mixed up with the Diggs clan. For all I knew, one of them was a murderer. Possibly the same one who'd been flirting with her.

"This Bob's awfully talkative with a complete stranger, isn't he?"

"Well, I'm not a complete stranger. We've met before, remember? Besides, he'd had a little too much to drink I guess."

Loose lips sink ships, I thought. And sometimes wicked stepmothers.

CHAPTER FOURTEEN

The day of Ivy Diggs' memorial was sunny and unusually muggy. Earthquake weather, my mother used to call it. My disguise of sunglasses and a black, wide-brimmed hat wouldn't seem out of place, but it would be uncomfortable wearing black in such warm weather. I had kept my mourning suit from Tom's funeral years before and had worn the simple black dress and jacket, perked up with bright scarves and jewelry, for business meetings and interviews. This was only the second time I had worn the hat. I hoped it would be the last. It looked as hideous and unattractive as I felt wearing it, but the brim and netting obscured my face so I wouldn't be recognized, unless someone mistook me for the Reaper's beekeeper.

I parked the Jeep in front of Happy Homestead Cemetery and slipped in among the group of people assembled in the chapel. There were enough black-draped mourners present for me not to be noticed, since everyone's attention was focused on Reverend Ramseth, who was delivering the eulogy. Everyone except for me. I was observing the assembly and taking mental notes.

The only one not present was the one Nona told me about: Bob, or Bobby, as I had heard him called on the *Dixie Queen*. I figured he must be in a bar somewhere, chatting up someone else's daughter instead of attending his stepmother's funeral. Whether or not he wanted to go, it would have been respectful to be there. I noticed more and more that people of his and

Nona's generation were not burdened with the same sense of duty as those in mine were. I grew up with codes of ethics like "Do unto others," "Children should be seen and not heard," and "Ours is not to reason why; ours is but to do or die." Although, I surmised from what I'd observed thus far that it wasn't a case of ethics that caused Mrs. Diggs to end up dead.

"We are gathered here on this glorious day in a place appropriately named Heavenly Valley to remember our dear, departed Ivy."

Frank was flanked by his daughter and a son. The grieving widower looked appropriately grief-stricken. Could have been an act, I thought, but it appeared genuine. I couldn't say the same for the other family members. Dora stood close beside her father, comforting him. She had a faraway look that conveyed she'd rather be someplace else. Ted's face showed as much emotion as a Sphinx. It seemed to me that he would have preferred to be someplace else, too. No great love lost there, apparently. But then, most men aren't prone to public displays of emotion, even at funerals.

The reverend continued his litany. "Loving wife and mother, Ivy will never be forgotten by those who loved her and a community that . . ."

Suddenly an odd sound emitted from somewhere nearby. When heads snapped in my direction, I realized it was coming from me. My purse was playing music! "Scotland the Brave" repeated several times before I could fish the cell phone out of the recesses of my bag and hit the right button to answer it.

"Who is this?" I hissed into the phone.

"Hey, Mom. Just testing to see if you figured out how to use your phone."

"Obviously I did, but your timing sucks."

"Why? Where are you?"

"Someplace where it's awkward to talk right now."

"You're not at that woman's funeral, are you? I saw where you circled her obit in the paper."

"Yes."

"Wouldn't it be better if you let Skip handle this business with Ivy Diggs?"

"Can't talk now. I'll talk to you later, okay?"

"You'd better."

The phone clicked. I shoved the cell phone back into my purse and made tracks for the car before I got any more dirty looks from the bereaved, if there really were any of those present at Ivy Diggs' mock memorial.

The second I got back to my car the cell phone rang again. Only this time it wasn't Nona.

"Skip, how did you get this number?"

"From Nona."

"She's probably shouting it to the mountaintops that her old-fashioned mother has finally joined the twenty-first century."

"Well, maybe it's a good thing. It makes it easier for me to keep in touch with you when I need to. Like now."

"What's up?"

"Just checking to see if you'd found out anything else about Ivy Diggs. I see they had a memorial for her today."

"I just left there."

"You did? What a nosy thing you are."

"Oh, come on, Skip. You know you wanted to go, too. You're just as nosy as I am. Nosier."

"Actually, I was planning to be there, but I couldn't get away from the office."

Skip wasn't fooling me one bit. He knew me well enough by now. "I can tell you're just dying to cross-examine me. Want to get together for coffee or something?"

"I've got a better idea. How would you and Cruiser like to go fishing this evening after I get off work?"

"Still determined to catch that super trout on the *Trout Scout*, huh?"

"I'll never give up until he's mounted on my wall."

"Okay, what time?"

"Meet me at the dock around six. We'll have plenty of light left."

After Skip hung up, I decided to try initiating a call on the cell phone. I dialed Professor Blayne.

"Blayne here," he answered.

"Hello, Professor Blayne, this is Elsie MacBean."

"Oh, hello there." I loved hearing that English accent again.

"I hope I'm not interrupting anything important. I just wanted to touch base with you about that demonstration you promised. When would be a good time?"

"How about right now?"

"Uh, well, sure. That would be fine."

"Splendid. Meet me at Diggs Marina in an hour then."

"I'll be there."

"Great. Dress casual and better wear your tennies."

The line clicked. I didn't own any tennis shoes. My Nike joggers would have to suffice. I hope I wasn't going to need them to keep a lead on the charming Mr. Blayne. I was beginning to get the idea that he was a ladies' man with a long line of conquests. Austin Powers, eat your heart out. Blayne had better teeth, though.

CHAPTER FIFTEEN

I spotted Crispin when I arrived at Diggs Marina. He wasn't hard to spot.

"Nice to see you again, Elsie," Crispin said.

"You, too, Crispin."

"Cris, remember?"

"Cris."

"Did you have any trouble finding the place?"

"Well, it does seem to be hiding from the rest of the world." The marina was located on private land and well secluded from throngs of tourists who frequented the Ski Run marina and beach. No smell of hot dogs and sweaty, sunburned bodies permeated the air at Diggs Marina. No jet skis were rented out here, but the Tahoe jet set knew where Diggs docked his fleet of expensive speedboats and yachts. Skip's *Trout Scout* outboard would look like a dinghy next to Diggs' stable of sleek thoroughbreds. But even those didn't impress me as much as what was locked inside the boathouse.

"Where else would you expect me to conduct my top secret project?"

"Top secret?" This guy was starting to seem more like 007 by the second.

Crispin unlocked the door and ushered me inside the dark building.

"I'm having you on. It's just that I'd rather keep this under wraps until I have gathered more data. If tourists spot this floating around in the lake, curiosity seekers might interfere with my studies."

He flipped a switch, and the fluorescent overhead lights flickered a little. I couldn't believe my eyes. "My gosh, you have a submarine!" Moored in the building was a fourteen-foot torpedo-shaped craft. Its color perfectly matched the cobalt blue of Lake Tahoe, which aided in camouflaging it from prying eyes.

"A mini-sub, actually. It's specially equipped with the DART system for my studies."

"This must have cost a fortune."

"A few bob," Crispin commented.

"Who pays for all this?" I asked.

"It's privately funded."

"By whom?"

"I'm really not at liberty to say. Top secret, you know."

"So, why are you telling me? I'm with the press."

"There's something about you that assures me you will keep it quiet if I ask you to, at least for a while." He looked deep into my eyes. "Will that be a problem?" Suddenly I felt like a cobra under the spell of a snake charmer.

"N-no problem."

"Jolly good, then." The spell was broken, but I still felt strangely under his power. Crispin gestured to the open hatch of the sub. "Care to take her for a spin?"

"I suppose so." I remembered the submarine ride at Disneyland where Tom and I took Nona when she was seven, but that one ran on tracks. This was a real sub. I just hoped he knew how to work the thing. I'd been on the lake many times, but this would be my first time in a submarine with a handsome Englishman. This aging Beatles fan was thinking how "fab" it would be if the submarine was yellow, but the minute I stepped down into the confined quarters of the DART sub, I knew I'd never want to live in a yellow submarine, not even with Crispin Blayne.

Crispin maneuvered the mini-sub away from the dock and it slowly submerged. He flipped a toggle switch on the instrument panel, and I heard an odd whirring sound above us.

"What's that noise?" I asked. I felt myself begin to flush. Whether it was claustrophobia or a hot flash was hard to tell.

"Relax, Elsie. It's just the periscope engaging. Here, have a look."

I peered through the spyglass. Crispin flipped another toggle and the periscope rotated slowly, revealing a diorama of Lake Tahoe's splendid scenery.

"I'll bet you've never seen Lake Tahoe quite like this before, have you?"

"Can't say that I have." A jet skier whizzed in wide circles a few hundred yards off. He didn't spot us, but Crispin retracted the periscope just to be sure he wouldn't.

"We'll be diving now," Crispin said. "We're heading toward Rubicon Bay."

"Is that the location of the fissure you were telling me about?"

"Yes. I'll be gathering mineral samples in the area. There's a solid wall of rock that extends fourteen hundred feet below the water's surface."

"Guess that's why you need this sub. It's a lot smaller inside than it looks on the outside, though."

"It's designed to hold two people, three at most. I usually have an assistant who comes along on these dives and helps me take readings. Perhaps you'd do the honors today."

"Sure. If you'll show me how."

"Certainly. There's nothing to it, really. It simply requires a good pair of eyes."

He had me there. I hated to do it, but I put on my bifocals.

Fortunately, they were the invisible kind. Through the sub's porthole, my eyes were seeing Tahoe from an entirely different perspective. This was a whole other world beneath our world that I had never known existed—a fantastic realm of subterranean peaks, windswept plains, perfectly preserved geological formations and artifacts from Tahoe's history.

"This is amazing!" I said.

"Indeed it is. This is the seamount. The terrain here is very much like that above us."

"Yes, I can tell that this landscape was once above water."

"The level of the lake used to be much lower than it is now. You can see the same varieties of plant life here as you see now on the surface."

I was amazed at the clarity of the water. The growth of plankton due to pollution had not yet sullied her waters, but the buildup of sediment from overdevelopment of the land above was slowly obscuring the landscape. A whirlwind of silt churned by the sub's propellers looked like an underwater blizzard in the illumination from the powerful halogen spotlights on the bow of the DART. As the sub dove deeper yet, my ears popped, and I felt my stomach lurch like I was dropping in an elevator shaft. With any luck, I wouldn't toss my cookies and turn this into a yellow submarine after all.

CHAPTER SIXTEEN

The DART sub submerged into Tahoe's waters and made way for Glenbrook, the gravesite of the steamer *Tahoe*. This was where she had sunk and come to rest on a sandbank at 375 feet below the surface on August 29, 1940, when D.L. Bliss scuttled his beloved craft rather than have her put on display for tourists to carve their names in or, worse, have it be sold for scrap.

From Emerald Bay to Rubicon Bay to Glenbrook, the lake is the final resting place for sunken craft and shipwrecks, some of which have yet to be located. Some were lost in turbulent squalls, others, like the steamer *Tahoe*, were scuttled when they became obsolete or unprofitable to operate. Many of these craft were used to transport cargo, mail, even gold and silver. Who knew what treasures lay far below us awaiting discovery?

The true site of the steamer *Tahoe*, hundreds of feet deeper than originally thought, had been located only in recent years with the technology of that time. The advanced navigation and detection systems of DART were capable of locating objects at far greater depths than had ever been reached before.

Silent as a ghost, the DART sub glided past the sunken lady of the lake. Every detail of her elegantly crafted woodwork was perfectly preserved; not a single metal bolt was corroded by time and the waters of the lake's depths, which would not be the case in salt water. Through the porthole I glimpsed the promenade decks. I imagined the ladies of her heyday in the 1890s, adorned in their finery, strolling on the arms of gents along the polished wood deck. I saw them admiring the breathtaking mountain panorama of a century ago from the benches that lined the promenade.

Still intact after so many years, the teak benches were covered with a dusting of fine white silt, looking as they might have when the 190-foot-long craft traversed the lake in a winter snowstorm. I had been on the lake when the mountains were coated in white, like great bears of the North, and the snow blew in horizontal sheets. Tahoe was a different world on those days, as white as goose down, as pure as a mountain spring. The scars of the white man's influence were hidden from sight, and Tahoe appeared once again clean and unspoiled, as my ancestors knew it.

Crispin brought me quickly back to the present with his announcement. "The clarity of this lake makes Loch Ness look like a peat bog."

"Didn't Jacques Cousteau explore this lake, too?" I asked.

"Almost all 39 billion gallons of it. It's purported that he led an expedition to what was believed to be the bottom of the lake at that time. In fact, we now know the lake is much deeper than was originally thought. Mr. Cousteau never revealed his findings or showed the film footage he took to anyone. He was simply reported to have said, 'the world wasn't ready' for what he found down there."

"Gosh, makes you wonder what he saw, doesn't it, Cris? I'd sure like to have a look at that film."

"So would I. No one knows where it is. It may have been destroyed. Cousteau may have destroyed it himself. That's assuming the story is even true. There are so many tales that surround high mountain lakes like this one, it's sometimes hard to separate fact from fiction."

"I know what you mean. Up here we have many Washoe legends as well as those perpetuated by pioneers of the last century. I admit that there are some pretty fantastic stories about Lake Tahoe, but I have no doubt some of them are true."

"Well, I hope that my newly collected data may confirm some of those truths."

As a Native American writer, I was naturally more intrigued with storytelling and fiction, but what we were about to discover was beyond any fantastic fiction I could ever have imagined.

CHAPTER SEVENTEEN

As we approached the 500-foot depth, the mysterious underwater world beneath Tahoe had grown as dark and sunless as a tomb. What I next witnessed I could only describe as something straight out of a Stephen King novel.

"It looks like we have some obstacles up ahead," Crispin said.

"Obstacles?" What could they be? Another underwater mountain range? An uncharted shipwreck?

"I'm not sure what this is, but it's going to make for some tricky navigating. I'll need to concentrate through this stretch. See what you can spy out the porthole."

"Will do." Only the increasing frequency of electronic blips filled the silence of the sub's cabin as we propelled forward. The silence was split by my gasp of horror.

"What is it, Elsie? What do you see?" My tongue wouldn't work, and even if it had, I couldn't have found the words to describe the surreal scene we had come upon.

Crispin slowed the craft to a crawl and peered outside the porthole, too. "Good Lord! Do you know what this is?"

We both fell silent as we gazed on a field of corpses seemingly suspended by some unseen hand like hideous marionettes. I had heard tales of the "body layer" of the lake where drowning victims sank and came to rest in the frigid waters. That was why they never surfaced and the lake never gave up her dead, as Skip so aptly put it. I never believed those stories to be true until now. Here they all were in an underwater morgue, the incorruptible dead of Lake Tahoe, preserved through the centuries.

Navigating through the ghastly underwater catacomb was like hell's history lesson, Rocky's horror fashion show—long, flowing dresses of the nineteenth century, flapper dresses of the Roaring Twenties, even Sixties' flower power and teeny weenie bikinis. There were bearded pioneers and trappers. Still others were in native Washoe dress. My grandfather had told me of how in burial ceremonies of yesteryear, our people's dead were hurled into the lake from the promontory of Cave Rock. Is this where they had come to rest?

Tattered garments of the dead billowed like sheets hung out to dry on a breezy day. Hollow eye sockets gaped from waxen faces, and lifeless limbs waved a macabre greeting in the currents of the lake. Some parts of the cadavers had been nibbled away by fish and crabs. I swallowed hard as I felt my stomach lurch and my gorge threatening to rise. I could stand no more.

"Please, Cris, let's get out of here."

"We should be out of it in a moment. I'm taking her down deeper."

I sighed with relief. I understood why Cousteau had kept his discovery a secret. I thought it best that it remain one. I only hoped Crispin felt the same.

Our small craft dove to even greater depths. I began to wonder what other strange and terrifying mysteries awaited us in the deepest, uncharted waters of the lake. After what I had observed thus far, I had begun to feel somewhat apprehensive—even fearful of what further escapades I may have let myself in for on this voyage to the bottom of the lake. I had also begun to feel claustrophobic in the sub's small cabin. Sweat beaded on my forehead, but this was no hot flash. This was just raw fear. Crispin sensed my discomfort and tried to distract me with conversation. "There's the new fissure I was telling you about, Elsie," Crispin said.

It looked far larger than he had described. From this perspective, the crevasse looked like the Grand Canyon.

"Will it get any bigger, you think?"

"That's partly what I'm here to discover. By studying the surrounding geology, I can tell where it's headed. There appears to have been considerable seismic upheaval here already."

The flash from a special underwater camera snapping photos of the area lit the surrounding terrain like midday. I was glad that Crispin had chosen not to photograph the underground burial site we had just passed through. It would have been somehow sacrilegious. Photographing corpses was more Skip's line of work. I wondered what he'd think about my being down here in a submarine alone with the handsome professor. Ordinarily I'd say he wouldn't have given a rat's flaming fanny, but his behavior ever since the Tahoe Terror incidents had me puzzled and, I confess, a little intrigued. He had become downright protective of me.

"Well, Cris, you'll let me know when I should relocate to Sacramento, won't you?"

"With the tsunami that would result from a quake of the same magnitude as Loma Prieta or greater, you could surf all the way there."

I laughed, but recalling some of the jolts we'd felt in the basin and surrounding areas, I knew he wasn't kidding about the devastation that would result from such a powerful quake. Rock and roll had taken on a whole new meaning for Tahoe residents in recent years. Mount Rose and Mount Pluto had been active volcanoes during the Cretaceous period. There's nothing to say they couldn't become active again. Mount St. Helens had surprised the heck out of a lot of Washingtonians in the 1980s by blowing her top.

As we approached the stone gorges of Rubicon, Crispin engaged the robotic arm to gather the mineral samples he said he had come on this strange journey for. The arm was fitted with a kind of vacuum that collected and stored the samples in a receptacle until they could be studied later.

The sub maneuvered with agility among the remarkable geologic formations. We passed through natural arches and underwater caves. One was nearly as large as Cave Rock on the East Shore.

"I need you to watch that DART scanner closely for me, Elsie, and tell me if you see any kind of change in the field. If you do, let me know so I can start taking a reverb reading."

"Will do."

I watched the pulsing iridescent green light sweep a black field. Nothing was happening. The sound of a steady blip, blip, blip filled the silence. Then the blips hiccupped.

"Hey! I think there's something out there."

He studied the monitor for a moment. "Oh, that's just a school of mackinaw. Probably some forty-pounders. They grow big out here."

"Wow, I'll have to tell Skip he's been fishing in the wrong place."

"Who is Skip?"

"He's the sheriff in these parts. Also a good friend of mine."

"You've known him a long time, then?"

"Yes, since before my husband died a few years back. He and Skip were best friends."

"I'm sorry about your husband."

"Thanks."

"What happened to him?"

"He was killed in a forest fire. Tom was a firefighter."

"I see. So, you haven't remarried?"

"Nope."

"Not even a boyfriend?"

Suddenly this sub seemed a trifle smaller than it had a moment ago.

"No boyfriend." I swung the spotlight in his direction. "What about you? You married?"

"Divorced."

"Must be pretty recent."

"How do you know that?" I pointed to his narrowed ring finger. "Ah, very observant of you."

"And what about you, Cris? Do you have a girlfriend?"

Crispin smiled at me in a way no man had smiled at me in a long time. "Not at the moment." I was diving deeper into the vast lake of his blue eyes when suddenly the blips on the DART monitor sped up noticeably. Both our heads snapped around to watch the monitor. The black field was almost entirely green.

"Blimey! We've got something big this time."

Neither of us knew then just *how* big.

CHAPTER EIGHTEEN

Again I peered out the porthole of the sub while the professor took readings and the aquatic camera snapped repeatedly. I watched the needle swing in wide arcs. I couldn't see anything through the porthole except the formations of this underwater rock garden, but the rapid blips and reverb readings told a different story. So did the sound picked up by the transducers linking the sub to the control base back at the docking area. We were both baffled by the sounds we heard—a distinct series of grunts and then a long, mournful groan.

"I've heard this sound before, Elsie."

"What do you think it could be?"

"I'm not sure, but it sounds very much like what I and my Scottish team heard during the exploration of Loch Ness last year. I just hope the camera out there is getting good snaps of what I'm seeing on this screen. I'll know more after I've had a chance to decipher the DART's readings and recordings." For the first time since our underwater cruise had embarked, Crispin looked a little worried. "I think perhaps we'd better head back now."

"Are we in any danger?" I'd nearly been shipwrecked once on the *Dixie Queen*. I didn't care to repeat the experience.

"I don't think so. Better to be safe than sorry, though."

The sub progressed slowly, cautiously back through the rock formations in the subterranean Grand Canyon.

Suddenly there was a terrible rumbling sound, like underwater thunder. Everything inside the sub began to vibrate.

"What's happening, Cris?"

"It must be an earthquake! Grab on to something!"

The sub began to shake violently. Powerful shock waves caused the small craft to buck like a bronco. I peered out the porthole to see what was going on. Fear gripped me when I saw enormous chunks of stone breaking away and plummeting to the lake bottom. A shower of debris pummeled the outer hull like hail. A massive one narrowly missed the sub's stern. Crispin somehow navigated the craft through the quaking labyrinth unscathed, and we were once again in quiet, unobstructed waters.

I was glad when we finally reached Diggs Marina and Crispin helped me out of the confining sub. The submarine ride at Disneyland was never this exciting!

"I'd be interested to know what you find out from your readings and the photos."

"Certainly. Perhaps we could meet for dinner one evening, and we can talk about it then."

"I suppose that would be okay." No matter how hard I tried, there was just no way I was going to keep this strictly business with Crispin Blayne, and I wasn't sure I minded one bit. "Why don't you call me later in the week and we can arrange something."

I said good-bye and headed for home sweet home. When I got there, Skip, Nona, and Cruiser were waiting for me. I gave Nona a big hug. At one point on my magical mystery tour, I wasn't sure I'd ever see her again. Cruiser whined until I knelt down to hug him, too. He repeatedly licked my hands and face. I was glad to be on terra firma again. The firma the better, in my opinion.

"Gosh, boy, I haven't been gone that long."

"Hey, where's my hug?" Skip laughed.

I gave Skip a playful bear hug.

"How was your meeting with the professor, Mom?"

"Pretty scary."

"Why?" Nona asked.

"Didn't you two feel the earthquake?"

"We had an earthquake?" Nona said, glancing at Skip.

"We didn't feel anything here, Beanie. Are you sure?"

"Of course I'm sure. I was scared to death way down there in that submarine with Crispin."

"A submarine? What submarine?" Nona said.

"Blayne has a submarine?" Skip said.

Me and my big mouth. "I wasn't supposed to say anything about that. I guess I'm still a little shaken from the experience. Don't tell anyone, you two. It's top secret."

"You got to ride in it?" Skip sounded like a ten-year-old boy when he said it.

"Yes, only I wish I hadn't, especially since there was an earthquake. It must have been at least a five on the Richter Scale."

"Well, come to think of it, Cruiser has been acting kind of strange all afternoon," Nona said. "But I just thought he was missing you."

"Changes in dog and cat behavior are good indicators of seismic activity," I said. "I'm surprised you didn't feel it, too. It must have been a pretty good temblor."

"Maybe it was too far down to be felt up here," Nona said.

"Could have been a subterranean quake, I suppose, but if you'd been down there in the lake where I was. . . . I think I need a cup of coffee. Anyone care to join me?"

"Count me in," Skip said.

"Make that three cups, Mom."

"Three it is."

Thunder rumbled in the distance as I filled the coffee cups

with hot Sumatra decaf and sat down to take a much-needed rest.

"Sounds like we might be in for a little storm," Skip said.

"Oh, I love a summer storm in the mountains," Nona said, sipping her coffee.

"Well, I'm just glad I made it back here before it hit. I wouldn't want to be caught out on the lake in a thunderstorm."

"So, what's-his-name really has a submarine, huh?" Skip said.

"It's Crispin Blayne," I said.

"Yeah, I know. Gee, where do you shop for one of those around here? Subway?"

"Har de-har-har. He didn't pay for it himself, silly."

"Who did, then?"

"He wouldn't say, but whoever it is has money to burn. That thing must have cost a bundle."

"Hmm. Top secret subs. You sure he isn't a double agent?"

"Very funny."

"Say, Mom, you didn't say whether you saw Tessie down there at the bottom of the lake." Nona laughed and nudged Skip in the ribs.

"I saw something down there, all right."

"You did?" Nona and Skip chorused.

"There's a lot down there we know nothing about." I wasn't about to tell them everything I'd seen from the sub's porthole. They'd never believe me. It was no wonder Cousteau had taken the secret to his grave.

"It must have been Blayne's sub the *Queen* collided with on July 4th," Skip said. "And it was probably the sub's periscope that snagged me under the water. I also think it's what our eyewitness, Boney Crider, saw. He described something with a long neck that protruded out of the water. You think just maybe he could have been describing a periscope?" Skips words

99

dripped sarcasm like Cruiser dribbles saliva.

"So, I guess that solves the mystery of our illustrious lake monster," Nona said.

"We're overlooking one thing."

"What?" Skip looked puzzled.

"I still think we have a killer out there on the loose somewhere. You're not forgetting about our floater, are you?"

"Which one? We seem to have a surplus of those these days."

"I'm referring to Ivy Diggs."

Skip poured another cup of coffee. "There's no proof that Ivy Diggs' death wasn't an accident."

"There's no proof that it was, either."

"But Mom, with all that bashing around the *Dixie Queen* took out there on the lake, any one of us could have fallen overboard. Even you almost did. Don't you think that's probably what happened to her?"

"No, I don't, and I'm going to prove it or know the reason why. A steak knife was missing from the table, and it could certainly have been used for more than cutting filet mignon."

"You think her husband did her in with a steak knife then threw her overboard?" Nona queried. "That sounds just too bizarre, especially with all those people around to witness it."

"I can't think of a better opportunity. It was dark and everyone was watching the fireworks display. No one was paying attention to anything that might have been going on at the stern of the boat. Besides, someone had to have taken the knife. That someone had to be on the *Dixie Queen* that night, and it probably wasn't a bus boy. Any way you slice it, Ivy Diggs was cruising for a killing."

"If Sierra Sherlock says it, then it must be so," Skip joked.

"Someone thinks they've gotten away with murder, and we're going to hound everyone who was on that boat for answers, Skip, until we get to the bottom of this."

"Okay, okay. We'll hound them, only isn't that Cruiser's job?"

Cruiser heard his name and ambled over to beg a biscuit. When I didn't deliver the goods immediately, he found a way to get my attention. He did a quick headshake, and a dollop of saliva flipped from his pendulous flews and landed slap in my coffee cup.

"Nice shot, fella," I said, grimacing.

Nona and Skip exploded with laughter as I dumped my coffee into the sink. Maybe next time we'd just go to a coffee shop where I could get a cup of Java sans slobber.

CHAPTER NINETEEN

After Skip left, I decided I had better get to work on a draft of the article for the *Tattler*. Deadlines loomed, and while the pressure of a due date usually stokes my creativity, today my word flow seemed dammed up. My concentration was poor and the unusual heat wave wasn't helping, either. The thermometer outside my door registered nearly 100, and my house doesn't have air conditioning. Ordinarily, there was no need for it at Tahoe, but climate changes being what they are, I could have used it today. I opened up all the windows to try to catch a cross breeze, but there was none to catch.

Nona had gone shopping, so Cruiser and I had the place to ourselves for a while. I enjoyed having her visit, but I still needed some alone time every now and then, especially when I was brainstorming articles or novel plots. There was something about this phase of life I was entering that made living on a desert island look pretty attractive sometimes. I often wondered how Tom and I would have fared together had he survived. So many couples' relationships founder around the twenty-five-year mark, due to either female or male menopause. Men were more notorious for having affairs and buying flashy cars. I thought of my crimson coupé and my infatuation with Crispin. Apparently, women weren't immune to such midlife foolishness, either.

I certainly had plenty of material for my article. More than I could squeeze into a 2,000-word feature. I wasn't quite sure

from what angle to approach the Tessie sightings without sounding like some kind of a kook. I still had no tangible proof of her
existence. Skip's theory was far more plausible than mine, but
too much tourism relied on such interesting local lore, and I
wouldn't want to be held responsible for an economic downturn
in our community that thrived on the tourist trade. Besides, the
Washoe side of me couldn't so easily dismiss these legends. And
the skeptical sleuthhound in me wouldn't brush aside Ivy Diggs'
disappearance.

I brewed some iced tea and sat down at my laptop to face the
vast white space on the screen. I answered e-mail for half an
hour, but finally ran out of mail to answer, darn it. After
Googling around a while longer, I decided it was time to quit
stalling and get to work. About the time my opening sentence
came to me, Cruiser waddled over and planted his chin on my
knee.

I patted him on the head and told him to go lie down. He
didn't. He always seemed to want my most attention whenever
I sat down at the computer to get some work done. I could find
enough ways to procrastinate without Cruiser's help.

"You already had a biscuit, boy."

And your point would be, oh lowly food slave? Cruiser gazed
pitifully at me with those sad-sack eyes. Is it any wonder basset
hounds are so often overweight? Who could resist such a plead-
ing look? I tried ignoring him and continued typing. He didn't
budge but held his ground, knowing that eventually I would
cave in and deliver the goods. I held out longer than usual this
time so I could at least get the first paragraph or two of my
article. But when he whined pitifully, that was all she wrote.

"Oh, Poirot's pedigreed poodle! I give up! I'm getting your
biscuit, already." Cruiser's personal food slave marched duti-
fully to the closet and raided his private yum-yum reserve, but I
would serve no whine before its time. Let's see, which doggie

delicacy would it be this time? Milk Bone? Too noisy. Bacon-flavored Beggin' Strip? Nah, that would be gone in a single bite, and he'd be back beggin' for another one in two seconds flat. Only one thing would hold him for long enough to give me some quality writing time—a rawhide chewy.

"Here you go." I tossed him the chew, and he disappeared into the living room for a serious gnawing session.

I turned on the lights in my office as black clouds shrouded the sun and shadows filled the room. Thunder rolled again, only it was not so distant this time. A flash of lightning lit the sky. At last my words were starting to flow, along with the cloudburst that pelted the back deck. Thunder slammed directly overhead. The lampshades were still rattling when Cruiser barreled into the room and hid under the bed.

"Relax, boy. It's only a thunderstorm." I called him to my side and gave him a reassuring pet, then resumed typing. The thunder was coming closer on the heels of the lightning flashes, which were truly spectacular. Cruiser returned to his hiding place, but I kept on typing until I felt a strange tingling sensation course through my body. The hairs on my arms stood on end. I'd had that sensation once before when the Tahoe Terror had stalked Nona and me, but never during a thunderstorm. It could mean only one thing. Lightning was about to strike. Close!

Quicker than a lightning bolt, I snatched from the wall the plug and phone line connecting my computer. The world outside my window flashed white, and there was a sound like a dump truck being dropped off a skyscraper. The lights extinguished. The darkened room paled with successive lightning flashes, and the thunder roared as though God Himself was bellowing down at me from above.

After a while the storm moved eastward, and I could count higher between drum rolls of thunder. Cruiser and I crawled from under the bed, and I stepped out on the deck to be sure lightning hadn't hit the house and the roof hadn't caught fire. The spear of lightning had missed my cabin by only a few feet and had struck one of the towering pines nearby. A curl of smoke rose from the charred wood. The bolt had split the tree in twain.

I plugged in my computer again and had just picked up where I'd left off when the phone rang. It was Skip.

"You okay over there, Beanie?"

"Yes, Cruiser and I are fine. A little shaken up, though. That was some little storm, Skip. A lightning bolt just missed my house. I may have to get some tranquilizers for Cruiser if we have any more thunderbumpers like that one." And for Mom, too.

"Didn't much like it, huh?"

"Not a bit. He hid under the bed." Skip didn't need to know the rest. "What's up?"

"You've raised a few questions in my mind over this Diggs case. I found out that the license plate of your tailgater is registered to Frank Diggs. I'm going over to talk to him. I figured you'd want to come along for the ride."

"You bet I do."

"Can you be here at the station in half an hour?"

"Cruiser and I are on our way."

I hung up the phone, abandoned my article once more, and loaded my co-pilot in crime into the car. The downpour had stopped, so it was easy cruising over to headquarters. I rolled down the windows, partly so Cruiser could hang his head out, and partly to ventilate the car. The rain-freshened air was the perfect antidote for eau de basset.

By the time Skip, Cruiser, and I were pulling into the circular drive of Diggs' Glenbrook estate, the sun's rays had pierced the clouds. I had to help Cruiser out of the back of Skip's patrol jeep. It was too high up for stubby legs. I tied him up to a tree outside so he could enjoy the fresh air while Skip and I went inside. Besides, I didn't think the Diggs would appreciate muddy paw prints on their carpet.

Skip rang the doorbell, which sounded like Big Ben thundering through the foyer. Soon we heard the sound of footsteps, and the door opened.

Dora Diggs gave us a cold stare. "Yes?"

"Sorry to disturb you, but we'd like to talk to your father," Skip said.

"About what?"

"About your mother's death."

"Ivy was my stepmother, not my mother."

"Your stepmother," Skip corrected. "May we please come in for a few minutes?"

"My father isn't feeling well today." The aperture in the doorway narrowed.

"This won't take long." Skip didn't wait for an invitation. I took his lead and stepped into the foyer.

"Very well, but please make it brief. Wait in here." Dora ushered us into the study and disappeared down the hall.

I surveyed the ceiling-high mahogany bookshelves filled with volumes of books of every kind. It even had one of those ladders that rolls on runners so you can reach the topmost shelf. "Wow, I'd love to have a library like this one, Skip. I'd spend the rest of my life reading."

"You will have."

I laughed. "Yeah, sure. As soon as I get that million-dollar advance for my great American novel."

I heard the sound of toenails click-clicking on tile. Suddenly, a little white dog appeared in the library and started yapping at me. It was the same dog I had seen in Ivy Diggs' lap the night of her presumed drowning. Dog lover that I am, I instinctively dropped to my knees to greet it. It ran to me and leapt up at my face, showering me with kisses. It seemed starved for attention, which didn't surprise me now that it didn't have its mistress to make baby talk to it and feed it from the table.

Voices echoed down the hallway. Dora reappeared with Frank. Diggs looked a bit ragged around the edges. His face was ashen. He didn't look any happier to see us than his daughter had. Dora helped him into a wing-backed chair and gestured for us to sit down. I couldn't help noticing the scars on her wrists. Aware that I had, she tugged her sweater sleeves down to cover them.

"Sorry to disturb you today, Mr. Diggs," Skip said. "We won't take much of your time. We just have a few questions about your wife's death."

Diggs' mouth bowed and his lips quivered. "Yes?" he managed to croak. His daughter looked distressed at her father's reaction. Bitsy responded to him, too, but Dora shooed her away. She went around to the other side of the chair and tried to jump up in Frank's lap.

"Bitsy, out! *Now!*" Dora raised her hand, as though to strike the dog. Bitsy shot off down the hall.

"How long was it before you missed your wife on the boat?" Skip asked.

"Ten or fifteen minutes, I suppose," Diggs said. "As I told the police that night, I left to use the restroom and when I came back, Ivy was . . . gone."

"Were you very angry with her?" I asked.

"Yes, I suppose I was. Ivy sometimes had a tart tongue." Dora's eyebrow arched. I remembered how Ivy had talked to Frank at their anniversary party. Yes, Ivy had a tart tongue, all right. "We had an argument, but if you're trying to insinuate that I killed my wife . . ."

"We're not saying that, sir, but we have reason to believe that your wife's drowning may not have been accidental. We're just trying to get to the bottom of it."

"How about you, ma'am. When did you last see her?" Skip asked Dora.

"I told the police before when they questioned us on the boat," Dora snapped. "The last time I saw her was when she threw her drink at Dad and stormed up the stairs."

"You never saw her on the upper deck?" I said.

"No, I was watching the fireworks with everyone else. I didn't notice where she was. There was a large crowd, and it was dark."

"Did you see anyone remove a knife from the table setting where you were sitting?" Skip said.

"No," Dora said.

Frank shook his head.

"You think someone stabbed Ivy?" Frank said.

"We have no way of knowing," I said.

Skip continued. "Her body was never found and autopsied, but a knife was missing from your table, which leads us to believe . . ."

"Oh, Ivy." Frank's voice hitched and he began to sob.

"This talk is upsetting my father," Dora said. "I think you both should probably leave now."

"Of course," Skip said. "We'd like to talk to the rest of the family, though, when it's convenient."

"You'll find my brother, Ted, at the showroom. He practically lives there. I don't know where Bobby is. Off fooling around, no doubt. Please leave now." She gestured toward the door. "Rest here, Dad. I'll be right back with your pills."

"I'm sorry if we upset your father," Skip said.

"Dad's been very ill lately. He has a heart condition, and all this hasn't helped. Ivy's dead, and she's still causing trouble." Dora mumbled the last sentence under her breath as we exited the front door. It wasn't intended to be heard, but I snagged it like a fish on a line.

"Tell me something, Miss Diggs," I said.

"What?"

"Did you get along with your stepmother?"

Bitsy saw her chance for escape and slipped through our legs but saw Cruiser and stopped to make his acquaintance.

Dora quickly snatched up the small dog, set it down in the entryway and gave it a firm nudge backward with one foot. Bitsy yelped her surprise.

"Mom had only been gone a couple of months before Dad met Ivy. They corresponded for a month or so, then next thing we all knew she was marrying him. She made his life, all our lives, miserable from day one. I hated her, and I'm glad she's dead!" Dora's eyes were daggers of malice. "Now, if you'll excuse me, I really have to go. My father needs his medication."

"But . . . hey, wait!" My words hung in the air like the last of the gray storm clouds overhead as the door slammed in our faces. The real storm, it turns out, was only beginning.

CHAPTER TWENTY

Skip and I stopped at Debbie's Diner for a quick snack before returning to our offices. Who should sashay over to serve us but the one and only Rita Ramirez, frizzy red hair and all. She'd earned quite a reputation in these parts, and that was before her involvement in the Tahoe Terror murders. She was cleared of any connection with the killings, but anyone else with a shred of dignity would have packed up and moved to a new town where no one knew her. Not Rita. She didn't seem to care what anyone thought. She still had her eye on Skip, too, which didn't seem to bother him in the least. Mind you, Rita had her eye on every man in the county. She was always on the lookout for someone to rescue her from waitressing.

"Hey, Skippy, what's shakin'?" Rita said, snapping her gum. Skip didn't need to answer. It was pretty obvious what was shakin' in Rita's low-cut blouse. "What'll ya have?"

Skip *uhm*ed and *ah*ed a bit as he surveyed first Rita, then the menu. "Uh, let's see. Bring me a chili cheeseburger, fries, and a Coke. What'll you have, Beanie?"

"I'll have the garden burger and an iced tea."

"Want the senior discount, hon?" Rita said.

"Not yet, sweetie," I snapped. Oooh, that Rita always knew how to get my goat. Of course, our subtle Venusian exchange of insults shot right over Martian Skippy's head.

Rita scribbled our orders on the tablet and hurried off to flirt with the businessmen seated at another table.

"Aren't you worried about eating beef these days?" I asked Skip.

"No, why?"

"Well, there's mad cow disease and hoof and mouth, and that's just for starters. Not to mention *E. coli.*"

"Well, if I suddenly start staggering around and mooing, you'll know the reason why." I laughed. "So, what do you think about the Diggs story? Did you believe them?"

"I'll reserve judgment until we talk to the rest of the family. I have to admit Frank Diggs was pretty convincing, though. If he really has heart trouble and is as feeble as he looked, it doesn't seem likely he'd be giving his wife the heave-ho over the railing or racing after you on hairpin turns. He seemed genuinely distraught, but I can't say the same for his daughter."

"It's clear that she didn't hold Ivy Diggs in very high esteem. You think it might be Dora who did her in?" Skip scratched his head. "Except, if she killed her stepmother, I doubt if she would have admitted her true feelings to us."

"She could have purposely done that to throw us off the track, the way a sly fox doubles back over its trail to confuse the hounds."

"I don't follow you."

"Think about it. She knows we'd think that she wouldn't tell a couple of investigators she hated Ivy and was glad she was dead if she really had killed her."

"Like you said, I think we'll be better able to sort this out once we've talked to the other members of the family. We'll pay a little visit to Diggs Dive and Expedition tomorrow, but first we're going on that fishing trip, kiddo. There's a forty-pounder out there somewhere with my name on it."

"To tell you the truth, Skip, I'd rather be boiled in whale blubber, but I'll do it for you. Cruiser can come along, too, right?"

"Of course, but better tell him not to forget his water wings."

"You kidding? What do you think those ears are good for besides dipping in his food bowl?"

We were still laughing when I heard the snapping sound that told me Rita was on the way with our orders. We both dove into our meals. Crime detecting can give you a real appetite, and my appetite was whetted for getting to the bottom of Ivy Diggs' disappearance, which was beginning to look more and more like murder.

But it was I who was about to have another close brush with death.

CHAPTER TWENTY-ONE

I managed to stall avid angler Skip on the fishing trip, but not for long. After my near burial at sea, I felt I'd had enough of Waterworld for awhile. However, very early the next morning, I found myself on the lake once again with Cruiser and Skip in the *Trout Scout*. At least we were cruising along in smoother waters, and I was on the water instead of in it. For a little while, anyway.

Cruiser was sporting his GPS transmitter and the new life vest I'd bought for him over at the Haute Hydrant. He was having the time of his life perched at the helm like a ship's figurehead, except no sailing vessel I had ever seen had one that looked quite like this. And who needed a mainsail when we had Cruiser's long ears to catch the wind?

Roses of dawn blossomed in the eastern sky as we set our course for Rubicon Bay. The spray of cold lake water on my face rinsed the sleep from my eyes. I had made the mistake of telling Skip about the school of forty-pound mackinaw that had appeared on the DART screen of the sub. He was itching to get at them and would never rest until he had one dancing on the end of his line.

"Is this where you saw them, Beanie?"

"Pretty sure it is."

"Well, only one way to find out."

Skip baited his hook and cast out the line, then settled in to wait. "Say, how about getting that thermos of coffee I brought along and pouring us a cup?"

"Who am I? Rita Ramirez?"

"Pretty please?"

"Okay, okay. Maybe it will wake me up. I don't know why I let you talk me into this. It's not like I don't have plenty of other things to do. Carla's waiting for my article. I'm going to have to request a deadline extension, and she won't be happy about it."

"It'll keep for an hour or two. You're such a workaholic, woman."

"Have to be. I don't have a man to support me, you know."

"Well, that's easily remedied. There are lots of guys who wouldn't mind being married to a nice gal like you."

"Did you ever think maybe I prefer being on my own?"

"Well, sure, but don't you get lonely living all by yourself?"

"I suppose I've gotten used to not having to pick up dirty socks and underwear and rattle pots and pans every night at five o'clock sharp. Tom always wanted his dinner 'on the table, Mable,' the minute he got home from work. I admit I miss cooking for two sometimes, but I don't miss adhering to someone else's schedule. I eat when I'm hungry, not because the clock strikes five. Besides, Cruiser gives me lots of company. The house is never empty with him around."

Cruiser barked in answer at the mention of his name, or at least that's what I thought until the ticking of the reel in Skip's hands told me otherwise. Cruiser continued barking. A distance off our port side we saw something. The still reflection of the surrounding mountains in the clear waters began to ripple, then the water began churning.

"What is that?" I said.

"Probably a school of fish feeding at the surface," Skip said. "Hey, guys, take my bait, will ya? Here, hold this a minute." Skip handed the fishing pole to me, started the engine, and steered the boat at low-throttle toward the strange phenomenon. It seemed to move away from us each time we neared it. I realized this was the same thing Boney Crider had described seeing on one of his fishing trips. Skip stopped the motor and all was silent. The boiling in the water had stopped. Whatever had been there was gone.

I tended Skip's fishing pole as we surveyed the area for any sign of what we'd just seen. Suddenly, the line went taut.

"Whoa, I've got something," I said, jumping to my feet.

"You sure have. Hang on, Beanie!"

"I'm trying, I'm trying. Jeez, this is a big one. I think this is the fish you've been waiting for your whole life, Skip."

Suddenly something tugged hard, and the rod horseshoed. Next thing I knew, I was dog paddling in the chilly waters of Lake Tahoe. Skip's fishing rod sank down into the depths of the lake. I hoped I wouldn't be following close after.

I was glad Skip always insisted his passengers, even canine ones, wear a life vest. I've never been a very good swimmer, which was probably why I usually declined to accompany Skip on these outings. This would probably be the last time, too, I thought, as I waited for him to pull the *Trout Scout* alongside me and fish me out of the frigid water. Then I saw a large shadow pass under me, just like I'd seen on the *Dixie Queen* last July 4th. Something was down there in the water. Something big. I was pretty sure it wasn't a school of mackinaw.

I thought perhaps it might be Crispin doing an early morning dive in his sub. The dark mass rose up from the depths toward me. What was it? Something scaly and thoroughly creepy brushed against my leg, and a chill zipped up my spine. Then I felt something tug at my leg. Suddenly, I was underwater, life jacket and all. I could hear Cruiser barking his head off from somewhere above as I felt myself being pulled down. This was it. I was going to die right here in the lake. I'd be floating around for eternity down in the body layer of Tahoe's icy waters with Ivy Diggs and all the other victims of the ancient lake's mysterious depths. Then just as suddenly, whatever had hold of me released its grip, and I surfaced, gasping for air.

I felt something take hold of me again, pulling me along on the surface. It was my water-phobic dog, Cruiser, dog paddling for all he was worth. I grabbed onto the webbed handle atop his life vest, which was intended for fishing your dog out of the water. Luckily, it could also work the other way around. Skip jumped in the water and took over for Cruiser. He climbed aboard first, then got a firm grip on my life vest and pulled me from the water. He did the same for Cruiser.

"A woman and her dog isn't quite the catch I had in mind for this fishing trip," Skip said, looking drenched and exasperated.

"This is not exactly my idea of a fun day out, either."

"Brave dog you've got there. I thought Cruiser was afraid of the water."

"So did I." I gave Cruiser a grateful pet. "You're full of surprises, aren't you, boy?"

"It's just a good thing you both were wearing life vests or you'd be fish bait by now."

"Sorry, Skip. I lost your good rod down there somewhere."

"Don't worry about it. I can get another one of those, but I can't replace you. Or Cruiser."

Skip unfolded the wool blanket he kept aboard the *Trout Scout* and wrapped it around my trembling shoulders, as I had for him in similar circumstances on the *Dixie Queen*.

"I really thought I was a goner this time. There's something big out there, and it's no mackinaw."

"I think you're right. We'd better get outta here while the gettin's good."

Skip tried to start the motor, but it wouldn't start. He tried again. The motor sputtered and coughed. We both felt a thump on the underside of the boat.

"Kill the motor, Skip. The sound is agitating whatever is out there." Skip turned off the motor and we surveyed the lake in silence, waiting for another impact. It came. Something collided so hard with the boat it nearly upended us. Skip fell backward and struck his head hard on the thwart.

"Skip, Skip! Are you okay?" I shook him, but he was out like a refrigerator light.

The sun crested the eastern ridge as I sat in the *Trout Scout* with Cruiser and my unconscious friend, expecting another attack from an unseen aquatic aggressor. In the golden light I saw something break the surface of the water in the distance. It was moving out on the lake, gliding on the surface in graceful circles, its scaly skin glistening like fool's gold in the morning sun. What appeared to be a fin rose up out of the water. Something long, snake-like, telescoped from the water and appeared to survey the area briefly before submerging.

I couldn't believe my eyes. Was I hallucinating or was I actually seeing Tahoe Tessie for the first time? Could this be a living, breathing prehistoric dinosaur? If only I'd had a video camera with me to record what I was witnessing. I did have my cell phone, but I'd never be able to figure out how to take a photo in time.

In the distance, I saw what I presumed was the creature's neck arch out of the water in a swanlike fashion. The long neck dipped down into the water a moment and surfaced again. I thought I saw the beast tilt its head back and down a huge fish, rows of sharp teeth glinting in the sun. There went Skip's trophy trout.

Suddenly, she humped up her body like a whale or a manatee, slapping her massive tail on the water's surface several times before submerging into the depths of the lake. No doubt a warning of some kind. Cruiser was barking his head off.

"Shhh. Boy," I whispered, fearing the creature might return.

The movement of the great animal's body in the water created shock waves of water that spanked the sides of Skip's small boat. Diamonds of light sprayed the air as what had nearly overturned us plunged back down to the depths of Rubicon Bay.

CHAPTER TWENTY-TWO

Cruiser's frenzied barking stirred Skip back to consciousness.

"Wha . . . what happened?" Skip sat up and rubbed the back of his head, wincing in pain.

"You fell and hit your head."

"Oh, yeah. Now I remember. That was a heck of a jolt back there. What hit us so hard?"

"You'd never believe it in a million years. Make that ninety million."

"These are deep waters out here. It couldn't have been a rock. Could it?"

"Try again."

"Oh, I get it. It was your mythical Tahoe Tessie, right?"

"There's nothing mythical about what I saw, Skip."

"Oh, come on. I thought I was the one with a concussion here."

"Very funny. Let's argue about it later, okay? Get us out of here before we both get hypothermia."

"G-g-good idea." Skip's teeth chattered so hard I could barely make out what he said.

He started the motor again, steered the tiller to bring us around and headed back for the dock. I surveyed the waters for any sign of our curious visitor, fearing she might return. Tessie didn't show herself again.

Skip and I were both shaken and chilled by our experience out on the lake. We had planned to visit Diggs Dive Shop and talk to Ted Diggs, but that would have to wait. Skip drove Cruiser and me straight home.

"What in the world happened to you?" Nona said. "You look like drowned rats!"

"We had an accident out on the lake," Skip said.

"An accident? Are you all right?"

I nodded.

"I think you should get into a hot bath. I'll get the water running. Get out of those wet things, and I'll go make something hot to drink."

My chattering teeth made it hard to respond. Skip answered for me.

"Good idea. I need to change, too," he said.

"You can use the shower to warm up, I said."

"I've got some extra clothes out in the car. Be right back."

A hot tub was heaven after the freezing water in the lake. Gradually, I felt the heat starting to quell my chills, and my teeth stopped chattering. I had soaked for about twenty minutes when I heard the door hinges squeak. Fearing it might be Skip, I snatched a towel from the rail to cover myself. Then I saw a shiny, black nose pop in the door and nudge it open.

"Cruiser, what are you doing in here, boy?" He took that as an invitation to come the rest of the way into the bathroom. A draft followed him in, which set me to shivering again. I picked up one of my soggy Nikes and threw it hard against the door to push it closed. Cruiser came over and sat next to the tub. I wasn't accustomed to having an audience at bath time. In fact, ordinarily I was the shower type, which was probably why Cruiser seemed puzzled by the fact that I was lying in a big bowl of water.

He reared up and rested his paws on the side of the tub. I

thought he was going to try to drink the water like he does out of the toilet. I playfully splashed warm water on his face to discourage him. He must have liked it, though, because the next thing I knew he had jumped right into the tub with me. "Cruiser!" A mini-tsunami of water sloshed onto the floor.

At first I was irritated because he had made a mess until I realized he must have been cold, too, from his icy dip in the lake. Either that or he was trying to rescue me again. After both of us had a good sudsing and rinsing, I climbed out of the tub, dried myself and wrapped up in the comfy old chenille robe I had inherited from my mother. Sopping up the puddle on the floor with a towel seemed like wasted effort because my soaking wet dog was about to make another puddle when I lifted him out of the bath. I dried Cruiser first with a towel and then with the blow dryer, which he loved, after he stopped barking at it. When bath time for basset was over, I felt like I needed another bath, but there wasn't a dry towel left in the house.

"What's all the commotion in here?" Nona said, peeking in the door.

"Cruiser decided he wanted a hot bath, too. After all, Skip and I weren't the only ones who went swimming in the lake."

"Well, coffee's ready whenever you are."

"I'm ready!" I stepped into my slippers and padded into the kitchen to join Nona and Skip. Feeling like a frisky pup again, Cruiser pranced along behind me. As I passed the living room, he took a detour and nose-dived on the carpet to finish drying himself, spreading a layer of damp fur from one end of the room to the other. I guess a hero hound dog like Cruiser was entitled to a good victory roll. That's why Mr. Dyson invented the "Animal" to vacuum up all that hair.

"Skip's been telling me about your big adventure on the lake this morning."

"How's the head, Skip?"

"Still hurts some."

"Serves you right for dragging me along on that fishing trip. You know I hate fishing."

"Don't blame me. How was I supposed to know it would end up like that?"

"What happened out there, anyway, you two?" Nona said.

"Something hit the boat and nearly upended it. That's how Skip fell and hit his head."

"What was it?" Nona asked.

"I think it was probably a floating log or something. Your mother thinks it was . . . Oh, I'd better let her tell you. It's just too incredible."

"Tell me what? Tell me what?" Nona was on the edge of her chair, like everyone else in Lake Tahoe would be if they ever saw what I had seen out in the lake. No one would believe it. Neither would I if I hadn't seen it plain as day.

Nona's eyes grew round as flying saucers as I related my fantastic account of the events that had occurred. I was pretty sure Skip would just file it along with all the other implausible reports surrounding the Lake of the Sky.

CHAPTER TWENTY-THREE

When Skip and I entered the establishment of Diggs Dive and Expedition, several people were admiring the racy new inboards displayed in the showroom. Skip instantly joined them. Others were shopping for diving equipment. One man was trying on a green wetsuit. When he slipped on a pair of diving goggles, he looked so much like a frog I half-expected to hear him croak. Speaking of nearly croaking, after my recent escapade in the lake, I knew that skin diving was one hobby I would never take up. I hoped that went for Nona, too, especially if Bobby Diggs was the one doing the teaching.

Finally, a pretty, young salesclerk came over to us. Her nametag said Monica. "May I help you?" she said.

"Yes, we're here to speak to Ted Diggs."

"He's around here somewhere. Wait here. I'll get him."

I wasn't sure whether it was the speedy-looking boat Skip was busy admiring or the shapely blonde who had just helped us. "Say, Skip. Think you'll get one of those babies someday?"

"Huh?"

"The boat, Skip, the boat."

"Oh. Only if I win the lottery. This one here costs more than my house."

My eyes popped when I looked at the price. "Jeez, Louise. Talk about sticker shock. I had no idea these things were so expensive. The *QE2* didn't cost this much."

Skip laughed. "I probably should be boat shopping, though. I may have to retire the old *Trout Scout* one of these days."

I tried not to look too relieved at that announcement.

"You wanted to see me?" Skip and I turned to face Ted Diggs. He surveyed us so coolly that I shivered.

"Yes, Mr. Diggs," Skip said. "My partner and I would like to ask you a few questions."

"About what?"

"Your stepmother's drowning," I answered.

Ted glanced around the showroom, looking ill at ease. "Let's step into my office."

Skip and I followed Diggs upstairs to his private office.

"Have a seat," he instructed. "Better make this quick. I have customers waiting. What do you want to know?"

"We have reason to believe that Ivy's death was not accidental," Skip said.

"You mean you think someone tried to kill her?" Ted looked appropriately surprised. Whether it was an act or not was hard to tell. He had one of those poker faces that don't reveal much emotion. It probably served him well in closing deals with wealthy patrons, but it could also be useful in diverting a homicide investigation.

"Yes, it's possible she could have been murdered," Skip said.

Ted's eyebrows formed golden arches. "Do I need a lawyer present for the rest of this conversation?"

"No, I don't think that's necessary right now. This isn't a formal inquiry."

"Then I don't have to talk to you unless I want to."

"That's right," Skip said. "You don't have to . . ."

"But it would sure help us out if you would," I interjected, smiling.

Ted didn't smile back at me, but he didn't get up to leave, either, which I interpreted as license to continue with our line of questioning.

"I get the feeling from talking to your sister that your father's marriage to the second Mrs. Diggs wasn't very well received by his children," I said.

"I guess you could say that. We tried every way we could to prevent Dad from marrying Ivy."

"Why?" Skip and I spoke in unison.

"Well, the age difference for one thing," Ted said. "She was young enough to be his granddaughter."

"How old is your father?" I asked.

"He's sixty. Ivy was in her twenties."

"Men his age frequently marry younger women," Skip said.

"Was that the only reason you were against the marriage?" I said.

"Dad only knew Ivy a short time before she marched him to the altar. We felt he should at least wait until the flowers on Mom's grave were wilted before he remarried."

"I suppose there are some things you just can't control," I said, thinking of the strange assortment of men that had paraded through my daughter's life. "Widowers don't usually fare well after the death of a spouse," I added. "Your father was probably lonely after your mother passed on."

"Yes, but when some young chick marries a rich old man with one foot in the grave, you know it's probably just for his money. And that was sure the case with Ivy. He was always buying her expensive clothes, jewelry, cars. She was like a vampire. Always draining him dry. Why, only a week before she drowned, he bought her a brand new Mercedes."

"Are you and your father partners in this business?" Skip asked.

"Yes, but he isn't working anymore. He's been retired a year or so. After he married Ivy, his health took a turn for the worse. No wonder. She'd drive any man to his grave. He had his first heart attack within a couple of months after their marriage.

Dora cared for him so my brother, Bobby, and I could run the business for Dad."

"How is business?" I asked.

"You could say we're keeping our heads above water." Ted snickered at his own pun.

"Think we could talk to your brother while we're here?" Skip asked.

"He's out teaching a class right now."

"A class?" Skip said.

"Diving lessons. He runs the diving school when he's in the mood to work, which isn't often. I'm in charge of the rest."

I was hoping Bobby's student wasn't my daughter, especially after what had happened to Skip and me earlier.

"Well, we'll try to catch him later, then," Skip said. "Perhaps you could give him a heads-up that we'd like to have a chat with him."

"I'll let him know," Ted said. "Is that all? I have to get back to work. This is our busy season." When Ted opened his desk drawer to retrieve some keys, I glimpsed a semi-automatic pistol. He noticed that I noticed and slammed the drawer shut.

"That's all for now," Skip said. "We might have more questions for you later."

"Well, please call before you come next time. I'd like to have my lawyer present if I'm going to be answering any more questions."

"That's your prerogative, of course," Skip said.

Ted ushered us out of his office, back down the stairs, and out the front door.

Skip and I headed back to his patrol car.

"Is it just me, Beanie, or did we just get the bum's rush out of Diggs Dive and Expedition?"

"You could say that. Must have been the mention of the 'M' word."

Skip looked at me quizzically, no doubt still focused on pretty Monica.

"Murder, Skip, murder!"

CHAPTER TWENTY-FOUR

Cruiser trailed close on my heels as I hurried to answer the phone. It was way past time for his midmorning walk, and he knew it. I snatched the receiver.

"Hello?"

"Elsie?"

"Speaking."

"Cris Blayne here."

"Oh, hi, Cris. How are you?" Antsy dogs notwithstanding, I sat down on the sofa to take this call.

"Jolly good. Listen, I have some readings from our dive the other day I thought might interest you. Would you like to get together and go over them?"

"Yes, those would be good for my article. I'm trying to wrap that up, so the sooner the better."

"How about this evening at The Cock and Bull pub? You know where that is?"

"Yes. What time?"

"Shall we say seven?"

"Fine, I'll meet you there."

"Cheerio."

The line clicked. I felt like a teenager who had just made plans for her prom date. But I was fifty years old. I wasn't supposed to be having such feelings anymore. Cruiser's wet jowls on my pants leg brought me quickly back to reality.

"All right, boy. I get the message."

I snapped on his leash and we were out the door. Sometimes my life seems like one long dog walk, but it is my duty as a dog owner to exercise my dog. Of course, Cruiser is a bit more demanding than most dogs about his walks. Three a day is the norm when I'm not working on books or articles or hot on the trail of a murder investigation.

One thing Cruiser would never have to be was a backyard dog, left chained to a doghouse, forgotten by his owners once the cuteness of puppyhood was past. Cruiser was a rescue dog, though, so I hadn't had him from puppyhood. I'll bet he was a cute one, though. Woe to the prospective guardian who is not prepared for the laidback personality and stubborn streak of the basset hound or the slobber stains on walls, windows, and draperies. Or rather, woe to the basset, because most likely he'll end up surrendered to a shelter, or left by the side of the road like Cruiser was. Cruiser was one of the lucky ones. He found a home with people who accepted and loved him for the adorably stubborn, slobbery fellow he is.

As Cruiser and I trekked up the trail behind my cabin, the wind rushing through the pines sounded like a mountain waterfall. Squirrels sassed at us from the safety of high pine branches. Dewy spider webs, still unbroken from the night's silent spinning, draped between the firs like diamond necklaces sparkling in the sun. The woods were blessedly silent, except for the occasional chatter of a chipmunk and the squeaky-hinge sound of the darting chickadees, tits and other tiny mountain birds. It was always hard to return to the stress-inducing drone of civilization after our sojourns in the forest.

As Cruiser and I emerged from the woods, I saw Nona on the back porch taking in the morning sun. Cruiser trotted up the steps to greet her, got his strokes, then went to his water dish to tank up.

"Hi, Mom!"

"Hi, Sweetie."

"Awesome day, isn't it?"

"Sure is. It's hot again today, though."

"I heard it could hit the high nineties."

"Good excuse for me to stay inside and work today."

"What are you working on?"

"I'm still trying to finish up that piece for the *Tattler,* and then I need to do a little mystery plotting."

"Well, you have plenty of material with everything that's been going on lately. How did things go at the Diggs' place?"

"Nothing conclusive yet, but one thing is certain. Ivy Diggs isn't being missed one bit by the Diggs family. All except for Frank. He's the only one who seems the least bit broken up about the loss. From the conversation I overheard on the *Dixie Queen* that night between those two, I find that hard to fathom. She talked to him like a dog. Sorry, Cruiser."

Cruiser looked up momentarily from his sunny spot on the deck, then dozed off again.

"You think one of his kids did her in?"

"I'm not ruling it out. They weren't in favor of the marriage to begin with. Tried to talk the old man out of marrying her so soon after his wife's death, but it didn't work. He married her anyway."

"I can't believe these senior citizens who chase after young things just to convince themselves they aren't getting old."

I hoped Nona wasn't referring to me, but then she didn't know the fantasies I was entertaining about my "date" with Crispin Blayne at The Cock and Bull. I might just have to take her along to chaperone her mom.

"Well, don't stay out here too long, honey. You'll cook."

"I could use some warming up after my swim."

"Swimming? Where did you go swimming?"

"Oh, I forgot to tell you I was taking a diving lesson today."

"Diving lesson? You went diving? In the lake?"

"Where else? The YMCA?"

"Very funny." I wasn't smiling when I said it.

"Why do you ask?"

"Gee, I don't know. Could it be because people are drowning almost daily in the lake and there's some kind of creature out there that could be the cause of it?"

"Oh, Mother. You're being ridiculous. There's nothing out there besides big fish."

"I know. That's what has me worried."

"Besides, Bobby knows what he's doing. I wasn't in any danger."

"You mean Bobby Diggs?"

"Yes. Him. Why?"

"He's a possible murder suspect is all."

"Don't be so melodramatic. He hasn't been accused of anything."

"Not yet."

"Please don't worry about me so much. I can take care of myself. If he gives me any trouble, I'll just sic Tessie on him."

The hours passed like minutes, as they always do when I'm writing. As usual, I had accomplished a lot once I actually sat down and got busy and put worries about Nona aside. It was just getting the seat of my pants on the seat of the chair that was always the biggest challenge.

I felt pleased with myself. Not only did I have a good draft of my article for the *Tahoe Tattler* but I also had the first chapter of my new mystery on paper. All I still needed to do was collect some numbers and technical tidbits to fill in the gaps in my article. Those I would get from Crispin tonight, I hoped. Nona had plans of her own for the evening, not with Bobby Diggs, I hoped. She probably wouldn't have told me if she had. At any rate, she wouldn't be serving as senior chaperone for her mother.

When I drove up to The Cock and Bull, he was sitting at one of the outdoor tables sipping a stout. He waved me over to his table and I sat down.

"Hello, Elsie. So glad you could make it."

"Cris. Good to see you again."

The barmaid came over to the table. She was dressed authentically in the fashion of English barmaids, complete with fake accent that sounded more like Valley Girl Yiddish.

"Oy, may I 'elp ya, marm?" she said, batting her eyes at Crispin, while she took my order.

"Do you serve margaritas?"

"Blimey no, marm. Just beer and wine."

Crispin rolled his eyes. I stifled a giggle.

"In that case, I'll have a glass of your house white."

The barmaid flounced off to get the drinks.

"Wonder what part of London she's from," Crispin said, smiling.

"I'd say somewhere near Bakersfield Street."

Crispin laughed. "The weather is so nice tonight, I thought it would be good to sit outside. Is that all right with you?"

"Sure." Crispin's lake blue eyes were staring straight into mine. I'm sure I wasn't the first woman to go swimming in them. *Remember, Beanie, stick to business.* "How are your studies progressing?"

"Very well. I'm still researching the samples I collected, but it's the snaps I think will interest you the most."

"Oh. Did you bring them with you?"

"Yes, I have them here in my briefcase." Crispin unfastened the straps on his weathered leather case and pulled out a folder. He produced a collection of underwater photos shot from the sub's camera mounted on the exterior. I saw the school of mackinaw the DART screen had picked up. There in one photo was the wreckage of the old steamer *Tahoe*. Underwater caves and fantastic geological formations were as clear as though taken on land, and so was the other photo he showed me. I wouldn't have believed what I was seeing if I hadn't already seen it for real.

CHAPTER TWENTY-FIVE

Crispin pulled his chair around next to mine. He was sitting so close to me I could smell his aftershave—English Leather, what else?

"As you can see right here, we have what appears to be the fin of a rather large aquatic creature," Crispin said. As he pointed at the photo on the table, his hand brushed against mine. It was like rubbing your feet on a carpet and touching metal. A bolt of electricity shot through me like the one that split the tree outside my cabin.

"It must be a huge animal," I said.

"Yes, it would be close to twenty meters long if my calculations are accurate."

"That's sixty feet! What kind of animal is it?"

"Until now I believed it might have been a plesiosaur, but now I'm thinking it may be an archeocete. It makes more sense that a warm-blooded animal could have survived in Tahoe's near freezing waters than a cold-blooded one like the plesiosaur."

"Do you really think it's possible that any could have survived for this long?"

"As you can see, it is entirely possible. They'll be thrilled about this."

"Who's they?" I asked.

"*National Geographic.*"

"I see." That explained all the expensive high-tech gadgets, including the mini-sub.

"They also funded my studies of the Loch Ness monster and other prehistoric creatures purported to exist throughout the world. Remember the movie *Godzilla*?"

"You mean the one with Raymond Burr?" I was announcing my age to Crispin. Me and my big mouth.

Crispin smiled as though he'd read my mind. "Both of them."

"Sure, what about it?"

"Well, there may be such a creature that exists somewhere in Tokyo Bay. Such legends have survived the centuries for good reason. That's next on my list of studies."

"I know all about legends. Native Americans have many such beliefs, but my ancestors probably also smoked all kinds of interesting things in their pipes just before they saw some of these mythical creatures." Just like Boney Crider.

"It's my mission to prove that they aren't just legends. Tahoe Tessie, as you call her, is out there, and these photos are proof positive."

"I believe you, but most people wouldn't. Photographs can be retouched, and computer programs can do all kinds of morphing tricks these days. I've heard that the famous head shot of Nessie is actually the tail of some smaller creature on a cleverly cropped photo."

"This isn't just a photograph, Elsie. This is an image generated by the DART readings, and those can't be altered. The program was designed that way, so the readings could not be disputed for any reason."

"Too bad you didn't capture more of the creature on here then. Most people would dismiss this as being part of a large fish, like a salmon or sturgeon." I looked at the photo again. "Are you sure this isn't a sturgeon? I've heard they can grow pretty large if conditions are right."

"Have you ever seen a sixty-foot sturgeon? Look at the size of this thing. We could generate a full representation from this. If we did, do you realize how immense this creature would have to be to have a tail that large?"

Crispin was right. Either there were anacondas in Lake Tahoe, or what I was seeing was the tail of a much larger creature than a sturgeon. But what he was telling me lived in our Lake of the Sky was no less fantastic to most people than the idea of an Amazonian anaconda inhabiting a North American mountain lake. I recalled the night of my birthday cruise and what I thought I had glimpsed in the viewing area of the glass-bottom boat. If I'd had a camera at the time, the photo wouldn't have looked much different from the one I held in my hand. It had to be the same thing I'd seen when I was with Skip in the *Trout Scout* and on the *Dixie Queen*. It had to be Tessie.

I hated to tell the professor, but I think his "secret" had already leaked out. I wasn't the only one who had spotted Tessie, or Nessie, or whatever it was swimming around out there frightening unsuspecting tourists and basset hounds. If Cruiser and I had seen it, others probably had, too. Boney Crider claimed he had, and it might have been the last thing Ivy Diggs ever saw. If only I'd had a video camera with me on the *Trout Scout*, I could prove to skeptical Skip what I'd seen was real. That was a problem easily remedied. An idea was simmering on the back burner of my brain. I hoped something was also simmering in the kitchen at The Cock and Bull.

"I'm getting hungry," I said. "I haven't eaten anything since this morning."

"Well, let's order up some pub grub, then. Have a look at the menu."

I surveyed the card a few minutes. The assortment was authentically English: bubble and squeak, toad in the hole, spotted dick. Sounded more like an assortment of Medieval plagues than menu selections. I finally settled for the shepherd's pie. It sounded the least disgusting of the lot.

While we waited for our orders to arrive, I made small talk. "How are you enjoying your stay here in Tahoe?"

"It's quite nice. The lake is beautiful. Reminds me a bit of the Lake District in England, although the mountains there are not as lofty, of course. It's quite spectacular, though."

"Is that where you're from?"

"No, I live just outside of London, but I was born in Cornwall. It's even more wild and beautiful than here."

"I didn't think that was entirely a London accent you had."

"My wife was a Londoner, though."

"Oh? How long were you married?"

"Two years. Then one day she just disappeared."

"Did you ever find her?"

"No. She vanished without a trace. She was presumed dead and an inquiry ensued. I was even placed under suspicion for her disappearance for a time until I could clear myself." Crispin motioned to the barmaid for another beer. "Sorry. I shouldn't be boring you with all this personal history."

"I'm not bored. Far from it." I sipped the last of my wine.

"Oh, you're empty. I'll get you another."

"Thanks. Make it White Zinfandel. The Chardonnay she brought me is a bit too dry for my taste."

"Sweet wine for a sweet lady." Crispin smiled and I felt my toes tingle. Or maybe it was just the wine. I knew one glass was my limit.

"So, you never saw your wife again?"

"Never."

"You think it's possible she may still be alive?"

"I don't know. If she is, she's probably living in France or Italy. Maybe Florida. Lots of wealthy men there. Zoë had champagne tastes."

"Are you wealthy, Crispin?" I wanted to bite my tongue. "I'm sorry. I'm being too nosy."

"It's okay. I do come from a very old family. The Blaynes owned a lot of land in Cornwall at one time. They still figure prominently in the region. Tin mining and all that, you know. My great grandfather did rather well for himself."

"Ah, so you come from mining country. Mining was big here, too, at one time. Silver and gold."

"Yes, I know. It's quite fascinating, really."

"Quite sad, don't you mean? They clear-cut every tree in this whole basin to shore up the silver mines in Nevada."

"Yes, I've seen photographs."

"Looked like the aftermath of Hiroshima," I said. "There's no end to man's greed or his willingness to decimate his own home in pursuit of wealth."

"Things aren't much different in England."

"If it weren't for conservationists like Lucky Baldwin, no trees would have been spared in the logging of timber." I thought it ironic that the man who was responsible for drawing droves of tourists to Tahoe and establishing gambling here also had a hand in its preservation. His daughter, Dextra, had Lucky's grand casino torn down, but gambling was here to stay.

Once the sun dropped behind the mountains, the air turned chilly. Crispin and I decided to go inside to eat our supper. The Cock and Bull has an authentic-looking pub upstairs, so we ate our meal in one of the cozy booths.

The shepherd's pie was delicious, made properly with lamb instead of the usual ground beef you get in most British-American restaurants. Unfortunately, Crispin ordered fish and chips. Ever since I had carried Nona, when Tom and I lived in the San Francisco Bay area, I couldn't stand the smell of fish. During my pregnancy, I tossed my cookies whenever Tom came home with the catch of the day. He soon learned to clean his own fish out on the back porch and wash the fish smell off his hands. I no longer threw up when I smelled fish, but it sure didn't add much to my meal with Crispin. Neither did Skip's surprise appearance in The Cock and Bull.

CHAPTER TWENTY-SIX

I saw Skip step into the pub and perch on one of the stools. I called out, but he didn't hear me. I waved when he glanced in the mirror behind the bar. He pivoted on the stool, stood up and walked over to our table.

"I didn't expect to see you here," Skip said.

"Ditto, Skip. What are you doing here?"

"I just got off duty and felt like a cold draft. It's been a hot one out there today." An awkward silence ensued. "Aren't you going to introduce me to your friend?"

"Oh, yes. Sorry. This is Professor Crispin Blayne. Cris, this is my good friend, Sheriff Skip Cassidy."

"How do you do, Sheriff," Crispin said in his clipped British accent.

"Professor."

Skip and Crispin sized each other up. I half expected them to start circling and sniffing each other like two dogs. Men! I felt obliged to run interference.

"Cris and I were just discussing some of his findings on the lake studies he's conducting."

"That so?" I could almost read the thought bubble over Skip's head.

"Why don't you join us?"

"Uh, no thanks. My drink is up, and I'm in kind of a hurry. I'll just leave you two to do whatever you were doing before I came in."

With that, Skip turned on his heel, paid for his drink and reclaimed his stool at the bar. I'd never seen Skip act this way before. I didn't understand why he hadn't just sat down with us. He didn't appear to be in much of a hurry, as he claimed. I wasn't on a date, after all. At least I hope he didn't think that's what it was. I hope Cris didn't, either. It wasn't really, was it?

I continued talking with Crispin through the rest of our meal, but I was keenly aware of Skip studying us in the bar mirror from time to time. I started to feel like I was out on a date and my big brother was spying on me. I wished Skip would just leave, but it was Crispin and I who ended up leaving. He wanted to play a round of darts, but I lied and said I had to get right home. It was only a white lie, though. I had work to do and a dog to walk before bedtime.

As Crispin walked me to my car, I noticed Skip heading for his patrol car, trying to look nonchalant. If I accused him of spying on me, he'd probably give me some cock-and-bull story, but I thought that was exactly what he was doing in the pub. And I just couldn't figure out his odd behavior around Crispin. Unless he was jealous. Skip? Jealous of me? Impossible. But then, that's also what most people thought about there being live prehistoric creatures in Lake Tahoe.

CHAPTER TWENTY-SEVEN

"Go on, boy. Let Mom sleep a little bit longer," I said, pushing Cruiser aside when he stuck a cold, wet nose under the covers. When he started whining for his breakfast, I knew there would be no snooze alarm for me.

I sat up on the edge of the bed and felt my temples begin to throb like someone was banging a ceremonial drum in the bedroom. I was feeling the effects of the two glasses of wine the night before. When would I ever learn? I had an article to revise, and with my head pounding, it would be difficult to be productive. Of course, it occurred to me that it wasn't the drinks that were responsible for my headache but just more Fun with Menopause. I wondered why someone hadn't created a game show for middle-age women like Memory Loss Jeopardy, What's My Mood?, or Wheel of Hormones.

"What's wrong, Mom?" Nona asked.

"Oh, just another of my stupid headaches."

"Can I get you some aspirin or something?"

"No, I don't think it would help."

"How did your date go last night with Professor Blayne?"

"Fine, except it wasn't a date, Nona."

"Skip must think it was. He called here twice this morning before you got up. He was asking all kinds of questions. I think he's checking up on you."

"I don't know what's gotten into that man. I never saw him act like he did last night."

"I didn't know Skip was the jealous type."

"Neither did I. Besides, there was no reason to be. I'll give him a call and see what's up. But first a cup of something strong and hot."

"It's already brewed. I made you some toast, too. And I'll feed Cruiser."

"Thanks, honey. I appreciate it." I forgave Nona for grilling me about Cris and was just glad someone besides me was serving as Cruiser's food slave this morning.

"How's the article coming along?"

"Not good. Carla wasn't satisfied with my first draft. Not sensational enough for her, I suppose. Or maybe there are just too many distractions with this Ivy Diggs investigation going on."

"What's the latest on that, anyway?" Nona buttered her toast thinly with diet margarine.

"Well, we talked to Ted Diggs. It's obvious thus far that Ivy won't be missed much by her stepchildren. Apparently, Frank didn't have much time to mourn his wife's death before Ivy came along. In fact, I suspect she may have been on the lookout for a man like him."

"Why is that?"

"There are lots of women who seek out lonely widowers, and the widowers are usually well off, as in Frank's case. Some of them scan the obituaries regularly to find easy marks."

"I thought only life insurance and junk bond salesmen did that."

"The buzzards start circling when there's a death in the family, and they aren't always strangers, either. When your dad died, I heard from relatives I didn't even know Tom had. This one wanted his gold pocket watch. That one wanted his bagpipes. Everyone wanted a piece of him."

"I suppose people are most vulnerable when they're grieving

for a loved one."

"You bet. Just ask any undertaker selling $10,000 caskets. Promise me you'll have me cremated when my time comes. You can just scatter Cruiser and me up in our sunny spot. That's where we've always been happiest."

"Oh, don't be so morbid, Mother."

"I'm not being morbid. Just practical."

"Let's talk about it later, okay?"

"No, we've never discussed it before, and now's as good a time as any. I'm not getting any younger, and you should be aware of my wishes before it's too late."

"For heaven' sake. You're only fifty!"

"Well, when he died, your dad was younger than I am. I was just lucky that all those things were already taken care of for me."

Nona's youthful flippancy faded at the mention of her father. "Don't worry. I'll see to it, but don't be like Dad, okay?" Her eyes glittered with tears.

I cupped Nona's chin gently in my hand. "That's the plan, honey."

"So, about this Ivy chick," Nona said. "You think she just married old Mr. Diggs for his money?"

"More than likely, considering the age difference."

"And you think he finally got fed up with her and killed her?"

"It was the first possibility I considered, but after having talked to some of the other members of the family, I think there are certainly alternative suspects in her death."

"You think one of her own stepchildren could have killed her?"

"Don't be so shocked, Nona. Blood may be thicker than water, but it gets pretty thin when a possible inheritance is involved. Money does strange things to people. It puts dollar signs in their eyes. I've heard of brothers and sisters at each others' throats, even extreme cases where they've committed fratricide over who gets the family jewels."

"Fratricide?" Nona's brows knitted.

"The killing of a brother or sister."

"That's pretty bizarre."

"It's entirely possible. From what I gathered, Frank let Ivy control the purse strings. It's one possibility of many. I haven't talked to all of the Diggs siblings yet."

"Who have you talked to so far?"

"Dora and Ted. There's still the youngest one, Bobby."

"You don't really think he had something to do with Ivy's death?"

"Well, he's been pretty elusive so far, which makes me very suspicious of him. I'm beginning to think he's avoiding being questioned about Ivy."

"I don't think so. He's pretty busy with his diving business and college classes."

"He didn't show up at her funeral, either, Nona. He's the only one in the family who wasn't there."

"I admit that is rather strange behavior."

"Yes, it is."

"Well, you, Skip, and Cruiser will get to the bottom of it."

"Yes, if Skip and I are still speaking. I need to call that funny guy and see what's eating him."

Out of habit, I started to reach for the wall phone.

"Mom, will you do me a really big favor?"

"What?"

"Will you please use the birthday gift I got you."

"I already made an appointment at Oh, Heavenly Lady for the spa day."

"Not that. I mean your cellular. Use it!"

"I am, honey, I am. Well, some of the time." I reached for my purse and pulled out the soft leather case that held the small phone. I flipped it open and dialed Skip's number. It rang a couple of times and I heard Skip's voice.

"Cassidy here."

"Hey, Skip. What's shakin'?"

"Just knee deep in paperwork as usual. What can I do for you?" Skip's tone sounded so abrupt and businesslike it took me aback, so I decided to keep my call strictly business, too. This just wasn't like Skip at all. I couldn't figure it out. What was going on with him?

"I wonder if you could help me with something?"

"What?"

"I want to plan a stakeout."

"A stakeout?" Skip tried to sound cool and professional, but he couldn't disguise the excitement in his voice. "Uh, okay. Who are we staking out?"

"Why don't you come over here for lunch? We can talk about it and plan the whole thing."

"Well . . ."

"I'm making some of my famous chili, Skip." I knew that would be too much for him to resist.

"Okay. I'll be there at noon or thereabouts."

"Fine, I'll see you then." I hit the off button on the cellular and slipped it back into my purse.

"Sounds like things are back to normal with you and Skip, huh?"

"You know Skip. Just say the words 'chili' and 'stakeout' and he's all ears."

"You mean more so than Cruiser?" Nona and I laughed.

The only thing I didn't mention to Skip and my daughter was that this would be a slightly different kind of stakeout than usual.

Chapter Twenty-Eight

"We're gonna have a what?" Skip sputtered through a mouthful of my killer chili.

"A Tessie watch."

"You've got to be kidding me."

"No, I'm not. I want to set up a surveillance camera over at Rubicon Bay near Boney Crider's place where we had our sighting the other morning in the *Trout Scout*."

"You mean where *you* had a sighting."

"Right. Anyway, I'm going to get some film footage of our mysterious lake monster or know the reason why. Then no one can dispute her existence."

"Is this an Alice B. Toklas recipe for chili you've cooked up here?"

"Very funny. So what do you think of my idea?"

"I think you'd better stop hanging around that old pothead, Boney Crider, is what I think. Didn't anyone warn you not to inhale during that interview you did?"

"I'm serious, Skip."

"I know you are. That's what worries me."

"C'mon. I wasn't in that boat by myself. You were there, too. You felt those jolts to the *Trout Scout*. That was no log we hit. Something was out there, and it was alive. You know I don't joke about things like this."

"Yes, I know you're not joking, but I can think of a dozen explanations for what you say you saw." Skip sprinkled more diced onions on his chili and sliced off some freshly baked cornbread.

"Okay, smarty. Name one."

Skip shoveled more chili into his mouth as he pondered my question. Cornbread crumbs collected in his mustache.

"When are you going to shave that bristly bottlebrush off your upper lip?"

"You mean you don't like my mustache?"

"No, I don't!"

Dashing Deputy Skip brushed the crumbs out of his mustache and twirled the ends between his thumb and forefinger. He probably thought he looked like Rhett Butler. I thought he looked more like Groucho Marx.

"Well, Skip?"

"Well, what?"

"I'm still waiting for that explanation."

"Hmmm. Well, it could have been one of those mackinaw with a thyroid condition you said I was supposed to find over there, which I'll never catch now because I don't have a fishing pole."

"I told you I'll get you another one."

"It also could have been some debris that surfaced and hit the *Scout.* As for your Tessie, it could have just been the light and mist playing tricks on you. Dawn and dusk do funny things to the lake, kind of like a mirage on the desert. I've been on enough early morning fishing trips to know that. Think about it. Most of the so-called Tessie sightings have been at those times of the day by fishermen who've already had a few beers."

"Sure, it could be any of those things, but I'm convinced it wasn't. You weren't down there in the water with it slithering around your ankles." An odd expression crossed Skip's face. "What's wrong?"

"Wasn't I? You forget the night on the *Dixie Queen* when I

went overboard. I felt something weird down there, too."

"That's right. I'd forgotten about that. You said it felt like something caught hold of you, then let you go. That was exactly the same thing I experienced."

"Well, I still think you're way off base, but like it or not I guess we're having ourselves a Tessie watch. We'll do it the same time as our other encounter, at dawn."

"No, I want to cover at least a twenty-four-hour period. She may not cooperate with our time schedule. I need to borrow some night surveillance equipment from you."

"No problem. I'll help you get set up, but I won't be able to stay with you the whole time. I have too much work piling up at the office, not to mention a homicide investigation. You haven't forgotten about that little detail, I trust."

"Of course not. We still need to corral the younger brother, Bobby, for questioning. Nona's been hanging around with him, and I don't like it."

"She has? Well, maybe she can help us out."

"Are you suggesting I use my daughter to lure a killer, Skip?"

"Of course not. I only thought since he's been so hard to pin down . . ."

"I don't want her involved in this business."

"I understand. Anyway, I think I know where we can find him," Skip said.

"Where?"

"I found out he's enrolled in some courses at the community college."

"That's right. He was talking to Nona about that the first time she met him on the *Dixie Queen*. It so happens I'll be over at the college later. In fact, I'll bet he's in one of Cris's classes."

"Say, Beanie. Just tell me one thing."

"Sure, anything."

"What's with you and this chalkboard duster, anyway?"

"Not a thing. I'm researching an article, and he's providing me with material. That's all. By the way, why didn't you come over and join us last night at the pub?"

"I would have felt too awkward. It looked like you were out on a date or something. Three's a crowd where I come from."

"Of course it wasn't a date. It was strictly business."

"Yeah? Since when do you conduct your interviews at pubs?"

I had to admit he had me there. I didn't usually do my interviews in dining establishments, and Skip knew that. What I didn't understand was why he would care.

"You've been acting kinda funny lately, Skip. What's up with you, anyway?"

"There's nothing up with me, except that there may be a murderer on the loose in Tahoe, and we still don't know who it is. This Crispin guy is a stranger in town, just like Medwyn was. You remember him and how that turned out. In fact, everything was fine around here before your nutty professor showed up."

"That's just a coincidence. Crispin's not a killer."

"What makes you so sure? He lays that accent on pretty thick. How do you even know whether it's authentic and he's who he says he is? You don't know him that well, do you?"

Like DART on Crispin's sub, I picked up on Skip's innuendo, but I didn't feel that I owed him any explanations about Cris and me. It was none of his business. Besides, there was nothing to explain about us. At least that's what I kept telling myself. "He just doesn't seem the type to me. Besides, what would be his motive? He didn't even know Ivy Diggs. What reason would he have to kill her? Anyway, he'd have to have been on the cruise that night."

"How do you know he wasn't? Half of Tahoe was on board the *Dixie Queen* for the July 4th cruise."

Skip was right. I didn't know for sure Crispin wasn't there that night, but until now I'd had no reason to wonder whether he was or not. "I can check, I suppose. That is, if they keep records of who goes on those cruises. I suspect they only count tickets. I don't recall anyone taking our names at the ticket booth, do you?"

Skip wiped his mouth with a napkin. "In our case, they would have. I paid for our tickets with a credit card. Could be that Blayne did the same."

"Not likely if he didn't want to be traced," I said. "I don't see a reason to do it, but I can ask for copies of the receipts if you think I should."

"Yes, go ahead, but please be careful you don't get yourself into trouble again."

"You don't have to worry about me. I'm a big girl."

"Nevertheless, I'd rather you didn't go nosing around in such things alone. We're a team, remember? You and me and that funny-looking hound dog of yours."

"I promise I'll be careful. I'll have my cell phone with me if I run into any Tessie trouble. Nona's orders."

"Well, I'm glad she's watching out for you."

"You two don't have to worry about me or Cruiser. Speaking of Cruiser, I'll take him along with me on the serpent stakeout. He's a pretty good watchdog when the chips are down."

Skip guffawed. "Especially when they're potato chips."

I glanced at Cruiser, who was conducting an under-the-table surveillance operation. Skip gave in and tossed him a piece of cornbread, which he caught on the fly. Not a crumb went to waste.

CHAPTER TWENTY-NINE

Silhouetted against the setting sun, the dark, craggy peaks of the western rim were prehistoric beasts looming over Rubicon Bay as I sat at the forest's edge with Cruiser. Those were the only things remotely resembling dinosaurs that I had observed in the past twelve hours I'd been sitting there with my borrowed surveillance camera, scanning the surface of the lake for any unusual activity. The only footage I had logged all day was of sunburned bathers, jet skis, and speedboats filled with rowdy tourists. Nothing unusual about that.

Nona had brought me some lunch around one o'clock, which I shared with Cruiser. The avocado, tomato and sprout sandwich, potato chips and six-pack of Diet Coke she picked up at the roadside cafe at Richardson Camp were a somewhat different repast than my Washoe ancestors would have partaken of on one of their hunts.

In days of old, I would have eaten freshly picked berries, seeds and pine nuts, perhaps some venison, rabbit or squirrel if the hunt were successful. After my belly was full, I would locate one of the many sugar pines that grew in the basin before the discovery of the Comstock Lode in Virginia City depleted nearly all of them. From one of the distinctive foot-long pinecones I'd have gathered some sticky sap and chewed it to freshen my breath or settle my stomach.

For thousands of years, the lake had provided the Washoe a refuge from the searing valley heat. Tahoe was the place where the fish once swam in numbers so great that tribal elders still tell of a time when men could reach into the lake and pull out trout by the handful.

For the duration of the summer months, our people gathered food and the women wove beautiful baskets from the pine needles and grasses—women like Dat-So-La-Lee, whose rare and exquisite handicraft is still highly prized among collectors. When she died, her genius died with her, but her art lives on and is a testament to the people who once thrived in the land of the Big Water.

When the alpine air turned crisp in the autumn and the first chill winds stirred the leaves of aspen trees, as golden as the ore that brought da bo oh (White Man) relentlessly westward, the Washoe returned to the valley below. In their wake, they left behind no smoldering campfires to burn the forests, no trash, not even a broken twig or a footprint to indicate that they had ever been here.

If there really were a prehistoric creature in this glacial lake that had somehow survived for eons, I wondered if any of my ancestors had ever spotted it, as I was hoping to now. Perhaps that was the source of some of the fantastic mythical creatures that were said to inhabit the lake. The terrible man-eating giant that devoured the enemies of the Washoe may have been more truth than legend. From what I had observed of Tessie thus far, she was probably a meat eater. Her serrated teeth also indicated that she was a carnivore, although she could possibly be omnivorous in order to have thrived on the plankton in the lake if fish were scarce. Nature has a way of making adjustments in her creations to adapt to the environment. Still, I had seen her scoop up that forty-pound fish like it was a sardine. If she was carnivorous, that could have been bad news for Cruiser and me.

Perhaps the eerie wail of water babies, the mythical creatures that terrified the Indians so much they dared not venture near

Cave Rock, was really the sound of the lake creature emanating from deep in the subterranean cavern said to still exist beneath the rock. To this day, Cave Rock holds many forbidden secrets for the Washoe people. It could be that Lake Tahoe was home to more than just the Wa She Shu and that bear, squirrel and coyote weren't the only animal life that still inhabited the area.

Dusk fell. The waters of the lake were once more serene, and the area was deserted except for Cruiser and me. The boats were all moored, and the tourists had flocked to Stateline to dine, drink, and spend their money amid the gaudy, pulsing lights of the casinos.

Speaking of drinking, I had drunk way too many soft drinks, and the call of nature was becoming impossible to ignore. I stood up and looked around for a secluded area. I spied some foliage off to my right and found a good place to relieve myself. Cruiser moseyed down to the edge of the lake to have a drink of water and then do a little tree marking of his own. This might not be the answer to the question of what a bear does in the woods, but at least I knew what a middle-aged, incontinent woman and her dog did.

I emerged from the prickly Manzanita and called out to Cruiser, who, as usual, was taking his own sweet time to answer me. I heard a rustling in the bushes, which startled me momentarily until out came Cruiser. He had something wrapped around his neck. I realized it was a silk scarf. Some woman must have lost it while hiking through the area.

"My, don't you look dashing." I laughed as I unwound the soiled scarf from Cruiser's neck, until I noticed something all too familiar about it. It was exactly like the Yankee Doodle Dandy scarf Ivy Diggs had worn on the night of her disappearance from the *Dixie Queen*. Then I noticed something else. The scarf was stained with blood.

CHAPTER THIRTY

I tucked the bloodstained silk scarf Cruiser had found into my coat pocket. Could it be the missing woman's scarf, or was it just another one that looked exactly like it? It was a silk Hermés scarf, and not everyone spent that much money on accessories. Even if some other prosperous woman had fallen on the trail and cut herself, would she use an expensive designer scarf to wipe off the blood? Possibly.

On the other hand, if it did belong to Ivy, how had it gotten here? Perhaps it had washed up on shore and the wind had blown it into the scrub brush where it lay until a certain nosy basset waddled by and ended up wearing it as an ascot. But if she had been stabbed and had bled on the scarf, wouldn't the bloodstains have washed off in the water? Not entirely, perhaps. I've always heard you can't wash out bloodstains, and now with advanced detection methods such as DNA tests, that is truer than ever. Crime labs even use lasers to detect the presence of blood or other bodily fluids. There was only one way to prove whether or not this was Ivy Diggs' scarf, and Skip would have to help me with that.

The forest was enveloped in darkness as the sun finally slipped into its rocky cavern on the west ridge. I'd brought along a down jacket and my trusty deerstalker to keep my ears warm. Once the sun went down at Tahoe, it could get pretty chilly, even in midsummer. Cruiser had a fur coat and built-in earflaps. Fortunately, the sand beneath me had retained the warmth from the sun. I nudged my coat collar closer around my neck and settled in with my hound for the night shift of the Tessie watch. A quicksilver moon cast a cold eye on the lake. Cruiser ambled down to the lake's edge to tank up with water again so he could finish hosing the rest of the shrubs in the vicinity.

I had almost dozed off when I heard Cruiser bark. I surveyed the surface of the lake but didn't see anything. I discovered Cruiser wasn't barking at the lake but at something he'd found in the sand. He was digging furiously, shoveling sand with his paws. Probably leftover food from campers. From the way Cruiser was going at it, I figured that must be one juicy rib bone he was after.

"Okay, boy. I'll help you." I knelt down and started digging, too. I dug until my hands hit something solid. I brushed away more sand to get a better look. At first I couldn't tell what it was, but I knew it was no rib bone. I had uncovered four oblong objects that were buried in the sand. Using my upturned deerstalker as a makeshift basket, I carried them back to my stakeout to have a better look.

I lit my Coleman lantern and brushed away a crust of dirt and sand from one of the odd things Cruiser had led me to. It was about a foot in length and very hard. At first I thought it must be a rock, but it soon became apparent that this was no rock. It took me a moment to realize that what I was holding was an egg. I held the ovum up to the light from the lantern. The shell was very thick, but I could discern the outline of an embryo inside it. The egg was way too large for one of the resident Canada Geese to have laid it, and as far as I knew there were no ostriches in Tahoe. Although ostrich farming had gained popularity, I had heard of no farms around here. I would have to show this to Crispin to see what he had to say about it.

I wrapped one of the eggs in Ivy Diggs' scarf and tucked it

gently in my backpack. I rinsed the other eggs in the lake water to help remove my scent and buried the clutch back where Cruiser had found it, covering the eggs gently with sand. Whatever animal had deposited these here would probably come back looking for them. I didn't want to disappoint her. I just hoped she couldn't count.

Skip would also be interested to know what I had found out here. He had provided me with some night vision goggles, a new piece of equipment I was sworn not to let anyone know he had lent me for this stakeout of mine. I had promised him, but I'd also made a promise to myself. I wasn't abandoning my post until I got something on film, even if it took me all day and all night, too.

Looking at the lake now in the eerie pearlescent light of the moon, I could envision Da-aw in its preternatural state millennia ago before human beings had evolved into the destructive creatures we've become, aliens to the natural world, harbingers of our own extinction. In my mind's eye I saw rivers of molten lava spilling from erupting volcanoes on what is now the North Shore, quakes and endless upheaval of stone forming the bedrock of Lake Tahoe. I could easily believe that Tahoe's depths harbored secrets that men and their technology would never fully disclose. Should I be trying to expose another one? My tenacious nature would not allow me to abandon my purpose now that I was committed to it. In the light of the full moon, I continued watching for any sign of movement out on the lake.

It was around midnight, and I had seen nothing unusual on Tahoe's calm surface. Looked like my Tessie watch was going to be a bust. I could already hear Skip's merciless ribbing about this fiasco. Cruiser had curled up at my side and was beginning to snore. I had nearly dozed off myself when a screeching sound jolted me awake. It startled Cruiser, too. I saw the shadow of outstretched wings brush the treetops above us.

"Settle down, boy. It's only an owl."

But Cruiser didn't settle down. His ears perked up. Then I heard a rustling in the bushes behind us. It sounded too large for a squirrel or coyote. I hoped it wasn't a bear. He may have caught scent of the remnants of the lunch in my backpack. The rustling sound grew louder. It was coming closer. I stood up, ready to make tracks if need be.

I sighed with relief when I heard a familiar voice.

"Beanie?"

"Over here, Skip."

"How's it going? See anything interesting out there?"

"Nothing yet. What are you doing here?"

"I just wanted to be sure you're okay. I brought you a thermos of coffee."

"Oh, thanks. I could use something warm. It's getting pretty nippy out here."

Skip sat down on a log.

"How are those new night vision goggles working out? I haven't had occasion to use them yet myself."

"They're pretty nifty. Here, try 'em." Skip slipped them on and I started to laugh. He looked funnier than Cruiser did in his goggles. "You look like a space alien."

"Say, I can see as clearly as if it was broad daylight. I hate to think what these gadgets cost the department."

"Plenty, I'm sure."

"Got to keep up with the techies nowadays in crime detecting, you know."

"Say, I did find something kind of interesting before you got here."

"Uh-huh." Skip gazed out on the lake, panning from one end to the other and back again.

"Did you hear what I said?" Skip didn't answer. He was

focused on the lake. Then I noticed his head snap back to one spot and do a Cruiser-style point.

"What is it?"

"Quick, aim the camera where I'm pointing and start shooting!"

I did as Skip instructed. The only sound in the night was the whirring of the video camera, and that same strange grunting sound resonating from somewhere out in the indigo waters of the lake.

CHAPTER THIRTY-ONE

"Did you hear that, Beanie?"

"Sure did, but I don't see a thing."

"False alarm, I guess. For a minute, I thought I saw something moving out there."

"Well, I'll leave the camera running. Maybe she'll show up again."

"Maybe, but I think your Tessie is camera shy."

"Probably so, since no one has captured her on film before."

"There's good reason for that."

"What do you mean?"

"She doesn't exist."

"Well, if she doesn't exist, then how do you explain this?" I pulled the egg I'd found out of my backpack, and carefully unwrapped it from the scarf.

"What have you got there?" Skip said, snagging an end of the scarf. He was more interested in that than the egg.

"Cruiser found that. I think it might belong to Ivy Diggs."

"What makes you think so?"

"It looks just like the one she was wearing the night she disappeared from the *Dixie Queen.*"

"That seems unlikely. It could belong to anyone." Skip examined the scarf. "What's this? Blood?"

"That's what it looks like to me. We need to find out if it's Ivy's blood."

"Okay. I'll have the lab do some tests." Skip folded the scarf and tucked it in his pocket. "What else you got there?"

I placed the egg in Skip's palm. "You tell me."

"It's an egg."

"Ever seen one like it before?"

"How should I know? Do I look like a chicken farmer?"

I hated to tell him, but with that straw-yellow hair of his and sitting there holding an egg he did look more like Old Mac-Donald than the county sheriff. I couldn't help it; I burst out laughing.

"Here, take this thing." Skip tossed the egg at me. I almost fumbled his pass.

"Hey, careful! Don't break it."

"What's the big deal? It's just a goose egg."

"I doubt that."

"Well, what do you think . . ." Skip stopped mid-sentence, then scratched his head. "Wait a minute. You're not telling me that this is a . . ."

"Yes, I think it might be. And it's not the only one I found."

"This is no dinosaur egg. That's impossible."

"Is it? Follow me." I led Skip down to the water's edge where Cruiser had uncovered the nest. Cruiser followed us and started digging in the sand again.

"No, boy! Leave it!" Cruiser obeyed my command and busied himself re-watering the plants he'd already watered.

I dug away the layer of sand and re-exposed the clutch of eggs, taking care not to touch them again. I held the lantern closer so Skip could get a good look.

"I still say they're goose eggs."

"Geese don't bury their eggs in the sand."

"They don't?"

"No."

"Well, something laid these eggs here."

"That's right. Something did, but it wasn't Mother Goose."

The first rays of dawn stabbed my eyelids. I forgot where I was for a moment until I heard the forest beginning to stir to life. Obnoxious jays bickering in the pines drowned the chatter of squirrels foraging for breakfast.

I felt Cruiser tucked close beside me, still snoring away. I was glad I'd had my hound dog with me for warmth. The campfire had died down hours ago. In fact, I felt downright cozy, considering I'd slept in the forest all night. I heard a louder snore, and looked up to see Skip's tonsils. He was leaning up against a tree with me snuggled against him. I sat up and tried to nudge him awake. I could more easily have awakened a hibernating bear.

"Skip. Skip. Hey, *wake up!*"

"Wh . . . wha?"

And I thought Cruiser was a sound sleeper.

Skip rubbed his eyes, stretched and yawned. "Is it morning already?"

"Yep. I think we'd better strike camp before the tourists show up."

"I've got to get to work, and I'd better take this equipment back with me before anyone misses it."

"Well, let me get the tape out first before you pack it up."

"Think you got anything on there?"

"I don't know. I sure hope so." Whether this had all been a huge waste of time remained to be seen. I felt a tingle of excitement at the prospect of being the first to capture the creature on video. Or maybe it was partly the fact that I also couldn't wait to share my prize Tessie tape with the handsome professor. That was sure to get his attention.

"Well, if you do, promise me something."

"What?"

"Let me see it before you call the *National Enquirer.*"
I laughed. "Don't you mean the *Tahoe Tattler*?"

CHAPTER THIRTY-TWO

Crispin and I sat alone in a dark classroom. After Skip's suggestion that Crispin could also be a possible suspect in Ivy Diggs' murder, I wondered if this was such a good idea. Still, I'd been in tighter quarters with him in the sub. If he had any ideas about getting rid of a nosy reporter, he could have easily taken the opportunity then and jettisoned me out into the lake with the rest of the corpses. Maybe he was just biding his time.

No, no. Skip had him all wrong. He was just jealous of Crispin, that's all. Of more concern to me was the fact that Skip might be entertaining ideas about us becoming more than the good friends we are, especially after our cozy night in the woods together. I was glad I had awakened Skip before he caught me snuggled up beside him in the forest. He might really have gotten the wrong idea. Anyone might have.

The light from the TV screen lit the shadows as Crispin loaded the video into the machine. I was excited to see what I had captured on film the night before. I could see the headlines in the grocery store checkout aisle gossip sheets already, right next to the photos of the two-headed baby and Elvis's ghost: "Prehistoric monster inhabits Lake Tahoe." I hadn't been this excited about seeing a movie since I was a kid at a Saturday matinee watching Captain Blood swashbuckling his way across the broad screen or Creature Feature King Vincent Price in *House of Wax*. I remembered wearing those silly 3-D cardboard glasses and ducking when objects seemed to leap off the screen.

Suddenly, I had a distinct craving for buttered popcorn.

"Are you sure you shot anything on here, Elsie?" Crispin said.

"I'm pretty sure I did. I heard the camera running, so I must have gotten something on film."

The film had captured something all right. Images of a man and a woman and a dog snoring away in the forest.

"I don't understand it. There should be something on that tape. Skip said Tessie must be camera shy. I guess he was right."

"Did you have the camera aimed at the lake?"

"I admit I'm no techie whiz, but I know how to use a camera."

"Hold on. I do see something else here."

Apparently the camera had captured other images besides Cruiser and me while we slept. There was a boat out on the lake, and there appeared to be some sort of rescue or salvage activity going on. The lights on the craft made it easy to discern the diver who periodically submerged and resurfaced.

"I guess they're still searching for drowning victims. We've had a few this summer at Tahoe." Looked like Tessie was a no-show. I felt embarrassed, but at least it had afforded me a good excuse to see the professor again.

"Well, I have a class to teach in a few minutes," Crispin said. "Students will be showing up momentarily."

"I'm sorry to have wasted your time with this, Cris."

"Not to worry. Do you mind if I keep this tape so I can examine it when I have more time?"

"I suppose not." I turned to leave. "Oh, I almost forgot. I have something else here that might interest you."

I picked up my backpack and pulled out the egg Cruiser had found.

"Hmmm. What have we here?" Crispin got up and flicked the lights back on. I handed him my unearthed treasure. He put on his glasses for a closer look.

"Good Lord, do you know what this is?" Crispin gasped. For a moment I thought he might faint. "It's a bloody dinosaur egg. Wherever did you find it?"

"Near Rubicon Bay. The same place Skip and I sighted the lake creature."

"I want to have a closer look at this under the fluoroscope. Come along, if you like."

I wasn't letting this egghead professor abscond with my egg. I followed Crispin out of the classroom and down the hall past his office to a lab filled with various kinds of equipment, none of which I could name and certainly would be no more adept at using than Skip's surveillance camera. I saw various rock samples in trays, which took me right back to my college geology class.

Crispin placed the egg in a contraption that looked something like an X-ray machine, apparently the fluoroscope of which he spoke.

"This looks like some pretty expensive equipment you have here."

"Yes, it is."

"I'm surprised the college can afford all these gadgets."

"They can't. The fluoroscope and all this other equipment are for the lake studies."

"What does this thing do, anyway?"

"Well, in medicine it's used in diagnosis for examining internal organs. It can detect cancer of the bones or ulcers in the digestive tract and osteoporosis. In this case, it will give us an accurate image of what's inside the egg. I'll just place it between this X-ray tube and the fluorescent screen, and we'll see shadows displayed here on the screen. The bones will look darker than the fleshy bits."

Crispin positioned the egg and turned on the fluoroscope. The contents of the egg were clearly visible.

"It looks like a bird to me," I said. "Are you sure this isn't some kind of a bird?"

"I can see why you might think that would be the case, but I assure you it's not. The skeletons of birds and dinosaurs are quite similar in structure," Crispin said. "That's why it has been conjectured in recent years that birds descended from dinosaurs. The skeletons are alike in some respects."

"I've heard that, but I find it hard to swallow that something so large could have evolved into something so tiny."

"But not all birds are tiny. Look at the condor. Or emus and ostriches. This egg isn't much larger than an ostrich egg."

"I thought that's what it was at first, but the shape was different. Besides, I've never heard of any ostriches in Tahoe."

"You're right. This is no ostrich egg."

"But weren't all the dinosaurs killed by a comet?"

"Not the comet itself, but the cloud of pulverized rock and debris from the impact that shrouded Earth from the sun and killed the vegetation that fed the dinosaurs."

"Then theoretically none of them could have survived."

"Theoretically. Still, at some higher elevations that are closer to the sun, and in deep lakes such as this one, the effects of such a cataclysmic event may not have been quite as severe. Perhaps some of the fish and plankton dinosaurs fed on might have survived. Even the dinosaurs themselves."

"So if a dinosaur does exist in this lake, she would be an omnivore?"

"That's possible, especially if she's mammalian." Crispin stopped talking and examined the screen more closely.

"What do you see?" He seemed transfixed. "What's wrong?"

"Come closer for a look."

I moved in closer until Crispin and I were shoulder to shoulder. I felt a thrill, but it wasn't from more physical contact with the handsome professor. He pointed to the screen, and I stood there dumbfounded. I couldn't believe my eyes, but we both saw it plain as day. The thing inside the egg moved. It was alive!

"This is amazing, Elsie!" Caught up in the excitement of the moment, Crispin suddenly pulled me against his broad chest and hugged me. Wrapping my arms around him, I felt the wooly fiber of his cardigan beneath my hands, inhaled his manly scent, and it was the pleasantest thing. For a moment, I imagined I was in Tom's arms again. I closed my eyes, enveloped in memories of long ago.

I expected Crispin to let go, but he didn't. He looked into my eyes. I felt myself swimming in the deep waters of his crystalline eyes, diving deeper and deeper. Then something amazing and utterly unexpected happened. He kissed me! He tasted like wild anise in a mountain meadow. I should have pulled away, but I didn't. So much for keeping things strictly business. Perhaps Skip had reason to feel jealous after all.

CHAPTER THIRTY-THREE

"May I keep this here to study?" Crispin asked, still holding the unusual egg I'd found.

"Just as long as you're not planning to fry it up with bangers for breakfast."

He laughed. "Well luv, I see the students are gathering for class. I had better be going. Thanks again for all your help with this."

Luv? Had I just heard him call me luv? "No problem, Cris. I'm more than a little interested in this myself." It wasn't every day that you were able to prove the existence of a prehistoric creature. For so many years people had reported sightings of such a creature, but none had been able to get the kind of evidence I had here. Skip would be so excited when I told him about this, and I'd enjoy serving up a big helping of crow for him, too. Of course, I wouldn't tell him about what else happened with the professor in his lab, or I might be having a little crow sampler myself.

Crispin walked me back toward the classroom. I felt myself clinging to every moment, not wanting to leave his company. Just as we approached, I saw a familiar blond-haired young man walking toward us.

"Is he in your class?"

"Yes. His name is . . ."

"I know who he is. That's Bobby Diggs."

"That's right. You've met him before?"

"Yes. He's the stepson of the woman who drowned in the lake recently."

"There was a drowning?"

"Yes, it was in the papers for days. Didn't you read about it?"

"No, I haven't had much time to read the newspapers."

"I have to. It's my job."

"Yes, I know. Well, you really must excuse me now, Elsie. It's time for my class to begin."

"Of course. When does class end?"

"Eleven-fifty. Why?"

"Oh, nothing. Just wondering."

I would wait outside until class was over, but not just to catch a glimpse of Crispin again. Bobby wasn't giving me the slip this time.

After the archeology class ended, Bobby shot out of the door so fast I had to run to catch up with him. Good thing I was wearing my Nikes.

"Mr. Diggs!" He kept going. "Bobby, wait!"

At that point he turned to face me. "Huh?"

"I'd like to talk to you for a minute."

"I'm in kind of a hurry."

"It'll only take a moment. I'd like to ask you about the accident on the *Dixie Queen* July 4th."

Bobby motioned for me to join him in a quieter spot away from other students. "What about it?"

"I need to know where you were when your stepmother fell overboard."

"You the police?"

"Not exactly. A private investigator."

"Then I don't have to talk to you, do I now?"

"No, but it would help me find out what happened to Ivy."

Bobby turned to leave, then paused and turned to face me

again. "Okay. Here's the thing. I don't remember that night too well. I'd had a few drinks, see?"

"Please try to think back. When did you last see your stepmother?"

Bobby pondered the question a moment.

"Well, I remember seeing her leave for the upper deck. Dad followed her up the stairs. I figured they were going to scout out a good spot to watch the fireworks. I tried to follow them, but I was feeling kinda dizzy, you know? Then the boat musta hit something 'cause people and stuff were flying all over the place. You remember. You were there, too."

"Yes, I remember." How could I ever forget?

"I fell and hit my head right here." Bobby pointed to his right temple, where there was a small scar, but it didn't look fresh to me. "Knocked me out for a few minutes. When I came to, the alarm was sounding and everyone was topside looking for Ivy."

"So you didn't see her again after she and your dad argued?"

"No. That was the last time I saw her."

"Where were your brother and sister all this time?"

"With Dad, I guess."

"How did you feel about Ivy marrying your father?"

"I didn't like it, and I didn't like her. None of us did, especially Dora. She despised the woman, but we all knew what Ivy was."

"Which was?"

"A hearse chaser."

"Hearse chaser?"

"You know. The kind of woman who marries rich widowers with one foot in the grave. Guys just like my dad."

When Bobby got into the black Mercedes with DIGG IT vanity plates, I suspected he knew something about chasing, too.

CHAPTER THIRTY-FOUR

On the way back from the college, I stopped at Debbie's Diner. I was just in time for the lunch rush, but I didn't have to wait long for service.

"Coffee?" the waitress asked. It wasn't Rita, thank goodness. Must have been her day off. I wouldn't have to endure her irritating behavior and thinly veiled insults, which always seemed to escalate whenever Skip was present.

"Yes, please." The young girl poured my coffee, and every drop of it spilled perfectly into my cup, unlike when Rita served me beverages. I'd never left Debbie's Diner without brown stains on my morning paper. I was thinking of joining the Red Hat Society and buying a purple dress just so I wouldn't blend into the wallpaper with all the other middle-age women in America.

What was it about a woman being over fifty years of age that made her suddenly invisible? Perhaps that was how a man like Frank Diggs had ended up with an unscrupulous woman like Ivy who, from what I had heard thus far, married him only for his money. Aging men are easy prey for younger women of questionable moral character. Male menopause is just as bothersome as the female kind, apparently.

In the days before my mother's final journey, she told me that life is full of transitions; it's all about learning to accept those transitions with wisdom and grace. She always did that. The answers to retaining self-worth in the face of old age do not come from a fat wallet, a plastic surgeon's knife, Botox injections, or a trophy mate. It just takes some of us longer than others to discover that.

Of course, hearse chasing, as Bobby had called it, is not limited to female predators. We've all heard of young gigolos who prey upon wealthy older women, feeding their vanity by heaping attention on them in exchange for money, clothes, and cars. Places like Tahoe, Florida and other retirement communities all have their fair share of younger men and women scanning the obituaries for widows and widowers.

"Have you decided what you'd like to order, miss?"

Miss? Boy, this girl was going to get a big, fat tip. Of course, I realized she was just buttering me up for one. You don't call fifty-year-old women *miss*, otherwise. "Yes, I'll have the veggie personal pizza, Mary Ann," I said, taking note of her nametag, "and you can call me Elsie." Her voice was soft and pleasant to the ear, a nice change from Rita's grating nasal twang and gum snapping.

"May I bring you anything else to go with that, Elsie?"

"No, thanks," I answered and went back to reading the newspaper.

My article about Tahoe Tessie had sold out all the papers in town within an hour of hitting the newsstands. The whole town was buzzing about it. In fact, the *Tahoe Tattler* had given front-page coverage to Tessie. I had no doubt that something this unusual would be featured in the checkout lanes right beside the alien autopsy photos.

Whether or not there were ever really any aliens to autopsy remained to be proven, but there was nothing phony about the dinosaur egg I'd found. That really existed! I'd touched it and seen it with my own two eyes, but I wasn't going to tattle about that, even though its authenticity had been confirmed by Professor Blayne, a cryptozoologist and respected authority on the subject. None of us, least of all I, had any inkling of the effect Tessiemania was about to have on our quiet, little mountain community or the attention it would draw, some of it from the wrong people.

The Ivy Diggs investigation was relegated to page eight of the *Tattler*. That was old news for everyone in town but Skip and me, and the supposedly grieving Frank Diggs. Apparently, he was the only one in the family who had shed any tears over Ivy, who, according to the Diggs children, was the classic evil stepmother. But Cruiser and I weren't about to let that trail go cold. At least not until I had ruled out all possible suspects in what I still felt was the real fantastic fish story around these parts.

In spite of what Bobby had told me, I couldn't dismiss the fact that he had been strangely elusive through this whole thing, declining to attend her memorial, never present when we had talked to other members of the family. I was beginning to get the feeling he might be hiding something. The rest of the family seemed to harbor some disdain for him, too, from what I had gathered thus far in talking to them. Every family has its black sheep, and apparently Bobby was the Diggs' main muttonhead. Perhaps it was the birth order theory at work here. Ted was the oldest, the successful one, who ran a thriving business and was clearly an "in charge" kind of person. Of course, I had to wonder if he had also been in charge of getting rid of Ivy. No one in that family was above suspicion in my book until I could prove for certain what happened to her.

Dora was the middle child. The in-between kid who always had to struggle harder for recognition, always overshadowed by the accomplishments of her older brother and usurped by the cute baby. Being also the only female, she was relegated to being caretaker of the younger child and now her ailing father. I wondered why the daughter of a family was always responsible for the care of aging parents, a traditional and chauvinistic role that had endured far too long. It had been the same in my family. When my mother's health began to fail, it was I and not my brother who attended to her needs, who stayed with her in the hospital. Apparently, the liberation of women has not yet extended to this area. We still have a long way to go, baby.

Whether birth order or being born female has more to do with being designated as caretaker is still open for debate, but from what I had seen and experienced, it made no difference. The only question no one has ever addressed in the birth order premise is, Which one of the children would be most likely to commit murder?

My cell phone rang. It was Skip.

"What's up?" I figured this was business as usual. I wasn't prepared for Skip's next question.

"How about I treat you to dinner Saturday night?"

"Sure, okay. McDonald's again?"

"No, I was thinking about the Lakeview Marina Bar and Grille."

For a moment, I was lost for words. What in heaven's name had gotten into Skip lately? This wasn't like him at all. He's the only man I've ever known, other than my Tom, who is so tight his wallet has a combination lock. First the staring contest at the pub, and now this. I had written that off to his protective feelings toward an old friend and partner in crime busting. After what had nearly happened to me on previous cases, I could understand that he might have a tendency toward watchfulness to be sure I didn't get mixed up with another creepy character. However, I couldn't find any word to explain Skip's dinner invitation other than what it was . . . a date.

"That's awfully expensive. You sure about this?"

"Sure I'm sure, if you're sure."

"Well, uh . . . sure. It's the best restaurant in town, in my opinion. Great view of the lake, too."

"Good. Pick you up around six-thirty."

"I'll be looking forward to it. Oh, by the way, what did you find out about that scarf?"

"Hold on. I've got the report here somewhere."

I heard the rustling of paper on the other end. No wonder Skip never managed to dig himself out of his Mount Everest of paperwork. I could identify. The stack of paper in my office wasn't exactly a Mount Everest, but it was at least a Mount Tallac.

"Ah, I found it," Skip said. "Let's see here, uh . . . yep. It's just as you thought."

"So, I was right, then. It is Ivy's scarf?"

"Affirmative, we have a DNA match on the bloodstain. Contrary to popular belief, dead men do tell tales—at least in the forensics lab."

And dead women, too.

CHAPTER THIRTY-FIVE

After the all-night Tessie watch, I was really beginning to feel a sleep deficit. In my twenties, I used to stay up all night long studying for exams or going to dusk-to-dawn drive-in movie shows, and it never phased me in the least. Not so anymore. I had never taken naps in those days, but now it seemed like a good idea. Even Cruiser was dog tired after our lakeside adventure.

"Come on, Cruiser. Naptime, boy." I patted the bedside to welcome him aboard the sleepy time train, and he climbed up on his raining cats and dogs quilt I kept at the foot of the bed for him. Of course, more often than not, when I awoke, I found him lying right next to me with his head on the pillow snoring away. I never scolded him, though. It was comforting to have a warm body lying next to me on cool Tahoe nights, even if it was a drooly basset hound.

My mind was so full of the strange incidents in recent weeks that before sleep overtook me I lay awake for quite a while, suspicions and theories churning in my head like the great paddle wheel of the *Dixie Queen*.

I was drifting in a small boat on the lake. The egg I'd found was cradled in my lap, wrapped up in Ivy Diggs' bloodstained scarf. Cruiser sat close beside me sniffing scents on the chill morning air. In the half-light of dawn, the Sierras were colossal primeval beasts rearing up against the sky. A fine, gray mist shrouded the lake's surface like a mourning veil. Where was my Tom? He should be here with me in the boat casting his line into the water. Except for Cruiser I was alone, adrift on the great lake of my ancestors.

In the swirling mist, I fancied I could see figures of Washoe women dancing in flowing white ceremonial dress, weaving baskets from alpine grasses in graceful motions of their hands, moving through forests and fields gathering seeds and nuts. Then the wind stirred, and the visions evaporated in the mist. I heard the soughing of the breeze in the sugar pines along the shore. Or perhaps it was not the wind I heard at all.

Through the mist I spied something ominously large and dark move through the water. I felt an overwhelming sense of dread wash over me. Pulling the flaps of my deerstalker tight over my ears, I tucked my legs closer to my body for added warmth. The creature in the water surfaced momentarily and peered curiously at me. She sniffed the air as though searching for something and emitted a long, mournful wail. Then she silently submerged in Tahoe's indigo depths.

Cruiser's nose began working furiously, as though he had scented something on the surface of the lake. The old notion about scent hounds not being able to track their quarry across water is a myth. Scents are carried to their sensitive glands on water as effectively as on any dirt trail.

"What is it, boy?" I said, stroking my trusty boating companion. He lifted his nose higher on the air and howled. *Aarooo!* Cruiser's baying was answered by a long, low bellow like a foghorn. Then I saw the lake begin to bubble and boil like water in a teakettle. The boat pitched until I was forced to brace myself by holding on to its sides. Cruiser barked incessantly at something in the water. Where was Skip? Would he come in time to rescue us before our boat was capsized and we were both drowned and lost in the dark depths of Tahoe, along with the lake's long dead?

The churning of the water grew more violent. I leaned over the edge to see what I could see. A dark shadow rose up from the depths. I heard a faint, eerie sound of bagpipes from somewhere beyond the impenetrable mist. Was I in Loch Ness or Lake Tahoe? Was it the famed Nessie I had seen gliding past the boat earlier? Was that what lurked beneath us now? I grasped the edge of the boat tightly with one hand and held onto Cruiser with my other hand, preparing for the inevitable upending of the boat. The thing was coming closer to the surface now. Closer. Closer. I shut my eyes and prepared for the worst. Then it came!

Something icy cold clutched my wrist like a vice, wrenching loose my grip on the boat. I glanced down and saw a woman's hand, whitish yellow and waxy, clenching mine. A tomb-like cold pervaded me as I saw her shredded garments streaming from her arm like seaweed as she rose up from the depths. Ivy Diggs stared at me through hollow sockets sunken in her ghastly white face. Grinning hideously, she grasped the bloodstained scarf from my lap. The egg fell to the floor of the boat and cracked open. Albumen spilled from the shell, and the two halves of the egg fell away to reveal its contents. Instead of a yolk, an eyeball gaped up at me. The corpse snatched it away and inserted it into an empty socket. Decaying matter oozed from around the cavity like yellow tears as the orb squeezed into place with a sickening plip!

I tried to scream, but no sound emitted from my throat. Staring at me with her gory eye, Ivy tried to pull me overboard. I struggled to free myself from her icy grasp, but she kept tugging and tugging. The sound of the bagpipes grew louder and louder. Suddenly I was yanked over the side, flailing helplessly in the dark water, sinking . . . sinking . . .

179

★ ★ ★ ★ ★

I hit the bedroom floor with a thud. Cruiser still had hold of my sleeve, and the cell phone was ringing out the tune of "Scotland the Brave."

"H . . . hello?"

"This is Oh, Heavenly Lady Spa calling to confirm your appointment for Saturday morning. That was for a full spa day, correct?"

"Huh?"

"Your spa day."

Still bleary-eyed and disoriented, I fished Nona's gift certificate out of my nightstand drawer and peered through my bifocals at the fine print. Nowadays everything I read is fine print. "Yes, and makeover, it says here."

"Fine. We'll expect you at eleven then, ma'am."

Ma'am! Could she tell I was fifty over the phone? "Thanks, dearie. I'll be there." Assuming I can find my walker.

"Fine, we'll be ready for you."

After I hung up the phone, I began wondering what I was letting myself in for. I hoped my nightmare wasn't only just beginning. What would I look like after this overhaul? I remembered the last time I'd had a "makeover." After the cosmetician was done with me, all I needed was a gypsy costume and trick-or-treat bag. But nothing I'd ever seen on Halloween was as frightening as the dream I'd just had. If that's really all it was.

CHAPTER THIRTY-SIX

Hurrying to the bedroom to get dressed for my spa appointment, I glanced at the mirror in the antique hall tree Tom had inherited from his family. I was glad I hadn't surrendered that treasure to greedy relatives when he died. I stroked my long braids and said, "Well, at least maybe they can do something creative with these, huh, Cruiser?"

When he shook his head, a glob of slobber landed squarely on the mirror—a constant hazard for basset owners. I had learned to tolerate wiping Cruiser's spit and snot off of every surface in the house. I bought Windex by the case at Costco.

Nona and I nearly collided in the hall. "Would you mind driving me to my spa appointment?"

"Something wrong with your car?"

"No. I just wanted some company is all."

"Not nervous about your makeover, are you, Mom?"

"A little, I guess." I twisted an end of one braid around my index finger. They had become a part of me, like Cruiser's ears were a part of him. Could you imagine what a basset would look like with cropped ears like a Doberman pinscher or a schnauzer? Perish the thought! But I knew my braids would be the first things to go once I was in the stylist's chair, and hoped I wouldn't look just as ridiculous.

"Oh, don't sweat it. Just relax and enjoy the whole experience."

"Easy for you to say. You didn't look like Bozo the Clown

after your last trip to the beauty parlor."

"Wasn't that in the sixties?"

"Not exactly. It was the seventies, and everyone looked like Bozos wearing gaudy polyester prints and those platform shoes."

"I've been to Heavenly Lady lots of times. They'll treat you right, and you won't look anything like Bozo. I promise."

"Okay, if you say so. Will you do me a favor and take Cruiser out for his afternoon walk while I'm gone?"

"But you just took him for a walk."

"That was his mid-morning walkies. I exercise him three times a day, sometimes four."

"You spoil that dog something awful, Mother."

"Vet's orders. Keeps us both svelte."

"Well, okay. I'll walk him up to the Rim Trail. That should wear him out for a while."

"Thanks, honey. See you later." I kissed her, gave Cruiser a quick pat on the head, and was nearly out the door when the phone rang. It wasn't the cell phone this time.

"Hello?"

No one spoke, but I could hear someone breathing at the other end.

"Hello, anyone there?"

More silence, then finally my caller spoke.

"Is this Elsie MacBean?"

"Speaking. Who is this?" Gads, I hoped this wasn't another telemarketer.

"Ted Diggs."

"Oh, yes. Mr. Diggs. What can I do for you?" I was hoping he had some information that would shed some light on my investigation of Ivy's murder.

"You can stop writing drivel like this, that's what you can do."

"What do you mean?" I knew exactly what he meant. It

wasn't the first and probably wasn't the last complaint I'd have to endure about that Tessie article I'd written.

"I'm talking about this article in the *Tattler* about some creature in the lake. What are you, some kind of wacko writing stuff like that?"

"No, I'm a reporter, Mr. Diggs. I was just doing my job. If you have some complaint about the article that was assigned to me, you should address it to the editor of the newspaper in a letter."

"Well, maybe I'll just do that, and maybe I'll slap you and the *Tattler* with a nice, fat lawsuit at the same time. This kind of nonsense could ruin my business. Since this article ran, no one is renting any boats, and no one is taking diving lessons, that's for sure. People are afraid to go anywhere near the lake."

"Well, it's nearly the end of summer. Doesn't that usually happen anyway?"

"No. We keep busy well into September, even October or November sometimes, if the snows come late. Things were just beginning to take off again after . . . well, never mind."

"I don't know what to say, Mr. Diggs. I wouldn't purposely try to harm your business. It's just the news, you know?"

"Well, I've got some news for you. You'd better stop writing any more articles like this or else . . ."

"Or else what? Are you threatening me?"

The line clicked.

"Who was that?" Nona called from the bedroom.

"Oh, no one, honey. I'd better make tracks. See you and Cruiser later. If anyone else rings, just let the answering machine pick up, okay?"

"Will do."

It was a perfect Tahoe morning. The sky was that incomparable sapphire blue I love so well. Cotton puff clouds skimmed the majestic peaks. I would hate spending this gorgeous summer day indoors, even if I was going to be Queen for a Day.

Oh, Heavenly Lady Spa was located in the Round Hill Shopping Center about a mile east of Stateline. The whole center had been recently refurbished and looked nothing like the place I remembered from years past with quaint antique shops and secondhand clothing stores. Only the Safeway remained as a landmark of the former mini-mall. Now, upscale boutiques and New Age gift shops occupied my old haunts, along with art galleries and, of course, the spa for all those "heavenly ladies" who graced their mansions in the sky.

It might have been the Gen-XYZ aura that made me feel so out of place when I walked through the double doors embellished with cut-glass angels in flowing gowns and tresses. Or it could have been the reggae music that conjured images of Jamaica and dreadlocks. Suddenly, I dreaded what might become of my locks! I almost did a U-turn right out the door, but it was too late. I'd already been spotted.

"How may I help you?" inquired the nubile receptionist. I glanced at her nametag. Buffy. This was slaying me.

"Uh . . . I have an appointment for a spa day and makeover."

"Oh, sure. I was the one who took your call earlier. Are you Elsie MacBean?"

"Yes."

"You're lucky we had this cancellation. We're, like, totally booked for the next two weeks."

"Totally, huh?" Sheesh, Heavenly Valley girl-ese. This wasn't a good sign. Maybe I should make a break for it and go to one of those old lady salons, I told myself, but I couldn't disappoint Nona. She'd be hurt if I let her gift go to waste.

"Just have a seat, ma'am, and we'll call you in a minute."

With an air of resignation at not only submitting to a midlife metamorphosis but again being referred to as ma'am by someone less than half my age, I snatched up a magazine and flopped down in a cushioned wicker basket that was intended to be a chair. The background music, a discordant blend of rap, rock and roll, and reggae, was beginning to grate on my nerves. I hoped that the massage came first.

One young woman at the counter had both eyebrows pierced and a silver bolt through her tongue and nose, not to mention her bizarre coiffure of multicolored cloth hair extensions that reminded me of a Raggedy Ann doll. This didn't bode well. I grew increasingly apprehensive of what I'd let myself in for. I flipped through the pages of impossibly perfect, computer-morphed models who wouldn't see a gray hair for another four decades.

Just then, I glanced up from the magazine to see an attractive, young brunette sitting across from me. I thought I recognized her from a writers' conference I'd attended. She sported a fashionable pair of ornate silver Brighton sunglasses just like the ones I'd recently admired at a boutique on the West Shore. She seemed suddenly aware of my gaze and quickly raised her magazine to hide her face. Growing flustered, she started flipping the pages of the magazine a little faster and then stood up and walked over to the display of nail colors and conditioners, making sure her back was turned to me. I was just about to ask her where we'd met before when Buffy returned.

"Your massage therapist is ready for you now, ma'am."

"Just call me Elsie, okay?"

I stood up and followed Buffy into one of the back rooms of the salon. While I was being pummeled on the massage table, I'd have plenty of time to try and remember where I'd seen that woman before.

CHAPTER THIRTY-SEVEN

For three solid hours I was steamed and creamed. During the deep tissue massage, I felt like I was going ten rounds with Mike Tyson, but after the facial and complimentary glass of wine during my pedicure, I had to admit I was feeling pretty mellow. Until it came time for the inevitable.

"Now, what should we do with these?" said Felicity the stylist, lifting up one braid, then another. How many more TV series ingénues would I encounter in this salon my daughter had sent me to?

"My, these are long, aren't they? Were we going for the *Guinness World Record* for braids?"

"No, we weren't." I hate it when they talk to you like you're a rest home resident.

"Well, they've got to go. We need an updated look for you, and a little color wouldn't hurt, either."

Not purple, I hope. When I'm an old woman, I may end up wearing the color purple but not on my hair. "Save my braids for me," I said. "You never know, Guinness might decide they want them, after all."

She draped me with a plastic cape and snapped it in the back. I had to shut my eyes when she wielded the scissors like a sushi chef. I heard the snip, snip of scissors—the deed was done. My braids lay on the linoleum floor like two dead snakes. My braid stumps were deftly loosened, and what was left of my hair fell in two dull brown curtains around my face.

"Now, what color should we go for?" She fanned a hair dye chart under my nose, and we agreed on Sedona Sunset, a reddish brunette, which she felt would brighten my complexion. Felicity disappeared for a few moments, and then returned with an evil-looking concoction. She dabbed the ice-cold brown muck on my head section-by-section until I looked like a sticky brown Q-tip. Then she mummy-wrapped my head in plastic and left me to simmer under a dryer. About the time my scalp felt like it was ready to peel from my skull, it was off to the shampoo station for a beauty baptism, deep conditioning treatment, and back into the hot seat for the rest of the transformation from crow to bird of paradise.

For the next half-hour, snippets of hair dusted my cape as a ring of newly dyed hair circled the base of the chair. After another hour of cutting, shaping and blow drying—the last time I'd been in a beauty salon, blow dryers hadn't been invented yet—she was done. Felicity twirled me around in the chair to face the mirror. For a moment I wasn't sure who was looking back at me.

"Is that really me?" Could this be the same fifty-year-old who came in the salon three hours earlier? I cupped a glowing russet wave of hair in my hand.

"Sure is. With a little makeup, you'll look awesome."

She was right. After another forty-five minutes with the aesthetician, as they call them nowadays, I did look awesome and not one bit like Bozo the Clown. She showed me step-by-step how to apply the products myself, and I was persuaded to buy what came to around $300 worth of foundation, blush, eye shadows, mascara, liners and lip colors. Small price to pay for a miracle, I figured. I paid the cashier. She bagged it all up with a free fragrance sample called Frolic and my souvenir braids, which were neatly tied off with blue satin ribbons.

I was just leaving the salon, admiring the results of my

marathon makeover reflected in the shop window when I spotted the same woman I'd seen earlier in the salon walking away from me through the car lot. She was wearing a scarf and sunglasses now. I saw her get into a brand new aqua blue BMW Z3; it still had Reno dealer's tags on it. Aware that I was staring at her, she peeled out of the lot. Before I could even get to my car she was long gone.

As I drove home, I couldn't get the woman in the Beemer off my mind. I had the nagging feeling we'd met someplace before, but where? I glanced at myself in the rearview mirror. I looked a good ten years younger. Skip wouldn't recognize me. Neither would Crispin when next I saw him, and I hoped it would be soon. At the stoplight, I pulled out the perfume sample from the Oh, Heavenly Lady Salon bag and spritzed it behind one ear then the other.

"Beanie, girl," I said to the younger-looking version of myself in the mirror, "I think it's high time you had a little frolic."

CHAPTER THIRTY-EIGHT

"Wow, Mom! You look awesome," Nona gushed when she saw me.

"Those are the exact words they used at the salon." Only it had sounded more like *awethome* when lisped through tongue bolts.

"I knew you'd look great, but . . . wow!"

"Thanks. You know, I feel great, too!"

"So, you're pleased with the results?"

"Oh, yes. I confess I had misgivings about it in the beginning, but I'm delighted with my new look." I gave Nona a big hug and kissed her on the cheek. "I appreciate your gift, honey. It was just the lift I needed."

"I'm so glad." Nona grinned from ear to ear. Speaking of ears, I couldn't wait to see what Cruiser's reaction was going to be.

"Where's Cruiser? I hope he still recognizes me."

"Asleep on your bed. He ran himself silly chasing chipmunks out on the trail. He was all worn out when we got back. So was I. We both took a little nap."

"I know the feeling. He'll follow that nose of his to the ends of the earth if you let him."

I walked down the hall to my bedroom to check on Cruiser. Of course I found him not on his quilt at the foot of my bed but lying right in the middle, head on my pillow, slopping up my last clean pillowcase. His head popped up when I stepped in.

Uh-oh. Caught in the act! His tail beat a happy-to-see-you tattoo on the bedspread. Or maybe it was just a ploy to persuade me to let him stay on the bedspread. I wasn't falling for it. I'd been known to let him lie on my duvet sometimes, like when his owies were healing from his tangles with Tahoe baddies. And he always crept up in the morning to wake me with a wet, friendly lap on the chin, but with the shedding problem, I wasn't planning on his making a habit of it. Of course, he had other plans . . .

"Cruiser, down, boy."

He thought it over a moment then grudgingly inched his way off the bed. When I headed back to the kitchen toward the Yum-Yum Nook, he trailed close at my heels. I tossed him a Milk Bone for being such a good dog.

"Any phone calls while I was gone?"

"I don't know. Better check the machine."

I played back the messages. There were two hang-up calls, then a message from Skip confirming our dinner at the Lakeview Bar and Grille. Nona overheard and immediately began quizzing me.

"You two going out on a date?"

"It's not a date, Nona. Just two friends going out for dinner. That's all."

"Okay, if you say so." Nona grinned.

"I say so."

"So, what are you going to wear for this friendly dinner that's not a date?"

Nona wasn't about to let up on this. Darn Skip and his big mouth. "I haven't thought about it, really. You know I don't go out much."

"Yeah, but that was before your makeover. Cruiser may have

to keep all your suitors at bay now that you're so trim and gorgeous."

I laughed, but in the back of my mind I was wondering what Skip would say when he saw the new me. I hoped he wouldn't laugh at my vanity and foolishness. And then there was Crispin Blayne. What reaction could I expect from him when next we met? I couldn't help hoping that might be very soon.

"I don't think any of the dresses I have fit me anymore since I lost weight. I may have to break down and buy a new outfit to wear."

"Oh, does this mean we're going shopping?" Nona almost sang the words.

"Yes, I guess it does." I could already hear the annoying screech of hangers on metal rods in the dress shops. I'd never be a member of Shopaholics Anonymous, but Nona never gave up trying to convert me.

"Could we go this afternoon?"

"I suppose so. We haven't been on a mother–daughter shopping spree in a while, have we?" I had plenty more work waiting to be done, but long ago I had learned to prioritize my life. Nowadays, family always comes before business.

"Great, I know just the place I want to go. There's a new shopping mall over in Incline Village I'd like to check out."

"I know the one, but I hadn't planned on a mall-a-thon."

"Aw, come on, Mom. Please?"

I sighed. Nona could spend an entire day in a shopping mall. I had written a promo piece on the new subterranean shopping Mecca before it opened. Fortunately for Cruiser and me, the new Crystal Bay Center also contained Petropolis, a pet-friendly facility, which includes a playground, doggie daycare, a dog-wash, a dog spa, and just about anything else a dog lover could imagine, and probably a few things you couldn't.

"The way things are going, Tahoe is going to be just one big shopping mall."

"I guess that's how it is with resort towns like this."

"I think that's how it is everywhere nowadays. Sacramento is the same way. The bigger the city gets, the more malls pop up. First there was Country Club, then Florin Mall and Arden Fair. Now there's the Galleria in Roseville and Brookstone in El Dorado Hills. And the people keep on coming. Urban sprawl at its best."

"I know how you feel about this place, Mom. I hope that doesn't happen here."

"Me, too. The only thing working in our favor is that most of the work in Tahoe is seasonal, except for gambling. It makes good jobs hard to find." The angry phone call from Ted Diggs came to mind. Boating was also seasonal. That got me wondering about the two hang-up calls on the answering machine. Could it have been him calling again to harass me?

"Kind of like good men, huh?" Nona said.

"There are still a few good ones left if you know where to look." I glanced down at Cruiser. He was giving me the soggy knee treatment, begging for another treat.

"When you find out where that is, let me know," Nona said.

"Why do you say that?" I thought about her experiences with Medwyn and Addison, but they were history, and no one was happier about it than I. Nona never went very long without a boyfriend, though. Six months was the longest I'd ever known her to be manless. Knowing what I did about her newest boy toy, Bobby Diggs, I feared her taste in men hadn't improved much since her Medwyn days.

"Oh, nothing." Nona went to fetch Cruiser another biscuit. "Funny how Cruiser has us trained to fetch for him on command, but I've never seen him fetch anything for anyone, not even a paper. A newspaper reporter should at least have a newspaper-fetching dog." I was wise to Nona's tactics. She was trying to deflect my inevitable questions about boyfriends by focusing my attention on the dog. She knows what a pushover I am for Cruiser. She wasn't fooling me for a minute with the food slave act.

"Having boy trouble, Nona?"

"Well, I've been dating a guy, if that's what you mean."

"Not that Diggs boy, I hope."

"Yes, I'm dating Bobby. Why?"

I thought back to that deadly evening of July 4th on the *Dixie Queen*. I remembered the collisions, screams of terror, sudden death, mysterious shadows in the deep, and the drunken, blond-haired man who had flirted with Nona, Bobby Diggs. Not to mention my harrowing race down the hairpins with Bobby's Benz hugging my rear bumper. I felt ill when I realized my daughter was dating a possible murder suspect and that she could be flirting with disaster.

CHAPTER THIRTY-NINE

"What is it with you, Nona?"

"What do you mean?"

"I mean why are you dating Bobby Diggs, for crying out loud?" I tried to keep my voice low, but the volume was rising steadily.

"Why shouldn't I date him?" Nona's brow knitted.

"He's just a murder suspect, that's all."

"He is not! What makes you think that?"

"Someone pushed Ivy Diggs overboard that night, and it could have been him. He was acting strange that night, and he's acted even stranger since."

"It could have been anyone in that party. For that matter, it could have been anyone on the entire boat."

"Just the same, I think you'd be wise to steer clear of him until we have further proof."

"You can't prove he did anything wrong because he didn't."

She was right, of course. I had no proof that he was anything more than a reckless youth with a lead foot and a love of liquor. All I had to go on was my nagging gut feeling that Ivy's death wasn't an accident and that someone close to her was responsible. After Ted Diggs' threatening phone call and the anonymous hang-ups, it could well be that he, not Bobby, was our lady-killer. At least I could be thankful Nona wasn't dating him, too.

"I know I have no proof, at least not yet, but I do know Bobby is a spoiled ne'er-do-well, the black sheep of the family. I also know you can do a lot better than him."

"Why do you always make snap judgments about everyone I meet? When will you ever accept the notion that I can take care of myself?"

"Oh, you mean like you did with Medwyn? You'd be dead meat now if Cruiser and I hadn't found you when we did."

"I'm not going to discuss this with you. It's really none of your business who I date, Mother. So just butt out of my love life, okay?"

Nona turned on her heel and huffed out of the house. The door slammed so hard behind her it shook the lampshade like a 7.0 earthquake. I heard car tires squeal as she backed out of the driveway and zoomed away. We'd been down this road before. Cruiser tucked his tail between his legs and slunk from the room. I had the satisfaction of knowing I was usually right about my daughter's questionable choice of men. And I was also standing alone in my living room. One of the conditions inherent in being right all the time.

I sat on the sofa crying when I felt a moist nose nudge my elbow. Cruiser edged up on the sofa and planted as much of himself as he could fit onto my lap. I wiped my tears on my t-shirt, leaving smears of mascara from the Oh, Heavenly Lady aesthetician's artistry on the sleeve.

"Oh, Cruiser. I'm sorry, boy. I know how you hate it when we argue." Stroking Cruiser's soft fur made me feel better, and his sympathetic brown eyes made me understand that at least one creature on the planet understood exactly how I felt.

I only hoped Nona would come back soon so I could apologize to her, too. I tried dialing her cell phone number, but she wasn't answering. She probably knew who it was and didn't want to talk to me. I couldn't blame her, I guess. I just hoped she wasn't off somewhere with that Bobby Diggs. Knowing my daughter, who is every bit as stubborn as my dog, she'd probably look him up just to spite me.

Maybe she was right and I didn't have anything to worry about, but until Skip and I could find out what happened to Ivy Diggs, I would remain my vigilant self for Nona's safety. I'd just have to be a little less obvious about it. I'd promised before not to be so overprotective where she was concerned, but no matter how old she got, I couldn't stop being her mother, and she would always be my little girl. But I didn't want to push my daughter away from me, either. I saw little enough of her these days. There was already a geographic distance between us. I didn't want to create an emotional distance, too. I only hoped she wouldn't beat a hasty retreat to San Francisco and never come back.

When the phone rang, I lunged for it, thinking it was Nona.

"Hello?"

There was no answer, but I knew someone was there. I could hear the caller breathing on the other end.

"Hello, is anyone there?"

Still no response. Angry, I slammed the phone down so hard I hurt my arm.

"I hate those crank calls!"

Now I was really wishing Nona would come back. Suddenly, the cabin seemed too empty, and I imagined the knotholes in the pine walls were eyes peering at me, like in my terrifying nightmare. I felt a wave of relief wash over me when I heard the sound of a car pulling into the driveway. Cruiser jumped down and trotted to the front door. When you saw Cruiser move that fast you knew it was for good reason, and it was. She had come back. I ran to the front door with Cruiser and opened it before Nona got to the porch. We both stood frozen in the doorway a moment. Her eyes were red, too. Then I stretched out my arms to my daughter and we embraced.

"I'm sorry, Mom," Nona sniffed.

"Me, too, Papoose." I stroked her silky chestnut hair. "I'll try harder to butt out from now on." The key word there was try, but for now it was enough. She seemed satisfied.

"And I'll try not to give you reason to worry so much about me. I shouldn't add any more heartache to your life than you've already had."

"You don't give me heartache, Nona. You're the greatest joy a mother could have, and don't you ever forget it, okay?"

She wiped her eyes and smiled. "Okay." There was a brief, heavy silence, and Cruiser looked worried that peace negotiations might be breaking down. Then Nona spoke. "So, when are we going to shop till we drop?"

"Now's as good a time as any. Let's go!" After that creepy phone call, I couldn't wait to get out of the cabin. "Come on, Cruiser, you're coming with us."

CHAPTER FORTY

The Crystal Bay Center drew patrons from Truckee all the way to Reno and beyond, as in the early twentieth century, when the Lake of the Sky attracted the wealthy to Tahoe in droves. Crystal Bay was more of an underground mini-city, really. I fully expected that if the environment continued deteriorating at its present pace, at some point in the near future we would all be living in a subterranean network of malls like gerbils in plastic tubes. Our survival in the second millennium appeared to hinge on the accessibility of a mall. I had already seen similar shopping Meccas in eastern states. I only hoped that would not be the fate of this natural wonder my Washoe ancestors had called home for so many thousands of years before European Americans ever knew it existed.

Of course, Nona was in her element. Nordstrom, Macy's, Ann Taylor, and a hundred other boutiques and dress shops would take more than a few hours for her to cover. But heck, what did I have to worry about besides my unfinished series of articles on Tessie and an incomplete mystery novel, not to mention an unsolved murder? When the going gets tough, the tough go shopping, and that's what we were about to do—Nona, me, and Cruiser, too.

I was glad I hadn't had to leave Cruiser behind while we went shopping, especially after that weird phone call. Under present circumstances, I preferred not to leave him unattended. Besides, Cruiser is accustomed to co-piloting with me just about everywhere I go, and more and more I favor places that are dog friendly. Unfortunately, those places grow fewer and fewer as cities become more crowded and tolerance for sharing space with dogs dwindles. I applauded the builders of Crystal Bay for incorporating an off-leash playground especially for canines. Tahoe finally had a few Fido-friendly venues, and I only hoped that dog owners would be their own best advocates by controlling their dogs in public and picking up after them.

I let Nona go her own way, and Cruiser and I headed for Petropolis. It wasn't hard to spot. This was Disneyland for Dogs! The entrance to the facility was well marked, I suppose you could say, with twin rows of blinking fire hydrants. They were set in a concrete avenue inset with intermittent drainage grates so that the area could be frequently washed down and disinfected. Much of the interior of Petropolis was designed the same way to facilitate the necessary cleansing of the area. Extensive measures were taken to keep things spotlessly clean and as fresh smelling as an alpine meadow in springtime. It would never do to have a shopper step in a steaming pile, although most of these pet-loving shoppers were not unfamiliar with such unpleasantries and therefore more tolerant of the inevitable "mistakes." You sort of get used to navigating dog areas like you're following an Arthur Murray dance floor diagram.

I guided Cruiser toward the fenced, grassy Petropolis Pup Playground in the hope that he would cavort with all the other dogs, but he came to a screeching halt when we passed the dog bakery called The Pawtisserie. I had to admit the aroma coming from within was too inviting to ignore. When we stepped inside the shop, I knew this wasn't just the usual kibble-and-bits feed store. It was downright elegant; from the multibreed patterned wallpaper with teal blue trim right down to the Dalmatian print carpeting on the floor. Its minimalist décor was Fido Feng Shui at its best. In fact, this bowser bakery was decorated more appealingly than most human bakeries.

Displayed inside glass cases was every doggie delicacy imaginable, even a bone-shaped birthday cake. There were carob-coated biscuits, carob chip cookies, cookies shaped like different dog breeds, and even treats specially made for dogs that were allergic to wheat and corn, which are common ingredients in most store-bought dog foods and munchies. Shiny aluminum pails placed strategically at dog-sniffing level were filled with various flavored canine cookies, which did not go unsampled by Cookie Monster Cruiser. Of course, I had to pay for everything he sampled. With most of the biscuits priced at a dollar apiece, I'd be broke in no time, so we didn't stay long in the Pawtisserie.

Next was the Bow-wow-tique, a designer clothing store for dogs. I had to admit this was the kind of shopping I could really get into. All kinds of outfits, from chic to silly to outright ludicrous, were displayed on hangers in sizes ranging from Chihuahua to Great Dane.

I browsed the doggie duds for a new sweater to fit Cruiser. Tahoe summers were notoriously short, and it would be no time before the weather turned crisp and winter would be upon us once more. A short-coated dog like Cruiser needs extra protection from the snow and cold. Would it be the Where's Waldo striped sweater, a leather bomber jacket, or the Aspen silver quilted jacket with faux fur? I was just trying the ski jacket on Cruiser for size when a tap on the shoulder startled me . . .

"Excuse me, ma'am?" I turned to face a young man. His badge said "Scott, Assistant Manager."

"Yes?" At first I thought he was going to chide me for trying the clothes on Cruiser.

"We're having a fashion show here in a few minutes. Would you like your dog to be in it?"

I had a lot more time to kill before Nona would be ready to leave the mall. "Sure, why not?"

"Great! Just go to the back of the store, and someone will get your dog outfitted for the show."

I led Cruiser into a storeroom filled with twenty or so dogs and at least that many fussing dog parents. Several store personnel were trying costumes on the dogs, fitting them for the right sizes. Some dogs were cooperative, but most would rather have been on the Pup Playground or sampling goodies in the Pawtisserie, including Cruiser.

CHAPTER FORTY-ONE

It was getting unbearably stuffy in the storeroom with all those panting dogs and their perspiring humans. Cruiser had been assigned to the "Low-Rider" group along with a dachshund and two bulldogs. My rebel bowser was wearing a bomber jacket. The fake sheepskin collar was drenched from the Niagara Falls of drool streaming from his tongue, which was nearly dragging the ground. If I sweated from my tongue like Cruiser, I'd have been drooling, too. I finally had to remove the jacket to keep it from being ruined before our curtain call. At fifty bucks a pop, I wasn't planning to buy two doggie designer outfits.

Nearly an hour had passed since I'd agreed to get involved in this four-legged fashion fiasco. Dogs were getting antsy, and owners' tempers were growing short as the wait wore on. It was easy to spot the potential stage mothers among us. One woman had the store assistant try ten different outfits on her pug before she was satisfied that Poopsie was the indisputable fashion plate of all of Petropolis. Of course, the only plate Cruiser had any interest in would have held a heaping helping of treats from the Pawtisserie. I thought of Ivy Diggs' pampered pooch and how, to her sister-in-law's supreme annoyance, she had fed the dog at the table like a child. People could really get carried away with doting on their pets—like entering them in fashion shows.

I could tell the harried employee was just about ready to slug the pug lady when at long last, we heard a voice on the loudspeaker announce the start of the fashion show. The pug led the pack with her owner, who was waddling down the Rover runway as "I'm Too Sexy" played over the intercom. Thankfully, the low-rider group was next. The door to the storeroom flew open with a bang, and the two bulldogs barreled out of there dragging their master. Cruiser and I were hot on their tails.

Appropriately, our musical accompaniment was "B-b-b-bad to the Bone." The store aisle-turned-catwalk, or in this case, dogwalk, was lined with colorful balloons suspended from large dog biscuits. Of course, Cruiser thought they were all for him. He grabbed first one biscuit then another, filling his mouth with as many treats as he could hold. Cheeks full of biscuits, he looked like a long-eared chipmunk storing his winter stash. As we proceeded, the collection of balloons bobbing behind us grew larger as Cruiser continued gathering biscuits. People were howling at the silly balloon-toting basset. Too bad there wasn't a clown division in this fashion show.

After the show, Cruiser and I couldn't wait to get out of there, so I made a dash for the register and paid for Cruiser's outfit. You'd have thought after all we went through for the fashion show, they would have given us the bomber jacket, since it was virtually ruined anyway. By the time we left the Bow-wow-tique, I had decided that my days as a doggie stage mom were definitely behind me. I was pretty sure Cruiser felt the same way about being a supermodel.

Even though Cruiser could have used a bath after that droola-thon—bassets can always use a bath—I decided to forego the dog wash and take Cruiser to the Pup Playground. As we entered the off-leash area, I grabbed some of the complimentary boo-boo bags, just in case Cruiser took a notion to relieve himself.

Several owners were playing with their dogs, mostly the ones with Frisbee dogs and ball-chasing dogs. Cruiser has never chased much of anything except squirrels or the dinner dish. Of course, I had to give credit where it's due. He had helped me out before with tracking a few criminals in Tahoe.

I sat down on a bench to rest with the other weary shoppers. I recognized several of the other people who had been cooped up in the Bow-wow-tique storeroom with their dogs. Cruiser did what bassets do best. He stretched out on the grass and immediately dozed off. If I'd had a bench all to myself, I'd have done the same. We had both shopped until we dropped, but our reprieve wouldn't last for long.

I had just shut my eyes when I heard Cruiser's dog tags jingle and felt a firm tug at the end of the leash. He was trying to get to the little bichon frise that had wandered up to make friends with him. There were several fluffy, white dogs in the play area, but there was something rather familiar about this one. I coaxed it to me, and it responded by yapping excitedly and jumping up into my lap to wash my face with its little pink tongue. Even though it was a far less drenching experience than getting Cruiser kisses, I finally had to push the dog away. I searched for an ID tag amid the nap of snowy fur and finally found one. The small, brass heart-shaped tag was engraved with the name, "Bitsy."

It was just too much of a coincidence that a dog named Bitsy that looked like Ivy Diggs' dog and barked like Ivy Diggs' dog wasn't Ivy Diggs' dog. But what I saw next was the last thing I expected to see in the Crystal Bay shopping mall—dead woman walking.

CHAPTER FORTY-TWO

A woman wearing a scarf and sunglasses came up and sat down beside me. She was the same woman I had seen before at the beauty salon and on the *Dixie Queen* the night of my birthday cruise, only this time she wasn't a redhead. She wasn't a brunette. She was now a stunning blonde. "Excuse me, but isn't your name Elsie MacBean?"

"Y-yes." Was I seeing a ghost or was this really Ivy Diggs?

"My name is . . ."

"I know who you are, Ms. Diggs. Only everyone else seems to believe you're dead."

"Yes, I know. And I'd like it to stay that way."

"Why?"

"I have my reasons."

"I'd love to know what they are."

"I'll tell you what you want to know, but not here. I'm afraid someone will spot me. I may have been followed."

"How did you know I was here?"

"I've been following you."

"What for?"

Ivy scanned the area warily. "Please, let's go someplace where we can talk in private."

"Well, all right. Where did you have in mind?"

"My place is close by. You have a car?"

"Yes."

"Good, then follow me over there. I don't want us to be seen

205

together. I don't want anyone to know I'm still alive or that I'm hiring a private investigator."

"Is that what you're doing?"

"Yes, if you're interested in the job."

I was already up to my earflaps in this case. I figured I might as well get paid for my time and trouble. The life of a freelancer is feast or famine, mostly famine. Tom's Social Security benefits don't cover as much as one might think. Today's fuel and power costs alone eat up that check in no time. On the bright side, at least you usually don't need air conditioning in Tahoe. I pitied the folks down in Sacramento this time of year. Cruiser wouldn't like it, either. Bassets don't tolerate summer heat any better than I do.

Should I tell Nona where I was going? No, I'd better not get her mixed up in this; besides, I'd never find her in this monster mall. I had the cell phone with me, though. I'd catch up with her later. She was probably so busy shopping she'd never miss me, anyway.

Cruiser and I tailed the two blondes in the Beemer, Ivy Diggs and a bichon frise named Bitsy. I hadn't driven on the north shore of the lake since last winter. If Tahoe was hauntingly beautiful dressed in winter white, summer transformed it to a virtual reality postcard of blue heaven. The water was so inviting that I might have wanted to leap right in if I hadn't already been doing so much of that lately. Never mind the fact that the lake, which is barely above fifty degrees, would turn my whole body into one giant goosebump.

I cruised along far enough behind Ivy so as not to attract attention from anyone who might have been tailing us. I was so busy appreciating the view of the lake, I almost lost my quarry but quickly spotted her car again just before it pulled into an upscale gated condo complex. She entered her security code into the keypad, and the iron gates opened wide; she buzzed me in right after her.

Ivy pulled into her garage. I had to park in a space a distance off, but it wasn't too far away for me to see where she went. She disappeared around the corner, and I got out of my car and followed her. I watched her climb up to the second floor to number 213, open the door, and leave it slightly ajar. I was a bit apprehensive about this whole thing. As I continued strolling down the walkway, the thought occurred to me that I might be walking into some kind of a trap. Could she and not Bobby Diggs have been the one who had nearly run me off the road at Emerald Bay in the Mercedes her rich husband had bought for her? Or were Ivy and Bobby in cahoots on this case? She said she'd been following me, but had she really been trying to kill me? Was there some reason she also wouldn't want me to know she was alive? What secret could she be hiding? Suddenly, I regretted not having told Nona or Skip where I was going.

As I marched up the stairs to who knew what in condo unit 213, I clutched the cell phone hanging on my belt like it was a .44 Magnum. For once I was glad Nona had insisted I carry the cellular with me. I didn't even own a gun, but I was sure wishing I had one now. At least I had Cruiser along with me to alert me to possible danger.

CHAPTER FORTY-THREE

I nudged the door to Ivy Diggs' condo open, not sure whether to expect an ambush on the other side. The only surprise attack awaiting Cruiser and me was an exuberant bichon frise named Bitsy, leaping for joy at her mistress's visitors.

"Come, Bitsy. Come to Mummy." Ivy coaxed her away with a tidbit and the little dog adjourned to her bed and busied herself with the treat. "Please have a seat, Ms. MacBean. Would you care for a spot of tea while we chat?"

"Yes, please." When I sat down on her white leather sofa, Cruiser tried to jump up with me, but I pushed him down. The bad thing about letting your dog on the sofa is that any sofa becomes fair game. Everything in Ivy's apartment was as white as a Tahoe winter, including the dog. If I bought a white sofa, it wouldn't be white for long. Mud-brown, claw-resistant, and slobber-proof leather is a much wiser choice for furnishings if you own a basset hound.

Momentarily, my hostess returned pushing a teacart and placed it between us.

"Do you take lemon or sugar with your tea?"

"Sugar and milk, please."

"Interesting. Most Americans don't care for milk in their tea. Just lemon, usually, if anything."

"My husband was of Scottish descent, so I learned the proper way to take tea."

"Oh, I see." Ivy played Mum to me, as the Brits say when

they pour tea, and Bitsy, too. After she poured my tea, she poured some into a separate saucer for the dog, lacing it with sugar and cream until it turned a rich butterscotch color. Bitsy lapped up the tea with her little pink tongue as Ivy made goo-goo baby talk to her obviously spoiled dog. *Thank goodness I don't spoil my dog like that,* I thought as I settled into the cushioned sofa with my cup of Earl Grey.

"Now, how may I help you, Ms. Diggs?"

"Someone is trying to kill me. I need you to find out who."

"Who would be trying to kill you if everyone already thinks you're dead?"

"Most likely the same person who came after me with a cutlery knife during my anniversary party then pushed me off of the *Dixie Queen.* Whoever it was knows the attempt on my life was unsuccessful. That's why I tried to alter my appearance by changing my hair color from time to time. I've been trying to keep a low profile since then, wearing disguises whenever I went out."

"Yes, I spotted you a couple of times when you were a brunette." Seems like if she didn't want anyone to recognize her, she would be driving a beat-up Volkswagen and living in less upscale digs, but I had the feeling that wasn't Mrs. Diggs' style. Clearly, she liked to have nice things. I wondered just how far she was willing to go to keep them.

"Someone is definitely after me. I should have moved out of the area entirely, but I love it here so. I figured if I relocated to the North Shore and changed my identity, I'd be safe."

So I was right after all. Ivy's disappearance that night was no accident. Someone had taken the steak knife and gone after her with the intent to kill her. Obviously, that person had missed the mark. But who was the would-be killer? It could have been Frank, a member of his family, or for that matter, any other passenger on the cruise that night. One thing was certain, though. It had to be someone who hated Ivy badly enough to want her dead.

From what I had observed, there seemed to be no shortage of enemies in Ivy's life. Everyone in the Diggs family hated her and her little dog, too. Maybe the perp was a cat person, or maybe the sight of a dog drinking tea like the Queen of England was just too much. It was almost too much for me, and I love dogs. I was surprised that whoever had tried to take Ivy out hadn't chucked her spoiled-rotten bichon overboard, too.

"Who told you about me?"

"I've heard about you. I know you've successfully solved murders in Tahoe before."

"Why didn't you approach me when I spotted you at the beauty salon?"

"I didn't know who you were. I realized that I had seen you on the *Dixie Queen,* too. I just thought you were some nosy stranger eavesdropping."

"I was." I took a sip of tea. Earl Grey was my favorite afternoon tea, but this was certainly no tea party. "So you didn't see the person who attacked you that night?"

"No. He came at me from behind."

"You say he. You think it was a man?"

"I don't know. Whoever it was is pretty strong. I didn't really have time to notice. I was overboard before I knew what hit me."

I thought about Dora. If she was strong enough to handle the dead weight of an invalid, she was certainly strong enough to give petite Ivy the heave-ho. And she certainly had the desire to do so.

"You have no idea at all who it was?"

"Well, I suppose it could be . . ." Ivy paused a moment, as though running through a long list of possible suspects. I half expected her to start counting on her fingers. Clearly, this woman had made more foes than friends in her lifetime.

"Maybe it might be better to try a process of elimination. Could it have been your husband?"

She gave me a vacant look I couldn't quite interpret, almost as though she really were doing ciphers in her head. Was she counting husbands?

"I doubt if it was Frank. His ticker is wonky."

I surmised what she meant. Thanks to Tom, I was good at translating British slang. "Yes, I'm aware of his heart problem."

"Oh, you spoke to Dora, then?"

"Yes, I've talked to all of Frank's kids."

"I'll bet they gave you an earful about me. They weren't too keen on my marrying their father."

"So I gather."

"I felt like I was living with a ghost."

"A ghost? How do you mean?"

"His first wife, Margaret. From the time Frank introduced me to his family, it was Maggie this and Maggie that. They were all quite unpleasant to be around."

"How so?"

"They squabbled constantly among themselves. The whole family is barking, if you ask me."

"Barking?" She had me there. Only dogs bark around my house.

"You know, barking mad. Crazy." She motioned little circles at her temple with an index finger.

"Oh, I see. So you believe that one of them might be the one who came after you?"

"Most likely. They all thought I was taking their father away from them. I suppose the fact that I was younger than my stepchildren didn't help matters much."

"Yes, that can cause problems, I've heard. What about the two brothers?"

"Ted was a hard one to read—strictly business. He's a worka-holic, and I think he was secretly glad when his dad took ill and stepped down so he could run things. He wanted control of the family business and would do just about anything to keep it that way. He and Bobby were always at each other's throats over the company. Bobby didn't like being bossed around by his big brother, and I don't think he cares much for work, to tell you the truth. He wants to play, and he wants more and more money to play with. He's still taking classes in college, too. The cost for that is dear these days. None of them liked for Frank to spend his money on anything for me. And they were furious that he named me as sole beneficiary in the event of his death."

"Did you request that he do that?"

"No. I mean I did ask him to make sure I wouldn't be left penniless in case anything happened to him. He was more than willing to do it. There was quite a difference in our ages, and he was ill, as I said. I knew his family'd leave me out in the cold if he were to die. This little Ivy bird has to feather her nest."

"Yes, I suppose you're right." I should have done more nest-feathering of my own over the years. Any smart woman does.

"To tell you the truth, I was getting fed up with the whole family. I think Frank was, too, except for that dotty daughter of his."

"Dora?"

"Yes. She and Frank are like this." She crossed her fingers. "She moved in to take care of her mother when she was dying. She kind of looked after everyone."

"Ah, the mother hen of the family."

"Keeps them all hen-pecked, you mean. They are really all she has. The only man who ever asked for her hand in marriage left her standing at the altar. The poor bloke probably ran scared when he found out what kind of family he would be marrying into. I think I would have done the same had I known beforehand. Dora tried to kill herself after he jilted her."

"I noticed the scars on her wrists."

"She wears long sleeves all the time to hide them."

I wanted to ask Ivy why she married a man who was decades older than she was, but I doubted if she'd tell me the real reason behind that. Perhaps she herself didn't know, unless it was as she said, nest-feathering. "If she's so protective of the family, do you think she could have been the one who came after you?"

"I don't know, but she hated me with a passion. That much I do know."

"Why didn't you call out for help when you fell overboard that night on the *Dixie Queen*? They searched for you for quite a while."

"I was afraid that if I got back on the boat, whoever had attacked me might try to finish the job. We were close enough to the shore that I could swim to safety."

"You could have drowned, though."

"I know. I did cry out a couple of times when I thought I might not make it to shore, but the boat was too far away by then for me to be heard." Ivy grew silent for a moment. There was more she wasn't telling me, but she wouldn't keep me hanging for long. "No, that's not entirely the truth. I wanted out of the marriage. I was miserable, and I saw it as my chance to escape and start anew. I figured if they thought I was dead I'd finally be free of them."

I suddenly felt sorry for Ivy. She was Nona's age, after all, and still had a lot to learn about life and people.

"Where were you injured, Ivy?"

"Right here." Ivy lifted her right sleeve and pointed to her shoulder. The wound was superficial and nearly healed.

"You must be a very strong swimmer."

"I am, but the water was so cold it was like knives stabbing me all over my body. I was getting pretty weak before I made it to shore."

"I know. Tahoe is beautiful, but it can be a cold, blue death if you're not careful."

"If it hadn't been for that old guy who found me, I might not be here."

"What old guy?"

"I think he said his name was Bones or something like that."

"Oh, you mean Boney Crider?"

"Yes, that's it. Boney Crider. Rather odd bloke. He lives like a hermit, all alone except for his dog."

"How did you get your dog back, by the way?"

"I stole her away. Those beasts were going to put my Bitsi-cums in the pound if I didn't rescue her. They hated my baby girl almost as much as they did her mummy, didn't they?" At the sound of her name in baby talk, Bitsy leapt up into Ivy's lap.

"Wouldn't that alert someone to the fact that you're still alive?"

"No, I don't think so. I made it look like she escaped under the fence."

"No one saw you?"

"It was after dark. I doubt it. At least I hope not."

The fact remained someone did know Ivy had not died that night on the *Dixie Queen*. Whether it was because of a bungled dog-napping or because someone had spotted her somewhere else around the Tahoe area, undeniably someone knew Ivy Diggs was still alive. Three in all, now. Me, Boney Crider, and the person who had tried to murder her during the July 4th fireworks display. I was starting to get the feeling that I was in very bad company, and I didn't like the feeling one itsy bitsy bit.

CHAPTER FORTY-FOUR

"Do you think you can help me, Ms. MacBean?" Ivy asked. Bitsy had finished her treat and was begging for another. Never one to miss out on handouts, Cruiser decided to get in on the action. Ivy gave them both a biscuit. I was glad they were Bitsy-sized treats. I didn't want Cruiser porking out again.

"If you're going to be my client, you may as well call me Elsie."

Ivy heaved a sigh of relief. I was seeing a different side of the woman everyone in her family seemed to detest. Maybe she had married an older man, but that didn't necessarily make her a hearse chaser, as Bobby had called her. Young women who married men decades older are usually in search of a father figure, generally because their own fathers were either neglectful, abusive, or absent entirely. On the other hand, what her in-laws said about her might be true. First impressions can deceive. Even second impressions, in some cases. Living with her day in and day out, they might have seen a side of Ivy that everyone else didn't see right off.

Was she an innocent little girl lost or just a cleverly manipulative and greedy young woman who knew what she wanted and would stop at nothing to get it? Was I being duped, too? Only time would tell. In the meantime, she had offered to pay me handsomely for my trouble. Cash in advance, with a bonus at the end of a successful investigation. I couldn't turn down an opportunity like this. Apparently, this little English bird had a nice, fat goose egg of her own in her nest. Of course, I would have to keep her existence and whereabouts under my beanie for the time being.

I was so intrigued with what Ivy was telling me, I had forgotten the time. Nona would probably be wondering what had become of me. She might think Cruiser and I had been the victim of mall-nappers or a car-jacking if I didn't get back soon.

"Okay, Ivy. I'll snoop around and see what I can find out. Here's my cellular number. Call me if you need to or if there's anything else you think I should know about."

"You will keep this confidential, won't you, Elsie? I know you work for a newspaper. If word leaks out, I'm dead."

"Don't worry. Your secret is safe with me." I could understand Ivy's concern. Being a reporter and a P.I. could make uncomfortable bedfellows, but she was overlooking the fact that her secret had obviously already leaked out, and evidently to the wrong person. I'd do my best to make certain it went no further.

When Cruiser and I pulled into the Crystal Bay mall parking lot, Nona was standing at the entrance looking rather cross. She slid into the back seat of my car and slammed the door shut. Whether it was annoyance at me for disappearing without telling her or the fact that she was relegated to the back seat because Cruiser was occupying the front one, I wasn't sure. Perhaps a bit of both. "Where on earth were you, Mom? I've been all over this whole mall searching for you. I thought you said you'd stay in Petropolis while I shopped."

"Sorry, honey. I had something else to take care of. I didn't expect to be gone long and didn't think you'd miss me."

"Well, I did, and I was getting worried about you."

"Did you run out of things to shop for already? I thought you'd be in there for hours."

"Well, I might have if His Slobberness hadn't come along for the ride." Cruiser must have recognized his title. He chose that moment to shake his head and shower the car with saliva.

"Aaaugh!" Nona sustained a direct hit. Fortunately for me, I was far more adept at dodging drool. I handed her a tissue and gave Cruiser's pendulous lips a swipe with his jowl towel.

"I wish you'd found us sooner. You missed the fashion show."

"What fashion show?"

"Cruiser was a supermodel on the catwalk at the Bow-wow-tique."

"Oh." Nona sounded thoroughly unimpressed. "Where did you two disappear to, anyway?"

I didn't want to lie to her, but I didn't want to tell her the truth, either. She wouldn't approve of her mother getting so deeply involved in the Ivy Diggs drowning case. So I made up a lie. Just a little white one.

"I ran into someone I knew."

"Who?"

"Someone I know in animal rescue. She wanted me to come and see a dog she's trying to place in a new home."

I glanced in the rearview mirror and saw Nona's eyebrow arch the way her father's used to when he doubted what I was telling him. I smiled at her, and she seemed to lose interest in her line of questioning, especially when I said we'd leave Cruiser in doggy daycare at Petropolis and go back for a second round of shopping. After meeting up with Ivy at the mall, I had forgotten all about the dress I'd come there to buy, but I knew Nona probably didn't buy my story about going to see a woman about a dog. That was better than telling her I was moonlighting as a P.I. for a dead woman.

CHAPTER FORTY-FIVE

For the first time since all this began, I felt like I might finally be on the right track in the Diggs case. Now I knew for certain that Ivy's disappearance had been no accident. It's my party and I'll die if I want to—that was the song that should have been playing at Ivy's anniversary party on the *Dixie Queen*. Someone knew she was alive and was intent on finishing the job that was started July 4th aboard the paddle wheeler. Ivy was marked for murder, only I still didn't know who had done the marking.

Cruiser was doing a little marking of his own as we made our way back up Lonely Glen to Boney Crider's Rubicon Bay hideaway. I didn't know if there was any point in talking to a crazy old hermit like Crider again, but I figured it was worth a shot. I wanted to find out more about the night he found Ivy. And I also had another mission to accomplish while I was there. After my disturbing dream, which I interpreted as a warning, I sneaked into Crispin's lab over the weekend and borrowed the egg back. I decided to put it back where Cruiser and I had found it. If I had learned anything from my Native American ancestors, it was that you don't go messing with Mother Nature. I thought it best that this discovery conveniently disappear. I was just glad I'd left that detail out of my *Tattler* article. I searched for my tape, too, while I was there but couldn't find it. Had Crispin found something else recorded on there, after all? If so, I'm sure he would have told me.

It was a Monday, and the beaches weren't as overrun with tourists as on the weekend. Cruiser helped me locate the spot where we'd discovered the strange eggs. No one was there to see a woman and her dog digging in the sand. I placed the egg with its mates, then covered it gently with sun-warmed sand. Whether they would ever hatch, having been twice disturbed, I couldn't be sure, but I would leave it to fate to decide. I'd think of something to tell Crispin later when he missed the egg.

After making our delivery, Cruiser dashed ahead of me up the incline to investigate wild scents on the trail, which wasn't unusual for a nosy guy like him. He had probably spotted a chipmunk or a ground squirrel, but as is the case with most rescued dogs, he never let me get too far out of his sight. Every now and then I would glimpse the white tip of his tail waving just ahead of me among the shrubs. He wasn't about to abandon his cushy life of gourmet dog treats and sleeping on my bed just to chase some nutty squirrel. I don't think he cared much for the designer doggie duds, but life is never perfect, not even for a pampered pooch like Cruiser.

I paused at a convenient vista point to catch my breath. The reports of a monster living in the lake may have reduced the number of boaters, according to Ted Diggs, but it hadn't reduced the number of amateur shutterbugs. Thanks to the *Tahoe Tattler*'s Capture the Creature contest for a clear, unretouched photo of Tessie, there were more tourists than usual for this time of year. Thank goodness the ad hadn't said "Wanted Dead or Alive." The only shooting done at Tahoe Tessie, should she be sighted, would be with a camera. At least I hoped so.

"Cruiser! Come here, boy!" I yelled. I turned to run up the trail to find him and nearly tripped over him. Puzzled, he looked up at me as if to say, "Why are you shouting? I'm right here."

I heard a dog barking somewhere nearby. Cruiser and I followed the sound. As we approached the Crider cabin, I saw his golden retriever outside the front door. Buster was barking frenziedly, but stopped when he spotted us and ran over to me. He grabbed the sleeve of my shirt and tugged until I followed him over to the front door. I knocked, but no one answered.

"Crider, you in there?"

Not a sound. I tried the door. It was unlocked. When I pushed it open and stepped inside the cabin, Buster dashed through the front room sniffing and whining. Then he made a beeline for the bedroom. I followed the dog and froze in my tracks when I opened the door. I reached for my cell phone and rang the sheriff's office.

"Sheriff Cassidy here."

"Skip, it's me."

"Hey, Beanie. Where are you?"

"I'm at Boney Crider's cabin over at Rubicon."

"Crider's place? What you doing there with that old pot-head?"

"I think you'd better get over here."

"You in trouble?"

"No, I'm fine, but it looks like Cruiser and I may have stumbled onto some trouble here."

"What's wrong now?"

"I don't know. Maybe you can tell me when you get here."

"I'm on my way!" The phone clicked.

While I waited for Skip to arrive, I surveyed the room. It was hard to tell in Boney's disheveled digs, but you could make no bones about the fact that there were clear signs a life-and-death struggle had taken place. But there was no sign of Boney Crider.

Chapter Forty-Six

Since this whole Ivy Diggs case began, there had been a drowning, a funeral, and a murder investigation, but thus far no corpse, not even when I found Boney Crider's place in even further disarray than usual but no Boney Crider.

The squeak of rusty hinges startled me, and I turned to see Skip enter the front door.

"Excuse me, ma'am. I thought you were . . . Beanie, is it you?"

"Of course it's me. Who were you expecting?"

"I didn't recognize you. What did you do to your hair?"

"I cut it, you goof."

"Looks like you did more than that."

". . . and added a little color."

"You look so . . . uh . . . different."

"Thanks." It was better than what I'd said about his mustache. I knew that was just Skip's attempt at a compliment, so I let it go and got back to the business at hand.

"Did you search the area for Crider?" Skip said, scratching his fuzzy upper lip.

"No, I thought I'd better wait for you to get here and size things up before Cruiser and I went snooping around. Didn't want to mess up any potential evidence."

"Looks like there was a struggle in here, all right. Everything's a mess."

"Everything was a mess before when I visited. This guy's a total slob."

"Obviously, he got away somehow because he's nowhere around here." Skip surveyed the room with a practiced lawman's eye, looking for anything that might be amiss. This place was a real test for his powers of observation.

"Who would want to kill a harmless old coot like Crider, anyway?" I began to wonder if the giant aliens Boney had spoken of had transported him to a parallel universe.

"We have no proof it's murder until we have a body, Beanie."

"Well, someone clearly had a bone to pick with Boney."

"That still doesn't mean it's murder. That's what you thought about the Diggs woman, but we've had no proof of that, either. I think you've been reading too many murder mysteries, girl."

Skip was right about one thing. Ivy Diggs hadn't been murdered. Not yet, anyway. I decided not to share my latest information about Ivy's resurrection with Skip, at least not yet. Ivy Diggs wouldn't want that. I didn't want it to leak out, either. I wanted to collect the money I had been offered to solve this case. I didn't get an opportunity like this every day.

Skip stepped outside with me. "The rest of the team should be along shortly. If there's a corpse to find, we'll find it, and if we do, I'll have the M.E. get right to work carving that old turkey."

"Delicately put." Skip and his gallows humor. I'll never get used to it.

"Want to come and watch?" He stifled a wicked chuckle. He knew I had no stomach for such things. I was like Cruiser. More into the tracking and sniffing end of crime.

"I'll pass, thanks. But you'll let me know the results of the autopsy if it comes to that."

"Sure."

"Well, I have some things I need to do."

"What about Crider's dog?"

I stroked the silken reddish-gold ruff of Buster's neck. Warm brown eyes met mine and spoke a silent query. "Boney must have been in a heck of a hurry not to take his dog along with him. He loved this old dog. Said Buster was the only family he wanted. We can't just leave him here, Skip."

"I'd take him, but my landlord doesn't allow dogs."

"I'll take Buster with me. I can probably find another home for a nice dog like this if need be, but he can stay with Cruiser and me until we find out what happened to his owner."

"What's King Cruiser going to think of that? He's not used to sharing his biscuits with anyone, is he?"

"No, but he'll adjust."

At least I hoped he would. He'd had canine houseguests before when I fostered Rags and Lang Po on the Sirius case, but they were little dogs. Cruiser might not take as kindly to a large male invading his turf. But he had met the dog before on neutral ground, and they seemed to get along okay. Cruiser is a pretty easygoing guy; however, he is still a guy. Boys will be boys, even if they're dogs.

The ride home went smoothly enough. I let Cruiser sit up front with me and put Buster in the back of the car. When we got home, I made the mistake of letting Cruiser out first and taking him inside the house. I came back for Buster and led him into the house, but Cruiser had already staked his claim. Cruiser's fur stood on end until he looked like a short-legged Rhodesian Ridgeback. He emitted a low growl.

"Cruiser, no!" I commanded, and he stopped growling. I knelt down and called him to my side. With one dog on either side of me, I petted them simultaneously, crooning "Nice Cruiser. Nice Buster. What g-o-o-o-d doggies!" Then I let them get better acquainted, if you know what I mean. After a good, long butt sniff, King Cruiser adjourned to his hairy throne, better known as the sofa, and the newcomer began exploring his new territory. I said a quick hello to Nona in her room and then went to my office to work for awhile. Before long I was so immersed in writing I wouldn't have noticed a parade of polka-dotted elephants.

I had worked for about half an hour when I heard a terrible commotion coming from the kitchen. I already knew what had happened before I got there.

Nona and I arrived in the kitchen simultaneously. For all the sound and fury, there were no bites inflicted. Just a lot of slobber, noise, and tooth gnashing. Buster had made the mistake of approaching the food bowl, the one that says "Top Dog." And the top dog didn't take too kindly to this interloper trying to eat from his personal dish. We pulled the two growling gladiators apart. I filled another dish with kibble and set it far away from Cruiser's dish. So the case of the quarreling canines was solved. If only my other cases were so easily cracked.

CHAPTER FORTY-SEVEN

The Lakeview Marina Bar and Grille had been voted best restaurant in South Tahoe for three years running. When we walked in the door, the foyer was filled with people waiting to be seated.

"I hope you made a reservation, Skip," I said.

Skip's woolly upper lip spread in a sheepish grin. "I'm sorry. I was so busy, I plum forgot."

"There's a forty-five-minute wait," the greeter said when we asked how long before we could be seated. We decided to kill some time at the watering hole.

Tourists were packed tan line to tan line in the bar. Every table was taken, but finally two stools opened up. I grabbed one and held the other for Skip while he went to the men's room. As I sat waiting for him, surveying the patrons across the bar, I heard someone ask, "I say, is this seat taken, Miss?"

I turned to face a handsome dark-haired gentleman.

"Cris! What are you doing here?"

"Same as you, luv. Having dinner. My, you're looking fetching tonight."

"Thanks. You don't look so bad yourself." Crispin was dressed in a tailored navy suit with a sky blue ascot that perfectly matched his eyes. Luv. He'd said that word again. I realized that it was not intended as a term of endearment when he used the same word to thank the barmaid for his drink. "We're still waiting to be seated. With no reservation, it's not looking hopeful."

"Oh, you're here with someone?"

"My friend, Skip. You remember him from the pub?"

"Ah, yes. The sheriff." Crispin stole Skip's stool. I was going to say something, but I figured he wouldn't be there long.

"What about you? You didn't come alone, did you?" I fished.

"No, I'm here with a friend."

I should have known Crispin would be here with a date. I'm sure he had lots of lady friends to choose from on any given Saturday night. Women just naturally flocked to such men like pigeons in Trafalgar Square. I felt a pang of jealously but wasn't sure why I should. Crispin was just toying with me, and I was mature enough and smart enough to know it. If only somebody would tell my foolish old heart.

"I guess you were wise to make reservations. Judging from this crowd, Skip and I will be eating our supper here at the bar."

"No other way to get in here on a Saturday night, I'm afraid. I'd invite you to join us, but our table only seats two."

"Oh, I wouldn't think of it, Cris. I wasn't hinting for us to join you."

Crispin laid his hand on mine. "Perhaps next time I can make that reservation for the two of us, instead."

"Perhaps." Now I was certain he was toying with me.

"Oh, incidentally, Elsie."

"Yes?" Was he about to ask me out on a date? I tried not to sound too eager.

"It's the oddest thing, but our dinosaur egg has gone missing."

"Really?" Imagine that. No wonder they call them egghead professors.

"Yes, I was keeping it until I could do more tests, but when I went into the lab this morning it was gone."

"A school prankster, you think?"

226

"Perhaps. It's a pity, though. Quite a rare find, that. At least I hadn't notified the *Geographic* about it yet."

"That is a shame." I don't think he suspected I was the egg-napper, at least I hoped not. I don't know exactly what possessed me to steal the egg, other than my disturbing nightmare. However, I didn't approve of tourists chipping off chunks of Cave Rock as souvenirs, either. I believed that what was native to Tahoe should stay in Tahoe. I'd had second thoughts about letting the professor keep the tape, too. It could be possible evidence in the case. What did he want it for, anyway? Tessie wasn't on it. Or was she? I hadn't viewed the entire reel. Could this have to do with the boat footage I captured on film? Had Crispin really wanted to destroy the tape? If so, why?

"Well, I see your friend coming to reclaim his seat. Cheers for now." He kissed my cheek and smiled. Good thing the place was air-conditioned or I might have melted into a puddle on the polished oak floor, but I played it cool. What else could I do under the circumstances?

"See ya."

I watched him stride across the room through the crowd to the stairs that led to the dining area. James Bond had nothing on the debonair and intriguing Professor Blayne. I was glad that Skip hadn't spotted him and especially glad he hadn't seen Crispin kiss me. Maybe this wasn't a date, but I didn't need a repeat performance of Skip's alpha male behavior at The Cock and Bull.

"They still haven't come to seat us?"

"Nope, not yet."

"Would you rather go someplace else, Beanie?"

"Everywhere else will be booked up, too. We might as well wait it out." I only hoped we wouldn't be seated next to Crispin and his date, whoever she was.

About then the hostess approached us. "I'm terribly sorry for the long wait tonight. The tourists have descended on us all at once. We do have a seating area outside, if you'd care to sit there. It's a different menu, though. Less expensive than the upstairs dining area but just as good."

That was all it took to make up Skip's mind about whether to stay or go. If I hadn't known better, I'd have thought he had purposely not made a reservation just to save money. He was so much like Tom in his spending habits, or rather lack of them, that sometimes it was almost like being with Tom again. Actually, I was rather relieved that Skip's and my "date" wasn't going to be champagne and candlelight. As it turned out, it certainly wasn't.

We followed our hostess to the grassy, tree-shaded area and sat down at one of the redwood tables shielded by gaily-striped blue and white umbrellas. The best part was that we would be able to watch the sun setting behind the back fence of mountains towering in the west and appreciate a perfect panoramic view of the lake from where we were seated. The spectacular swirl of clouds above us looked as though stirred by the finger of God.

"Well, this isn't so bad, is it?" Skip said.

"No. It's very nice out here. Kind of like a summer picnic."

"I'm glad they couldn't seat us indoors." Skip didn't know it, but I was, too, for other reasons.

Besides, in my way of thinking, this setting afforded far more ambiance than any restaurant with linen tablecloths could provide. If given the choice, I always preferred being out in nature. It was my Native American heritage, I suppose. What better dining atmosphere could there be than a golden sunset, the wind rustling through the pine trees and a flock of Canada Geese paddling past us begging for breadcrumbs?

"You look nice tonight."

Imagine that? I hadn't even had to set my hair on fire for

Skip to notice my appearance. I wondered now if perhaps he had seen Crispin with me after all, hence the uncharacteristic flattery.

"Thanks, Skip." I gave Skip a peck on the cheek, because when Skip gave someone a compliment, even a little one, I knew he really meant it.

"What made you decide to cut your hair, anyway?"

"Nona gave me a makeover at a salon for my birthday."

"That was good of her."

"Yes, it was time for a change. She just gave me the push I needed."

"What happened to your braids?"

"I donated them."

"Donated them? Who to?"

"Needy bald people." Skip looked puzzled and I laughed. "You know, like people who've lost their hair to chemotherapy or alopecia."

"Oh." Skip swept a hand self-consciously over the thinning hair on his crown then jerked his hand away as a young, attractive blond server approached the table.

"May I get you both something to drink?" she said.

"Sure. I'm parched. Want your usual margarita?"

"Yes, please."

"On the rocks or blended?" asked the server.

"Blended, no salt."

"And for you, sir?"

Skip grinned at the pretty young blonde. What was it with him and waitresses, anyway? "What kind of beer you got on tap?"

"Just about any kind you can name."

"Okay. Let's see, I'll have a Rolling Rock." Skip gave her a wink. I thought his head would do a 360-degree spin as she sashayed back to the bar.

It's a good thing this was no date we were on. If it had been, I'd have bashed him over the head with his own beer bottle. Crispin might have been escorting another lady, but I doubt he ever would have behaved in such a manner.

A little girl toddled after a mallard duck waddling between the benches. She squealed with delight when she tried to catch the bird, but it stayed safely out of her reach. When she got too close, the duck took flight and alighted in the marina, making golden rings in the water. He dipped his bill in the water three times, then did a full body shake to disperse the water over his back. His tail feathers formed an abalone shell-colored fan in the waning sunlight.

I happened to glance at the second floor windows of the restaurant and spotted Crispin. He was talking with someone. I couldn't see who was with him because a corner of the building blocked my view. However, I did have a perfect view of the marina, the docking area for million-dollar yachts. I could envision Crispin at the helm of one of them, expertly navigating the lake as he had in the mini-sub. I was in imminent danger of imagining this guy as another Errol Flynn, swashing buckles and all. I tried to focus on something else, anything else.

In the distance I saw the *Dixie Queen* steaming toward Emerald Bay. I could only hope that their dinner cruise would be less eventful than ours had been. That turned my thoughts once again to the Diggs case. Skip and I were more alike than I cared to admit. It was hard not to think of crime solving, even in ambient surroundings like these.

"Did you ever find Boney Crider?"

"Nope. Not a trace of him."

I remembered my bizarre interview with Boney that day at his cabin. Maybe he had transported himself to another galaxy after all.

"Where do you think he could be?" I would later regret having brought up the subject of his disappearance. Skip wasn't one to stop with shoptalk once you got him started.

"No clue, at least not yet. You were right about one thing, though."

"What?"

"Someone did try to kill him. Whether he succeeded or not, we don't know because we still haven't found a stiff."

"Boney appétit." I was sorry I'd brought up the subject before dinner.

"I still don't get why someone would want to off a harmless loon like Boney Crider. He kept to himself. Never bothered anyone."

"Don't know. He always minded his own business as far as I knew. I can't imagine him getting mixed up in anything illegal. Unless he was growing a little pot garden in the back woods."

"Even if he was, this was certainly no drug hit. Too slapdash for that."

"Yes, I agree. It probably wasn't related to drugs, but if somebody wanted him dead, there had to be a pretty good reason. Could be that he knew something and someone wanted to shut him up."

"But what could he have known, Beanie?"

"Good question."

"He hardly ever left his cabin."

"Maybe he didn't have to."

"What do you mean?" Skip scratched his fuzzy upper lip, which was coming to mean the same thing as when he scratched his head.

"Sometimes you don't have to go looking for trouble, Skip. It comes looking for you."

CHAPTER FORTY-EIGHT

By the time we had finished eating, it was nearly 8:30, and the sun was sinking fast. I glanced up at the restaurant window where I had seen Crispin earlier. He was gone and someone else was seated at his table. I felt somehow disappointed.

The red of the sunset turned the lake briefly to liquid fire before the spreading veil of night turned a magenta sky to indigo. At sunset it grew chilly, as Tahoe nights do. A strong wind picked up, and the billowing umbrellas twirled like whirligigs. When the servers began lowering the umbrellas one by one, we took the hint that it was nearly time to leave. Skip called for the check, and I asked for a bag for the leftover bread. I wanted to feed the geese before we left.

The young blond girl who had served us was struggling with one umbrella that had come off its runner, trying unsuccessfully to keep it from falling all the way down.

"Can somebody help me?"

Of course, Sir Galahad Skip leapt to the damsel's rescue and lifted the umbrella back up onto the track. She thanked him and then continued folding umbrellas and upending chairs.

Before Skip could make his next move, I tugged on his sleeve. "Let's go feed this bread to the geese before we leave."

"Yeah, sure." Skip lost interest in the blonde and followed me to the boat ramp.

We walked out onto the end of the floating dock. I wobbled a bit as it pitched with each wave, and Skip hooked my arm to keep me from falling in the water.

At first there were only three male ducks that quarreled amongst one another over the handouts. Then I heard a distant honking sound. Word had gotten out, and the geese were on the way. Soon there were a dozen birds in the water, all vying for our leftover bread.

"Hey, you guys, slow down! I only have so much bread, you know."

Skip laughed. "Got enough there for me to feed them, too?"

"Sure." I handed him a couple of slices of the French bread and he got into the act, tossing the pieces farther out for the smaller, less aggressive birds. That was Skip, always looking out for the underdog, or underduck in this case. Perhaps it was because he had been an underdog himself on the force for so many years before he finally made it to Sheriff and earned some long-deserved respect.

Skip might be a shameless flirt, but he was still a hero to me. Cruiser, Nona, and I wouldn't have survived our previous Tahoe escapades if it hadn't been for him.

I tossed the last of the bread into the water and was brushing the crumbs from my hands. The buttered bread was greasy, so I stooped down to wash my hands in the water. As I did I heard a pop, pop, pop! I thought it must be kids shooting off leftover fireworks from the Fourth of July until something whizzed past my ear. Behind me there was a grunt and a loud splash as Skip hit the water. The ducks and geese honked their surprise and took flight. The bullet had missed me but struck him instead.

"Skip!" I knelt down and reached out my hand. The water stained red with his blood. At first there was no movement. "Skip, Skip!" Then he reached out a hand to grasp mine, and I hoisted him onto the walkway. The bullet had hit him in the upper chest. He cried out in pain when I pressed my palm on the wound to allay the bleeding. The blond server he had flirted with moments earlier ran over to see what the commotion was about.

"Is everything okay?" she asked. Then she saw the blood.

"He's been shot. Call 9-1-1!"

"Someone's been shot! Someone's been shot!" She ran back into the restaurant, screaming all the way. The few patrons left in the patio area where we were sitting earlier scattered like the birds we had been feeding moments before Skip took the bullet from the sniper. I had the nagging feeling it had been meant for me.

I heard the sound of a lone boat engine revving as a white cabin cruiser sped away from the marina. I tried to get a good look at who was steering the craft, but it was too dark to see clearly. I did get a glimpse at the name on the side of the boat, though—*Mag*-something, but I had more important things to attend to; namely, my friend, Skip.

CHAPTER FORTY-NINE

"Hang on, Skip. Help is coming." *Oh, please, don't take him, Great Spirit.* Within minutes I heard the sound of sirens as the ambulance pulled into the marina parking lot. The paramedics worked over him, taking vital signs, one inserting an IV and dressing his wound while another one took down what little information I could provide.

Skip managed to raise his head to ask me, "Wh-Who did this?"

"I don't know. It was too dark to see. Save your strength. Don't try to talk."

Skip's head lolled back, and his eyes shut. His face was so pallid.

"Is he going to be all right?" I asked one of the paramedics out of Skip's earshot.

"He's lost a lot of blood, ma'am, but he's in good hands."

"Yes, I know."

In five minutes they were lifting him onto a stretcher and loading him in the back of the ambulance. I held Skip's hand as long as they would let me. I wanted to ride with him, but I knew it would only hamper the paramedics.

"Don't worry, Skip. I'm right behind you. See you at the hospital."

He smiled wanly at me and squeezed my hand. The doors shut, and lights flashed in the darkness as the ambulance pulled out of the marina lot and sped away. I hurried to my car and followed it to Barton Memorial Hospital's emergency room.

The staff whisked Skip into the ER and deposited him in one of the cubicles. The staff asked me to step outside so they could attend to their patient. As I did so, the paramedics were bringing in the occupant of another ambulance. One of the paramedics yelled, "We've got a cardiac arrest here," and the ER staff swarmed over him. Soon I heard an erratic blip, blip of the heart monitor.

"Have you been able to contact anyone who knows this guy? He didn't have any ID on him when the paramedics found him down by the lake," the doctor asked one of the nurses.

"Not yet. We'll keep trying."

"Look at his face! This guy looks like he's seen a . . ."

"Excuse me, miss," I said to the nurse as she stepped out of the cubicle. "I know this man."

"You do? Who is he?"

"His name is Frank Diggs."

Behind the curtain I heard the unsteady blip on the heart monitor become one steady tone. I heard the doctor shouting, "Clear!" as he repeatedly tried to jump-start Frank's heart. Then I heard him pronounce, "He's gone. Better notify his next of kin."

I stayed with Skip in the ER until the doc had finished treating his wound and transferred him to a hospital room. I was relieved that he would be okay and glad he had a private room so he could get some rest. He was clearly exhausted by his ordeal.

I leaned down and whispered in his ear. "I'll be back to see you tomorrow morning."

Skip opened his eyes long enough to mutter, "Okay" before falling into a deep sleep.

I kissed his forehead. "Rest well, my friend." Closing the door behind me, I headed for the admitting area.

"Here's my number. Will you please call me if there's any change in Mr. Cassidy's condition?"

"Certainly."

As I headed for my car, I saw the Diggs family rushing into the ER. Unfortunately, they were too late.

It was nearing midnight by the time I drove up my driveway. I saw the front curtains rustle, and Nona peered out. She would be distressed to hear what had almost happened to me, but even more distressed to hear about what had actually happened to Skip. As I drove home, thoughts of the incident ran through my mind. Who had taken a shot at us? Why? I'd certainly heard of drive-by shootings, but float-by shootings? Only in *CSI Miami* episodes.

Nona and Cruiser met me at the door. From Cruiser's welcome you'd have thought I'd been gone for months, but then that's the great thing about dogs. Every time you walk in your front door, it's a homecoming celebration returning war heroes would envy. All that's missing are flag waving, fireworks, and a ticker tape parade. I worried that with all the nearly disastrous incidents recently, one day there might not be a homecoming at all and my beloved Cruiser would be orphaned. Neither Skip nor Nona could keep a dog where they lived, but it was a comfort to know that Nona would see he was placed in a loving home if anything ever happened to me. I tried not to think about those things, but it was good to make arrangements just in case.

"That must have been some dinner date you were out on, Mom. I expected you home hours ago."

"Well, it didn't turn out quite as expected."

"Oh, yeah? Anything interesting happen I should know about?" I was in no mood for teasing so I gave it to her straight up.

"Someone shot Skip at the marina."

Nona's smile dissolved. "What? You're kidding!"

"I'm not kidding."

"With a gun?"

"No, with a whale harpoon. Of course with a gun!" The one thing I didn't tell her was that the bullet might have been meant for me. She'd never let me out of her sight again.

"Is he . . ."

"He's going to be fine. They'll be keeping him at Barton Memorial for a while. We'll go see him tomorrow."

"Do you know who the shooter was?"

"No, I couldn't see. It was too dark, and the boat was too far away. I did see part of the name on the side of the craft, though."

"What did it say?"

"It was hard to tell, but the dark lettering on the white yacht made it a little easier to make out in the dusk. All I had time to see was the first few letters before it sped away. It looked like M-A-G. Magellan, Maggie?"

Nona's face blanched.

"What's wrong, Nona?"

"Ted Diggs owns a white yacht."

"How do you know that?"

"I told you before, Bobby took me out on it."

I would talk to Nona more later about her "friendship" with Bobby Diggs, but right now I had more pressing matters on my mind. "Go on."

"It was called the *Maggie May,* after Frank Diggs' first wife."

CHAPTER FIFTY

When Nona and I arrived at the hospital the next morning, Skip was sitting up in bed reading the paper. I was relieved to see he looked far better than he had the night before, but he was still hooked up to an IV, which was laced with powerful antibiotics to stave off any infection that might try to set in during the healing process. My native ancestors once used the au natural versions of the same medicines used in hospitals nowadays.

"Good morning, Skip. How are you feeling?"

"Hey, girls! Glad to see your two cheerful faces. I'm doing much better, thanks."

"Oh, thank goodness. I guess those pretty nurses are taking great care of you, huh?" Nona and I exchanged smiles.

"I don't know about that. The night nurse looked like Mrs. Doubtfire in drag."

"Mrs. Doubtfire was already in drag," Nona said.

Skip laughed. "Say, Beanie, I see here we already made the Police Blotter section of the *Tahoe Tattler.*" Skip pointed out the section to me. Looked like I was getting more than my fifteen minutes of fame in the *Tattler* these days.

"News travels like Saint Elmo's Fire in Lake Tahoe. It's not exactly New York City, you know. There's usually not that much crime to write about up here."

"That used to be the case. Not so nowadays," Skip said.

He was right. There had been plenty of material lately, thanks to Tessie sightings, drownings, random shootings, and a dead woman named Ivy who wasn't really dead but soon might be if I couldn't figure out who was behind all this.

"At least we can eliminate one person from our list of suspects in the Diggs case, Skip."

"Who?"

"Frank Diggs."

"Why is that?"

"Because he's dead."

"Dead? How?"

"He died of a heart attack last night. Diggs was admitted about the same time you were brought in."

"So, if he's not the perp, then who is?"

"I'm still trying to find that out." I just hoped whoever was trying to finish Ivy off wouldn't finish us off first. I didn't like the idea of Skip being used for target practice and liked even less the idea of being a sitting duck myself.

"Well, I hope you find out soon. This is starting to get a little too personal to suit me."

"I know. I'm going to do some nosing around of my own while you're laid up here in the infirmary. I think it's time I paid the Diggs family another visit to see if I can get to the bottom of this once and for all."

"Just promise me you'll be careful. Frank Diggs may be out of the picture, but there's still someone out there who means deadly business."

"I promise. Don't fret about me. You just concentrate on getting well. I can take care of myself."

"Yeah, so you're always telling me."

"Don't worry, Skip," Nona piped in. "Cruiser and I will keep an eye on her for you."

About that time a young, attractive nurse came in the room with a tray and prepared to draw blood from Skip's arm.

"How are we doing this morning?" she said.

"I'd be doing better if you wouldn't keep drawing more blood from me than I lost."

"Yeah, I don't want to have to give him any more of mine," I said.

"Your friend saved your life, Mr. Cassidy. She has the same rare blood type you have."

"You have Washoe blood in you now, Skip."

"Guess I'm your blood brother, huh?"

The nurse smiled and began prepping his arm for the withdrawal.

"Well, we'd better get going, Nona. I think we're getting in the way here. I'll check in on you later."

"Sure thing. See ya, girls."

"Now, you'll just feel a little stick." I heard the nurse say as the door shut behind us.

"They just love saying that," I said to Nona. "I almost fainted dead away during that transfusion. Anything for Skip, though."

"I know, Mom." Nona laughed. "I'm sure Skip would do the same for you."

"I hope so. He's such a chicken about some things."

"He would. He worries about you more than you know. He told me something once, but he made me promise never to tell you."

"Well, now I have to know. Spill."

She hesitated a moment. "I'm not sure if I should. He'd be mad if he knew I told you, but under the circumstances . . ."

"What?"

"He told me that one time when he and Dad were out fishing, Dad asked him to watch over you if anything ever happened to him."

"That sounds like your father all right. He was a worrywart, just like Skip. They're alike in many ways."

"Do you think you and Skip might ever end up . . . together?"

"You mean married?"

"Uh-huh."

I didn't really know how to answer that question. Sometimes I wondered if what was between the sheriff and me was more than just a strong friendship, but it was hard for me to think of him in any other way.

"Well, I'm not really in the market for marriage right now. I don't think he is, either. We have our own lives."

"Yeah, you're probably right, but I hope you're not going to stay alone forever."

"But I'm not alone, dear. I have you, Cruiser, and my good friend, Skip."

"That's not the same thing as matrimony."

"Gee, this is a switch—you pressuring me to get married and settle down? I thought that was my maternal prerogative."

"I'm not pressuring you."

"Good, then let's change the subject. What say we go have lunch someplace? I'm starved." I could never solve a mystery on an empty stomach.

"Sounds like a plan."

Nona and I headed for my favorite health food restaurant, Sierra Sprouts. I rolled down the car windows, and the cool alpine air whisked through my hair. I turned up the song playing on the stereo to eardrum-popping volume, and we started singing along with Cindy Lauper about girls just wanting to have fun. Anything to get all this murder off my mind.

CHAPTER FIFTY-ONE

It seemed to take us forever to drive to Sierra Sprouts. Traffic was bumper to bumper on Lake Tahoe Boulevard. The tourists had all but taken over our town, which probably had more to do with the promise of a possible Tessie sighting than the summer season. Every motel sign said NO VACANCY. The beaches were littered with trash from all the curiosity seekers armed with camcorders. If there were only a way to get all these people to go back to wherever it was they came from. But my ancestors had hoped in vain for that, too, when the first white men had appeared in their peaceful, unspoiled valley. Seeing the long wagon trains with the settlers climbing out of them, the Washoe had thought that a terrible serpent was giving birth to the white man. Now there was a serpent of another kind lurking in the deep waters of Tahoe.

Thanks to Tessiemania, business everywhere was booming, even at the little amusement park where Tom and I used to take Nona when she was little. The place was packed with kids of all ages, most of them lined up for a new rollercoaster ride called the Tessie Twister. A silly-looking green sea monster slithered on undulating tracks along a crudely painted diorama of the lake. As we drove past, I could hear the delighted squeals of the children above the mechanical beast's bellow, which sounded nothing like the real thing. That would have sent the kids running from the park in terror, and their parents, too.

I suddenly wished I could somehow turn time backward to

the happy days when Nona was little and Tom was still alive. Oh, to have just one more day with him. If only there were a time machine ride at the carnival, I'd jump right in and crank the handle into reverse.

"Want to stop and ride the fairy wheel, Nonie?" That's what she had called the Ferris wheel as a child.

"Very funny, Mother. Besides, that one's for little kids."

"Right. Not big kids like you, huh?"

"It takes one to know one."

"Smarty pants." I cuffed her on the head.

We ordered fruit smoothies and vegetarian burritos. I had just sat down to eat when my cell phone rang. I was getting better at finding the right button quickly. No one in the restaurant seemed to notice the musical ring of my phone, perhaps because everyone else was already yakking a mile a minute into their own cell phones.

"Hello, Elsie?"

"Cris. How are you?"

"Quite well, thank you. I was wondering if you'd like to come over to my place later this afternoon for a little chat."

"Sure, what time?"

"How about 4:00? I'll put on a kettle."

"Fine, I'll be there."

I hung up the phone. Tea for two with the professor. My pulse skipped a beat at the thought of seeing him again, although I doubted if it was mutual. It was probably something to do with the lake studies again or our old friend, Tahoe Tessie. Only one way to find out, I figured.

"So, you're seeing the professor this afternoon, huh, Mom?"

"You heard what I said, Nona." I knew she was getting at something. Maybe it was the noisy, crowded restaurant or just another midlife mood swing, but I was in the wrong frame of mind for her merciless teasing. I don't know what it was about Crispin, but he wasn't a teasing matter to me. Could I be falling in love with him? Or at least lust?

I dropped Nona off and headed straight for Crispin's place. I was a little early for our rendezvous, but I hoped he wouldn't mind. I hadn't been to his place before and wasn't exactly sure where it was. A newer home, it was contemporary in style and had an unobstructed view of the lake. I don't know why, but I had expected a tweedy English professor to reside in an ivy-covered cottage or a pub with tarred beams, like The Cock and Bull. There aren't too many of those in Tahoe, though.

I rang the bell and Crispin came to the door wearing a terry bathrobe that matched his lake blue eyes. His hair was boyishly tousled, and a raven forelock brushed his intelligent brow. I felt my heart do a flutter kick in my chest.

"Do come in. I apologize for my appearance. I just stepped out of the shower."

"Sorry, I'm a little early." Truthfully, I wasn't one bit sorry I was early.

"Not to worry. You can make yourself comfortable upstairs whilst I change."

Don't change a hair for me, Crispin, lad.

Although the exterior of the house looked ultra modern, the interior was very "Tahoe" in style. The floor plan was reversed, with the living area upstairs to afford a view of the lake. We climbed up the Tyrolean-styled peeled pine staircase. A river rock fireplace was the focal point of the great room, flanked by enclosed built-in birch wood bookshelves to match the flooring. The bookcase was filled with tomes of every kind to be enjoyed while lounging in the overstuffed leather sofa and loveseat. The rest of the room was decorated in an outdoorsman motif, including a glass-topped coffee table with a hand-carved, painted wooden relief of trout swimming in a mountain stream.

There were matching end tables. Even the lamps had carved wooden fish circling their bases. Skip would love those! A state-of-the-art kitchen with chrome fixtures and black granite counters faced the expanse of windows overlooking the beauty of the forest and lake beyond.

"My, this is a very nice place you have here, Crispin."

"Oh, it's not mine. I'm just staying here until I finish up my work."

"When will you be leaving?"

"Soon, I expect."

My heart sank. "Do you have to go so soon?"

"Yes, I'm afraid so. Just a couple more details to attend to, then it's back to the university for me. I'm off for London next week."

"Details?"

"On the lake studies."

"Oh, yes. Of course. You sounded a bit mysterious there for a moment."

Crispin laughed. "Care for some tea, Elsie?"

"Sure. What kind do you have?"

"Any kind you like. I have English Breakfast, Assam, Earl Grey . . ."

"Earl Grey, please."

"I've put the kettle on, but I need to finish dressing. Would you mind pouring if it comes to a boil before I get back?"

"No problem."

Crispin descended the stairs that led to the master bedroom. I half wanted to follow him, but instead I sat admiring the view out the picture window, feeling a bit downcast about his imminent departure. Perhaps I should have been more forward about my feelings for the professor. After all, he had shown some interest in me. He'd kissed me! Now he was leaving Tahoe without ever knowing how I felt about him. Even Cruiser knew when to make his mark and claim his territory.

I slid a copy of the *Tahoe Tattler* from the coffee table, wondering if he'd been reading my articles. As I did so, I heard something hit the floor. It was Crispin's wallet. I picked it up to put it back on the table, then hesitated. It was wrong of me to snoop, but it's what I do best. If I wanted to know more about him than he had told me thus far, there was one sure way. Someone once said the way to a man's heart is his stomach, but it's really his wallet.

I flipped through the plastic sleeves. There was his British driver's license, temporary California license, credit cards, Royal Auto Club card, a few Euros, and a couple of C-notes. I started to close the wallet when I noticed a photograph hidden in a slot in the leather wallet. I had trouble sliding it out but finally managed to remove it far enough to see it was a photograph of a woman, a very attractive, young redhead. For a moment, I couldn't believe my eyes. What was Crispin doing with a photo of Ivy Diggs?

CHAPTER FIFTY-TWO

"Find anything interesting?"

"Huh?" I'd been caught in the act. I slid the photo back into his wallet and handed it back to him.

"Do you make a practice of going through men's wallets?"

"Only when I'm trying to find out more about them." Apparently, there was much more to know about Crispin Blayne than I had first thought. "I didn't know you knew Ivy Diggs."

"Who?"

"The woman in this photo."

"Oh, that's my wife, Zoë."

"But this woman's name is Ivy."

"I'm sure you're mistaken."

"No, I'm not. I know my client when I see her."

"Client? I don't understand. Are you a private investigator?"

"Yes." Elsie MacBean, P.I. I liked the sound of that. It sounded better than Elsie MacBean, stringer for the *Tattler*. However, I knew how dangerous this kind of work could be if you weren't careful. I hoped I wasn't about to get myself in trouble. Skip was right. I really knew nothing about Crispin except that he was an egghead Brit and something of a lady-killer—not literally, I hoped.

"How can you have a dead woman for a client?"

"Because she's not dead."

The whistle of the boiling teakettle screamed like Ivy had the night she fell overboard. Once again I heard the warning blasts of the *Dixie Queen,* and the incidents of that night played like a DVD in my head. I tried to envision everyone I had seen on the boat that night. Was Crispin lying to me? Sure, I believed he'd come here to study the lake, but could he also have tracked Ivy or Zoë, or whatever the heck her name was, all the way here to kill her? Perhaps he and Ivy had some unfinished business between them. Deadly business. Suddenly, I was beginning to feel a trifle uncomfortable here alone with Crispin. I didn't want to end up tea-totally dead.

Crispin took the kettle off the burner, poured the boiling water into a china pot and covered it with a cozy.

"What's the story with you, Cris?"

He turned to face me. His eyes were winter ice on the lake.

"What do you mean?"

"Did you know your wife was on the *Dixie Queen* July 4th?"

He hesitated before answering. "Yes, I knew she would be there."

"Is that why you followed your ex all the way from England to Lake Tahoe? To spy on her? Or to kill her?"

"Certainly not! I told you before why I came here."

"All I know is what you've told me, but I get the feeling you're hiding something."

Crispin turned back to the ritual of pouring tea, but I knew he was stalling for an answer.

"All right, I'll admit that there were times I wanted to give her a proper whacking, but killing her never entered my mind."

"Then why were you following her?"

"When they tried to blame her disappearance on me and accused me of murder, I hired a private investigator of my own to find out what happened to her. I've been following her for months, but I didn't know she had remarried. We weren't even legally divorced, and there are some other matters."

"Do you have children or something?"

"No. No children."

"What, then?"

"I had hoped that we could reconcile, but then . . . well . . . you see, Elsie, I still loved her."

My heart sank like the scuttled steamer *Tahoe*. Whether it was because I thought I was falling for someone I believed might be capable of murder, or because he was in love with the woman I suspected him of trying to kill it was hard to say. If he was the foiled killer, he did indeed have some unfinished business to attend to. I just hoped he might not first take it into his head to attend to a nosy reporter-turned-P.I.

CHAPTER FIFTY-THREE

I decided to forego the Tahoe tea party with Crispin, just in case he had lured me to his place under false pretense. Besides, I'd already had enough tea for two, starting with his ex-wife Zoë, aka Ivy. I'd caught him in a lie, and that put a whole new light on things. I made some excuse about having to see a vet about a dog and made a hasty departure. For all I knew he might have slipped something into my cup of Earl Grey. I really didn't want to think the worst of Crispin, but until I could prove he wasn't a suspect and that what he told me about his reasons for following his ex-wife was the truth, I was taking no chances. Skip had barely escaped with his life. I didn't want to place anyone else in jeopardy.

I was coming up empty on this case. I had a lot of hunches, but still had no positive proof of who was trying to kill Ivy. Frank was out of the picture, and everyone else seemed to have an alibi. But someone had come after her with the intent to kill and was now after me, too. With Skip laid up in the hospital, I felt vulnerable. I would have to watch my back from here on.

I'd have to retrace my steps on the Diggs case. One step forward, two steps back. Cha, cha, cha. I had to talk to Ivy again, and I still wanted to talk to the Diggs clan once more, too, starting with Ted and Bobby.

First things first, though. It was way past Cruiser's walkies time, and I couldn't expect Nona to dog sit the whole time she was visiting. I decided to go pick him up before heading over to

Diggs Marina. I figured there were plenty of places to exercise him on the way there. Cruiser knew them all and would give me the usual elbow nudge with a wet, cold nose when I came to one of his favorites. That always got my attention.

When I arrived at the old homestead, Cruiser was waiting at the door for me along with his new housemate, Buster. My excuse to Crispin was the truth. I needed to take Cruiser to see Doc Heaton for his booster shots soon. I'd have the vet give Buster a checkup at the same time, just in case I had to place him in another home. Cruiser and Buster had managed to coexist peacefully since they had sorted out the alpha dog debate over the food bowl, but I didn't know if it would work as a permanent arrangement.

Nona was waiting for me, too. She was a Fourth of July firecracker ready to explode, not with anger at me for leaving her to be a dog nanny, but with questions about my visit with Crispin. I wasn't sure what I should say about it, if anything. After all, it really wasn't any of her business, just like it wasn't my business to tell her not to date spoiled rich men's sons or freaks with nose rings and blue, spiked hair. Besides, I preferred to keep my concerns about the professor under my beanie for now. They were only suspicions, after all. I had no proof of anything.

I tried to divert the inevitable cross-examination by heading straight for the hall tree and Cruiser's leash. He followed hot on my heels, howling his excitement. You never picked up the leash around my house unless you meant business. Once the signal had been given, there was no turning back.

Evasion wasn't going to work this time, though. Nona knew I was avoiding her questions, and that made her all the more intent on asking them.

"Well?" she said.

"Well, what?"

"How was your afternoon with Remington Steele?"

"Very funny."

"Seriously. How did it go?"

"Okay."

"Just okay? Anything wrong, Mom? You look troubled."

"It's nothing. I need to walk this dog. Cruiser isn't going to let up until I take him for his walkies."

"Want me to come along?"

"No, I want you to stay put."

"Okay. We can talk later." She plopped down on the sofa. "I'd go with you, but I'm pooped from pup sitting."

"Sorry, honey. I didn't mean for you to come up here and run a kennel for me."

"It's okay. I don't mind, really."

Nona was just like her dad. All the complaining about Cruiser was just camouflage for the affection she felt for him.

"Hey, Buster, want to come along with Cruiser and me?" I coaxed. Buster looked at me, then ambled over next to Nona and curled up beside her.

"Looks like you're not the only one who's pooped."

"Looks like. Your adoptee has seemed kind of listless all day."

"He's probably missing his old friend, Boney."

"Probably so." Nona stroked the dog's head as he propped it on her knee.

She was right. I had noticed that Buster wasn't the same dog I had seen the first time I visited Crider's cabin. He hadn't shown much interest in food, either, but I thought that was because of Cruiser's reaction when Buster came too near his bowl. I hoped he wasn't harboring a health problem. He wasn't a young dog, but I suspected the retriever was just grieving for his master. If Boney didn't turn up soon, I would have to get Buster settled in a permanent home so he could adjust to his new life. Being bounced from foster home to foster home is no better for a dog than for a child. He was a nice dog and I had no problem being a foster parent to two dogs, but I was pretty sure Cruiser would never fully accept another male in his territory.

"I'll leave Buster here with you. He seems content for the moment." I also figured he'd be good protection for my daughter in my absence. Barking dogs scare trouble away.

"Maybe I should give up modeling and start up a doggie daycare center," Nona joked.

"I shouldn't be too long."

"Okay, but hurry back. I get worried about you when you're gone too long."

"No need. I can take care of myself."

"Got your cellular with you?"

"I've got it right here, see?" I brandished the phone like a pistol, then hooked it back on my belt. "Cruiser has his, too."

"Good. While you're walking Cruiser, I'll offer Buster some canned food. Maybe that will spark his interest a little."

"Good idea. There's some gourmet stuff in Cruiser's Yum-Yum Nook."

"Russian Caviar, no doubt, knowing that spoiled hound of yours."

"Well, if spoiling a dog is a crime, I'm guilty as sin."

We laughed, but at a deeper level we both understood that there were far worse sins afoot for us to be concerned about, not the least of them murder.

CHAPTER FIFTY-FOUR

Although Tahoe might have opened a new dog mall and a dog park or two, other parts of the community were becoming less dog friendly in the wake of dog attack incidents in the Bay area and elsewhere. You could even lose your home insurance if you owned a blacklisted breed. Never mind the fact that the problem had more to do with stupid, irresponsible owners than vicious pets. NO DOGS ALLOWED signs on beaches and parks in our area are testament to the wave of anti-dog sentiments. Fortunately, bassets aren't on the black list and there are no leash laws in the forest. Yet. There are plenty of places to pull off the main road and explore wide-open spaces and, happily, still enough undeveloped areas left, in spite of the relaxed building restrictions in Tahoe.

Cruiser knew the moment I pulled off the road that he was in for some adventure. When I opened the passenger door he was out in a flash, ready for action. There was a well-worn path from others who had stopped here to take a walk, most likely with a canine companion or two. As many a dog had before him, Cruiser made a beeline for the nearest cluster of foliage and lifted his leg, then busied himself reading the assortment of pee-mail other dogs had left behind.

The late afternoon sketched charcoal shadows on the sandy trail. A lizard skittered across the path, making reptilian grooves in the sand similar to the much larger ones I had seen on the beach with Cruiser and Nona. I began thinking about all the strange events of the last few weeks that began with my sighting of something most people claimed didn't exist—a prehistoric creature living in Lake Tahoe. I knew I hadn't imagined it, just like I hadn't imagined my recent brushes with death. Someone was out for blood. Mine.

I didn't know who the culprit was, but I still had plenty of suspects to choose from, including Crispin Blayne. It served me right for acting such a fool at my age. I was too old to be chasing after the likes of him, just as Frank Diggs had been too old for Ivy. She was certainly not above reproach, either. It was obvious to anyone that she'd married Frank for his money. Attractive, young gals like Ivy usually didn't marry men in their sixties with bad tickers for any other reason than financial gain. It's probably the same reason she'd married Crispin, who was obviously well heeled.

Crispin said his wife had disappeared without a trace, exactly as Frank's wife had from the *Dixie Queen*. How did I know that this wasn't all an elaborately staged "accident" that Ivy had almost pulled off. Was she evading a vindictive ex? It was clear that she was intent on reinventing her identity, perhaps for better reason than vanity alone. Could Ivy have been the one who tried to kill Boney and taken a shot at me at the marina to get rid of the only ones who knew she was still alive? She admitted she'd been following me. Maybe she had me busy searching for her killer just to throw Cruiser and me off her scent.

How did I know I hadn't been followed for weeks and that someone wasn't waiting for the right opportunity to bump me off? Maybe she had hired a hit man to run me off the road at Emerald Bay and take a shot at me outside the restaurant. Perhaps the killer was waiting for another opportunity to make an attempt on my life when I was alone, like I was now with Cruiser on this secluded alpine trail.

The forest seemed a lot darker than it had a moment ago.

And way too quiet, until I became aware of an odd sound among the trees. At first I thought the high-pitched sound was from the tiny mountain birds that flitted among the branches of the pines, but I realized the sound was not one heard in nature but a metallic sound, like a door swinging on squeaky hinges. The sound was coming closer. Someone was nearby, but I couldn't tell who it was. All I could make out among the lengthening shadows of the trees was the silhouette of a large man against the waning sunlight.

Cruiser's fur spiked and a rumble emanated from his throat as our forest intruder clawed his way through a tangle of pine branches. All the while I heard that insistent metallic screech stabbing the silence of the deep woods.

I tensed as Cruiser's warning growl grew louder. The interloper was nearly upon us. I had no weapon, but at least I had my cell phone, as Nona had advised me. I was just about to punch 9-1-1 when the man hidden among the trees stepped into a patch of sunlight.

"Boney Crider!" Did I have it all wrong from the beginning? Was Crider somehow involved in this case? Was the harmless hermit act just a front for something more sinister than smoking an illegal substance?

"What are you doing here, Boney? I thought you were dead."

"I nearly was, but I managed to escape."

I remembered his comment about transporting himself to other galaxies and wondered just how far he'd escaped to.

"You did a pretty good vanishing act. Where have you been keeping yourself all this time?"

"I've been lying low. Had to. I didn't want my attacker coming back to finish the job. But I've lost Buster. I hope he wasn't hurt."

"Don't worry. Buster's safe at my house, but he's been missing you."

It was the first time since I'd met him that I'd seen Boney Crider smile—for the love of a dog.

"Why would someone want to kill you?"

"Because I know too much, I guess."

"Like what?"

"I know about the operation on the lake."

"Operation? What do you mean?"

"They're secretly bringing up a treasure from an old wrecked steamer over in Rubicon Bay near my place. I was doing a little salvage work of my own out on the lake one night when I saw the boat and a diver pulling something up out of the water. They didn't want anyone else knowing what they were up to or they wouldn't have been out there in the middle of the night. Lucky for me there was a full moon that night, or maybe it was unlucky. They spotted me."

"You said 'they.' Who are 'they'?"

"I don't know. I could only make one of them out clearly."

"Who was it?"

"The same one who attacked me. Bobby Diggs."

As surprised as I was to stumble across Boney Crider while walking my dog in the woods and by what he had told me about Bobby Diggs, the ringing of my cell phone surprised me more. It wasn't a sound I expected to hear in the forest, but I also didn't expect the voice I heard on the other end.

"Hello, Elsie?"

"Ivy? What's wrong?" She sounded distressed, out of breath. "Where are you calling from?" Silence. I was probably losing the signal way out here in the forest. "Ivy? Can you hear me?" Drat these techie contraptions.

"I hear you." There was a hitch in her voice. "C-come to

Diggs Marina right away."

"Diggs Marina? Why there? What's up?"

"I can't talk now. Please hurry!"

"I'm on my way."

I couldn't ignore the urgency in Ivy's voice. Had Bobby come after her, too? It was risky going alone into an uncertain situation without police backup, but duty called. I was duty bound to go to my client's aid. Boney had wandered off into the woods, so I dialed Nona to tell her where I was going. Someone should know. There was no answer, but I left a message, hoping she'd get it soon.

Cruiser also left one last message at his bush as we turned back for the car and headed for the marina. I had no idea what to expect once I got there. I was no proponent of firearms, but I was wishing Skip had given me a handgun instead of a Swiss Army knife for my birthday. If only Skip weren't laid up in the hospital, I wouldn't need one. I was glad that at least I had my trusty K-9 unit along with me.

CHAPTER FIFTY-FIVE

It was dusk by the time Cruiser and I arrived at Diggs Marina. The place looked deserted. I knew cell phone signals could be spotty at times, but there was no mistaking that Ivy had asked me to meet her at the marina. I was here, but where was she?

Cruiser sniffed around as I searched the dock for Ivy Diggs. I was feeling pretty edgy and in no mood for a game of hide and seek. I was just about to give up and leave when I spotted a flash of white among the berths. It was Ivy's dog, Bitsy. Cruiser saw her, too, and took off after the little dog with me hot on his heels.

The bichon ran up to one of the boats and leapt aboard. Cruiser followed her up the gangplank. I realized this was the same craft I had seen at the Lakeview Marina that night—Diggs' yacht, the *Maggie May*. "Cruiser, come back here!" As usual, when in pursuit of anything from biscuits to bichons, he completely ignored my summons. I would have to retrieve him. Cautiously, I boarded the sleek, white cabin cruiser.

I followed Cruiser aboard the *Maggie May* and heard Bitsy's frantic barking. The sound led me to the cabin where I found Ivy bound and gagged.

"Hang on, Ivy. I'll get you out of there." She tried to say something through the knotted handkerchief in her mouth. As I reached for my cell phone to dial 9-1-1 for help, a rumble like thunder rose from Cruiser's throat. Suddenly, the cellular flew from my hand into the lake as I felt a crack to the back of my head. A burst of fireworks exploded before my eyes a moment before I tumbled headfirst into the cabin, out cold.

When I came to, I was lying bound and gagged beside Ivy in the cabin of the *Maggie May*. Stars were strewn across a dark sky, but I realized they were the ones orbiting right before my eyes. The full moon's rays pierced the dark through a gap in the door. I felt the thrum of the boat's powerful engine beneath me, then an echoing thrum of pain from the blow to my skull. I tasted the sweetness of my own blood as it trickled down the side of my face.

Someone was steering the craft on a course charted for deep water, which is exactly what Ivy and I were in now. If we were to avoid being Tessie tidbits, it was up to me to get us out of this. But how? Skip couldn't come dashing to my rescue this time. He was laid up in the hospital. No one else knew I was on this boat. Not even Nona. The cell phone she had insisted I carry with me was somewhere down there with the fish and whatever else lurked in the dark waters of Tahoe.

Where was my dog? I managed to loosen my gag. "Cruiser, where are you?" Only a fanatic dog lover like me would be worrying about her dog at a time like this. I didn't hear him or Bitsy, and that worried me. Had our captor thrown them overboard? Cruiser might have managed to tow me back to the *Trout Scout,* but he was no water dog. Then I heard a snoring sound coming from a corner of the hold. "Cruiser?" When he didn't respond to my summons and neither did Bitsy, I knew they'd been drugged to keep them quiet.

It began to get chilly. I noticed a wool blanket rumpled up beside me, so I tried to pull it over far enough so I could cover myself up for warmth. As I tugged on the blanket, what it had been concealing was slowly revealed. I let out a screech of horror as a moonbeam illumined the bloodless face of Bobby Diggs' corpse.

CHAPTER FIFTY-SIX

I knew my terrified outburst had alerted our abductor when I heard footsteps rushing toward us from above. When the door opened, the cabin flooded with light from the full moon. Glinting in the moonlight was the quicksilver of a semi-automatic pistol aimed at us, the same kind of weapon I'd seen before in Ted Diggs' office.

Ivy and I were ushered up to the deck of the *Maggie May* and ordered to sit while our legs were tightly bound. Crispin's handsome features appeared menacing in the ghostly wash of moonlight as he sneered at Ivy Diggs, then at me. I was seeing the dashing Professor Blayne in a whole new light.

"Well, Zoë, or Ivy, or whatever you call yourself these days. Looks like this is right where we left off, isn't it? You're about to disappear again, only this time it's for good."

Ivy struggled against her bindings, to no avail.

"What a silly little fool you are. Did you think you could toss me aside so easily as the rest? The only reason you married Frank Diggs was for his money, same as ever. Now it looks like I'm the one who's about to do the tossing of you and your meddlesome detective over the side of this craft. Good of you to help me lure her aboard for this moonlight cruise."

"So it was you behind this all along, Crispin."

"Yes, but unlike that wastrel Bobby Diggs, I'll finish the job properly. He had his chance to steer your investigation off course and you off a cliff, but he mucked it up. If you want something done right, you simply have to do it yourself."

"Even murder, it appears." I only wished that I'd had my recorder along with me to capture this confession on tape. That would be helpful when Crispin Blayne was put on trial for murder. I just hoped it wouldn't be *my* murder!

"Bobby Diggs was rather useless to me in the end, but he played right into my hands. Such a greedy fellow was helpful in retrieving the booty from the sunken steamer while helping protect my plans from nosy Parkers, including his own family. Rather foolish of him to think he'd actually get any of the treasure, though."

"You took a big chance confiding in a reporter, didn't you?"

"Having a reporter who believes in mythical lake creatures helped. I was worried that you might foil the operation with all your poking around in Ivy's disappearance, but your helpful media exposé of Tessie turned out to be the perfect cover." He didn't mention that he also must have known that I was under the spell of his charm, as many women probably had been.

"So you used everyone to your advantage, including me, to help cover your tracks while you retrieved a long lost treasure in the lake, not to mention dispensing with your wife."

"It nearly worked, too, didn't it, Detective? You had people running scared at first with your Tessie tales, which was just what I wanted to happen so I could complete my survey of the submerged wreck without any impediment. A pity you write for the *Tattler* instead of the *Times*."

I had to agree with him there. The *Times* paid better, too. "A pity, indeed."

"Unfortunately, people are a little too curious for their own good these days." Crispin revved the engine and steered the *Maggie May* for the deepest waters of the lake.

I wanted to scream for help, but who would hear me out here?

The deck beneath me grew harder by the minute, and my left leg began to ache. It felt like something was poking my leg through the pocket of my jeans. Probably my keys. Then I remembered what it was—the Swiss army knife Skip had given me for my birthday. Bless him! I knew it might come in handy sometime, but never like this.

I stretched my fingers as far as they would extend, but it wasn't quite far enough to reach the knife. I nudged Ivy and she looked at me with eyes that conveyed a mix of fear, desperation and cunning. Perhaps it was the same cunning that had landed her in this dire situation and entangled me in the middle of it all. But at the moment, I was glad to have her along for the ride. Maybe she could help me get us out of this fix.

When I pointed my index finger toward my pocket, she understood immediately what I was getting at. She scooted closer to me, with her back to me, watching Crispin all the time to be sure our abductor wasn't aware of what we were up to. She reached her hand into my pocket and managed to loop a finger on the round metal key chain loop of the knife. Slowly, cautiously, she inched the knife from my pocket. Then she lost her grip on it and it fell back into the bottom of my pocket. She tried again, but one of the utensils was hung on a loop of thread at the bottom of my pocket. She gave the knife a sharp tug, and the thread snapped. The thrust brought the knife up and out of my pocket in one swift motion, but Ivy lost her grip again and the knife fell. I caught it in my upturned palm just before it clattered onto the deck. We shared a sigh of relief.

With both hands still bound behind me, I managed to unfold a blade on the knife. I flinched as I nicked my finger getting the blade locked into position. A cut finger was the least of my worries right then. I began sawing at the bindings on my wrists until finally I felt them loosen just enough to free my hands. I was just about to work on the rope around my ankles when I felt the craft slow to a stop. The boat began to buck with each wave. Under normal circumstances I'd have been as sick as a dog, but fear and determination to survive took precedence over any sensation of seasickness.

Crispin approached us. His tall frame silhouetted against the moon, he posed a frightening query. "So, who's first to go for a dip?"

Ivy managed to loosen her gag in an attempt to reason with her husband. "You don't want to do this, Crispin. You have too much to lose if they catch you."

"But they won't, luv. I have my getaway perfectly planned."

"Please stop and think about what you're doing."

"I have thought about it, and I've decided to shut the both of you up for good."

"Sheriff Cassidy knows where I am," I lied. "He's on his way right now."

He paused to listen for the sound of a motorboat. "I don't think so, Elsie, old girl. Nice try."

Nobody called me old girl and got away with it. Crispin knelt down to tighten our gags. If I was going to make a move, it was now or never. In one swift motion I brought my free hand from behind me and sunk my Swiss army knife in his shoulder. He screamed in pain and lost his grip on the gun. It was knocked across the deck along with the knife. I lunged for the gun. Slapping frantically at the deck with one hand, I stretched to reach the gun, but it was too far from my grasp. Crispin quickly rallied and scrambled for the gun. He snatched it up. He also picked up my knife and tossed it overboard.

Crispin motioned me toward Ivy with the gun. "Over there with her." I obeyed. He rebound my wrists, though not as tightly as before. He was in a hurry now to be done with us, just in case I had been telling the truth about the sheriff. He jerked Ivy up to her feet, then me, and motioned us both to the starboard side. He attached weights to our ankles.

He lifted Ivy up with ease and sat her on the railing. Then he lifted up the weight and heaved it over the side of the boat. The curl of rope unraveled like a spool of thread. An instant later, Ivy was yanked over the side. As she went overboard, she managed to latch onto the lower rung of the boat's railing with her bound hands. She held on as long as she could, digging her long, manicured nails into her palms until they bled, but she was losing her grip. Crispin whacked at her hands a couple of times with the butt of the gun and missed. Then he connected. Ivy's scream pierced the silence as the gun smashed down on her fingers. I heard a sickening crack as they broke like twigs, but she still held her grip with one hand.

"This time it's going to be different, luv. This time you're going all the way." One by one he peeled Ivy's fingers off the railing until she finally released her grip. I heard the splash as she hit the water.

Then Crispin's attention turned to me. "Upsie daisy now, Elsie," he said, wagging the weapon toward the place where Ivy had been only a moment before. I climbed atop the railing and perched there, awaiting my fate as I peered into the deep, dark water. Where was Skip when I really needed him? Who would save me now? Still training the gun on me, Crispin lifted the weight attached to my ankles, carried it to the starboard side of the *Maggie May,* and prepared to toss it overboard. Ivy was gone. One down, one to go. My turn to die.

CHAPTER FIFTY-SEVEN

"You're next," Crispin said.

He fumbled momentarily with the heavy weight he'd roped to my ankles. As he prepared to heave it overboard and me along with it, I busied myself trying to loosen my wrist bindings. He was so intent on the task at hand he didn't notice.

The next few moments seemed to pass in slow motion. Still struggling to free myself, I watched him heft the weight higher, higher. As he was about to release it, he was suddenly distracted when the cabin door flew open with a bang. Cruiser bounded from his dungeon, tearing across the deck toward Crispin at the ready to protect me from harm. Admittedly, full throttle for a basset isn't all that fast, but it was fast enough to take Crispin by surprise. Evidently, whatever he had given the dogs to knock them out had not been administered in a large enough dose for a breed the size of a basset hound.

When Cruiser threw his full weight against Crispin, it was just enough to throw him off balance and topple him over the side of the *Maggie May*. As he fell, he let go of the weight still attached to my ankles. In one swift motion we plummeted from the deck in tandem into the frigid water. I heard Cruiser's frenzied barking as I took one last precious gulp of the rarified mountain air.

My wrists were already freed as I went overboard, and I latched onto Crispin's leather belt, dragging him down with me in a kind of bear hug. I'd often fantasized about embracing him, but never like this. We were pulled deeper and deeper into the big water where my long-dead ancestors slept. I feared I was about to join them in the great Lake of the Sky. I had lost my knife. No way to free myself now.

Crispin tried to break free of my grasp, but I hung on to him like Cruiser would to a juicy bone. If I was going down, so was Crispin Blayne. If anything, it would slow our descent and perhaps buy me enough time to think of a way out of this predicament.

Now my captive, the professor struggled to free himself. In the fading glow from the boat's running lights at the lake's surface, I saw the terrified look on his face as a string of bubbles expelled from his mouth. I imagined he was seeing the same expression of panic on my face, watching life slip away in iridescent pearls of air. He managed to unfasten his belt to free himself from our death plunge. The belt fell away in my hand, and Crispin was unleashed from my grasp. I kept on sinking.

My lungs began to burn as my need for oxygen increased and soon grew desperate. I dared not expel what breath remained; there would be no more. I began to hallucinate, or so I thought. I saw a dark mass moving up toward me from Tahoe's depths. Was this the lake bottom already rising up to meet me? I hadn't sunk that far already, had I? I felt something brush against my ankles. Then there was a slight tug on the rope, as though a giant fish were hooked on the end of the line. There was a sharper jerk. What was happening down there?

Suddenly, I had the sensation of a terrific weight upon me being released, and I was carried swiftly upward. Faster. Faster still. Then I saw a light above me. Was this what it felt like when you go into the light? Was I dying?

CHAPTER FIFTY-EIGHT

The light above me grew brighter and brighter as I was borne upward from my watery grave by some unseen force. I had not felt the moment of death. I still felt every sensation of the living—the icy water rushing along my body, the pain from the bindings still gouging my ankles. The light grew blinding. I must be nearly there now. I thought of my beloved Cruiser. What would become of him now? Then I fancied that I saw his dear, wrinkled face looking down upon me from above, his brow furrowed with worry. I had always heard that your life flashes in front of you before you die, but I didn't know that it was your dog's life.

As I broke the water's surface, the first gulp of cold alpine air hit my lungs like a slap on a newborn's bottom. I guzzled more of the colorless, odorless elixir of life, blessed oxygen, realizing I was not dead but soon would be if I didn't get out of the hypothermic waters of the lake.

The bright beam of a flashlight guided me to the boat's ladder, and I grabbed the bottom rung.

"Take hold of my hand," Ivy said. Somehow she had survived her plunge into the lake and had managed to free herself from her bindings.

I grasped her good hand, and she helped me the rest of the way up the ladder and onto the deck.

Cruiser trotted over to me and I knelt down to hug him. "Oh, Cruiser. My good boy." Not usually overly demonstrative,

Cruiser licked me up one side of my face and then the other. Bitsy dashed straight to Ivy and did the same. Apparently, the thrashing of the boat on the choppy waters of the lake had revived her.

I untied my remaining bindings. There were angry rope burns on my ankles. "I thought you were a goner for sure, Ivy. How did you escape?"

"I don't know. The rope just snapped. It must have caught on something sharp down there."

"Let's get back to the dock."

I started the ignition, but the engine didn't turn over. I tried several more times. Nothing.

"That's just great!" I said.

"What?" Ivy said.

"The engine won't start."

"Is it out of gas?"

"The gauge says there's fuel. It must be flooded."

"How are we going to get back? Row?"

"I suppose we'll have to wait until morning and hope someone spots us." I sure wasn't about to swim back to shore. I'd had enough of dogpaddling in Lake Tahoe to do me for a lifetime, and besides we were too far out. We'd never make it alive in that frigid water.

The wind picked up and it grew much colder. The moon slipped behind a dark cloak of clouds, and a heavy night mist settled on the lake. A storm was brewing. "Ivy, why don't you look and see if there are any more blankets so we don't freeze to death out here."

"Oh, very well."

I knew she didn't relish going down into the hold with Bobby's corpse, but she went to search for what we needed to survive this uncharted death cruise Crispin had taken us on. After all, it was because of her that we were out here in the first

271

place. I tried turning the engine over a couple more times, just in case there were enough fumes left in the tank to get us back to the dock. It coughed to life briefly, then died again. I stood shivering on the deck, trying to think of some way to get us back to safety when I heard something scrape against the side of the boat. I followed the source of the sound and leaned over the railing to see what it was. I peered into the mist but couldn't see anything at first. I screamed as an icy hand clamped like a vice on my wrist. Nightmares do come true!

Rung by rung, Crispin climbed up the ladder, murder flooding his cold blue eyes. Suddenly, I remembered the gun that had dropped on the deck during our earlier struggle. I wrenched myself free of his grasp and scrambled over to where I remembered last seeing it. I snatched it up then ran back to the side of the boat. Crispin had managed to climb farther and had hooked one hand on the railing, trying to pull himself up, but his wounded arm made it difficult. I cocked the hammer and pointed the gun straight at him.

"Don't move another inch or I swear I'll shoot."

What he didn't know was that I'd never even held a gun before, let alone fired one. There's a first time for everything.

CHAPTER FIFTY-NINE

Crispin froze, not sure whether I would fire the pistol but not really wanting to find out. The standoff would have lasted until dawn if it hadn't been for what happened next. The boat began to pitch and buck in the water. The storm seemed to be picking up fast. Too fast.

Ivy was suddenly at my side. She thought I didn't notice her brush away tears. I assumed they were from the mounting pain of her injured hand, rather than Crispin's betrayal and our desperate situation. Perhaps it was all of the above. "What is it? What's going on?"

"I don't know." The surface of the lake looked like a smoothie in a blender. Waves clapped violently against the *Maggie May*. This wasn't just a storm. What was happening? Was it another subterranean earthquake?

Suddenly, I recognized the electronic strains of "Scotland the Brave" emanating from somewhere out on the lake. It was my cell phone! The sound was moving closer and closer. Then I saw something enormous moving out in the dark waters, headed straight for us like a tidal wave. I feared we would be capsized.

"Hang on!" I cried. Ivy and I grabbed onto the railing and braced for a collision. But it never came. At the last moment the wave seemed to sideswipe the craft and dissipate. The boat rocked gently like a cradle, then I heard a shriek of terror. Gingerly, I peered over the side of the boat, fearing what I might find. Crispin was gone!

"We're safe now, Ivy."

"Thank heavens. What was that?"

"You don't want to know. Did you find any blankets for us?"

"Yes, I found some . . . they were covering this." Ivy held a solid brick of gold in her hand. "There's a lot more down there, too." I thought I saw dollar signs ring up in Ivy's green eyes.

"That must be the sunken treasure Crispin spoke of. So that's what he was after—a lost shipment of bullion from the Gold Rush."

"You mean that's what he was after besides me," Ivy said with a shiver.

"Hand me one of those blankets. Better wrap up in one yourself." I made myself a human burrito in the thick wool blanket Ivy had found and prepared to wait out the night until help could arrive. I stood watch on the deck just to be certain our foe wouldn't make a comeback, but I suspected that was the last we would see of Crispin Blayne.

As I waited, I heard another sound coming from somewhere out on the lake. I skimmed the flashlight beam across the water and thought for a moment that I saw some movement in the mist. Was it Tessie? Had she returned to scuttle us for good? The thrumming sound grew louder. Then I saw a light flash back at me.

"Someone's out there!"

"Who?" Ivy said, peering into the darkness with me.

The light grew brighter as the outboard drew closer and pulled alongside the crippled *Maggie May*.

"It's Crider, and Nona's with him. Thank goodness!"

Boney Crider helped us and the dogs disembark the *Maggie May* and climb aboard his smaller craft. I hugged Nona tightly. "How did you know we were way out here?"

"Cruiser's collar led us here," she said.

"What?" Ivy squawked.

"Of course," I said. "The GPS tracker on Cruiser's collar pinpointed our exact position so they could find us."

"Guess you're glad I bought Cruiser that collar now, aren't you, Mom?"

"You bet I am. I guess you could say he's a dog of a different collar."

I was making jokes to break the tension of the fact that we were still not out of danger out here on the water. Somewhere out there in the depths of Tahoe lurked something that could still mean to harm us.

Boney circled back for the east shore and the safety of the dock. As he did so, I heard the sound of the engine of the *Maggie May* growling in the distance. Ivy heard it, too.

"It's Crispin! He's alive, and he's coming after us. This time he'll kill us all!"

Finally, the engine turned over. Crispin revved it full throttle and steered his cruiser of death straight for us!

The *Maggie May* was gaining on us fast. Boney's underpowered craft could never outpace the powerful cruiser. Smoke was billowing from the engine as we tried to keep ahead of our pursuer.

"He's catching up." Ivy screamed. "Go faster. Faster!"

"I'm giving her all she's got," Trekkie Boney exclaimed like Scotty in a *Star Trek* episode. "She's just no match for his craft." If only the captain could beam us up out of this danger.

We were all hollering at the tops of our lungs for Boney to speed up. Even Cruiser was at the helm of the outboard, baying as though he were a coxswain on a rowing skull. Bitsy joined the fray, barking along with Cruiser.

The *Maggie May* was rapidly closing the gap between our two craft. When it looked like the race was nearly lost, I heard a sound like a ten-car pile-up on an interstate. I turned to see the *Maggie May* literally airborne. She came back down into the water with a terrible crash, breaking up. A moment later the cruiser exploded and was engulfed in flames. Boney slowed our overtaxed engine before it burst into flames, too.

We watched in stunned silence as though we were watching the sinking of the *Titanic*. The flames were gradually extinguished as the *Maggie May* slowly submerged to rest at the lake's bottom with the other shipwrecks. Like those unfortunate craft that had gone before, she bore her ghostly passengers and long lost treasure into the mysterious, uncharted depths of Lake Tahoe.

CHAPTER SIXTY

The summer season was winding down, and the campgrounds had begun to empty. Tessiemania quickly fizzled when tourists grew tired of attempting unsuccessfully to film the lake's elusive reptilian resident. The *Tahoe Tattler* abandoned its Capture the Creature photo contest; however, I had no doubt that the newspaper's sideshow carnie turned editor-at-large would find something else in Tahoe to sensationalize for the sake of newsstand sales. Carla was probably already hard at work on the two-headed pygmy alien story.

As my Washoe ancestors had done at summer's end, Tahoe's flood of tourists broke camp and began the long descent down the winding mountain pass. Assured that Cruiser and I were safe from further harm, Nona left for San Francisco to resume her modeling work, saying she could shake, rattle and roll there just as easily as she could here after a 6.0 earthquake rocked the region from Truckee to Markleeville. The temblor had sent them all packing, as Crispin would have said. Ivy had returned to London to start her life anew, hopefully on a better course. She took her darling Bitsy along with her, which wouldn't make Cruiser very happy, but Boney promised to bring Buster over sometimes for a play date.

"Well, I guess Britannia no longer rules the waves around here, eh Beanie?" Skip said.

"What do you mean?"

"I mean your geeky professor showed his true colors."

"You thought he was geeky?"

"Aren't all eggheads geeks?"

"No, not all. In fact, Cris was about as far from geekdom as you can get."

"You kind of liked hanging around with him, didn't you?"

I couldn't deny that I had been infatuated with the handsome professor, but women were allowed some middle-age crazies, too, weren't they? I admit I'd nearly gone off the deep end over Crispin Blayne, though. Literally. Whatever it was I thought I had felt for him, I would never admit it to Skip. A woman's heart is as bottomless as the Lake of the Sky and what lies hidden at its depths is best left there.

"Not nearly as much as I like hanging around with you and Cruiser. Anyway, that was before I knew he was a murderer. I suspected that something wasn't entirely cricket with Crispin. I just didn't know how sinister his intentions were or how devious he was."

This afternoon's crossing of the lake was a lot calmer than the last one Cruiser and I had shared. Sporting his new life vest and Born to Cruise hat, my faithful four-legged shipmate made a rather comical figurehead, hanging ten—paws, ears, flews, dewlaps and whatever other appendages you'd care to name— off the bow of the motorboat. Judging from his happy, panting face, he was clearly relishing the speedy cruise home from Skip's favorite fishing hole off of Rubicon Point. I wasn't sure if the spray misting my face was lake water or drool from Cruiser's windblown jowls, and I didn't much care. It was just good to be with my two best and truest friends in the whole world, and to be alive.

I don't know how Skip had talked me into coming back out on a boat yet again after my harrowing experiences on the lake in recent weeks. With Boney Crider's tip on this fishing spot, Skip was determined to catch his trophy fish. I guess there's no limit to what I'll do for a friend like Skip, but at least I had insisted he commission a larger craft than the *Trout Scout* for this sunset fishing excursion.

"This is a pretty nice tub you've got here, Skip. Where did you rent it?"

"I bought it from Diggs. I decided it was high time I invested in a new fishing boat."

"Must have been expensive. I thought you were saving every penny for retirement."

"Life is short. In my line of work you never know if you'll actually make it to your golden years."

"So the *Trout Scout* is officially retired?"

"Semi-retired. I'll use her for fishing the streams and rivers." I was glad to still count Skip among the living after nearly losing him to a stray bullet. Skip's wound had nearly healed. He was going to be okay, even though he wouldn't be fly-fishing for a while. But he had lived to fish another day, and for that I was grateful.

"Think we'll see any more of your friend, Tessie?" Skip, ever the skeptic, guffawed.

I smiled. "I suspect we've seen the last of her for awhile."

"Do you really think she ever actually existed?"

"According to the *Tahoe Tattler*, she does."

"Rag sheets have been cranking stuff like that out for years."

"Well, I was the one doing the cranking on this story, and I did my research. I admit that the *Tattler* is more interested in sales these days than solid facts, but you haven't forgotten about the dinosaur egg I found, have you? You saw that with your own eyes." I also knew what I'd witnessed out in the lake on my previous fishing trip with Skip.

"Yes, if that's what it was. I still think it was an ostrich egg. Maybe next we'll be searching for Big Bird in Tahoe."

"Maybe it was the giant Ang bird of Washoe legend who laid an egg."

Skip laughed. It was so good to hear him laugh. I joked about it with him, but I would always believe that the egg belonged to Tessie, and I knew she was still out there somewhere. No one could convince me that my sighting had just been a hallucination or some menopausal flight of fancy. In fact, I think Frank Diggs had seen the same thing just before his heart attack. The poor man had died of fright! Boney Crider claimed to have seen Tessie, too, but who would ever believe him? I would, that's who! I'd probably never convince old skeptical Skip of any of it, though. No use wasting my breath. I'd recently discovered that's too precious a commodity to waste.

"Think you'll stay on with the *Tattler*, Beanie?"

"I'm not sure. I do have my reputation to consider. I enjoy being a reporter, but the generous fee Ivy Diggs paid may enable me to focus on writing my books for a while, at least until the money runs out."

"Gee, too bad you didn't get to keep any of that treasure you found on the *Maggie May*."

"It's been returned to where it rightly belongs."

"Well, maybe you can moonlight as a P.I. You're getting a pretty good résumé built up for yourself."

"Yeah, I guess you're right."

"The way things have gone for me lately, I could use a little help from time to time. I still have some mending to do from this last escapade," Skip pointed to the spot on his chest where the bullet had struck.

"I know. That was a close one."

"Too close!"

"Technically, we're related now, you know."

"What do you mean?"

"We have the same blood after the transfusion they gave you

at the hospital."

"Guess that means we won't be getting hitched one day, huh?"

"Probably not, but we can be good friends, just like we always have been. You know you're my best friend next to Cruiser."

"Doggone right I am!"

I knew Skip was joking about marriage, but a new side of him had surfaced while Crispin was around that had me perplexed and a little flattered. It was nice to know I wasn't too old to turn a head or two. Perhaps our relationship was deepening in some ways, but I wasn't ready to give up my independence for any man just yet. Not even Skip.

"I could use some referrals if you care to send some my way."

"Sure. Whenever I can. The Tahoe community just keeps growing and so does the crime. Law enforcement isn't growing along with it, though. They need to hire more officers, but the funding just isn't there."

"There seems to be plenty of money to build new tourist attractions like shopping malls and ski trams."

"There's always plenty of money for that in a resort town like South Tahoe, Beanie."

Tahoe wasn't about to get any less populated. With predictions that in a decade one-third of the population of the entire country would be living in California, it stands to reason that some of that immigration would end up here. Like it or not, the Lake of the Sky would always be a year-round E-ticket attraction for outsiders. As long as people kept coming, crime would keep coming right along with them. Skip was right. The way things were going, there would never be a shortage of cases for this Sierra sleuth and her slobbery sidekick to solve.

I could buy every treat in the whole Pawtisserie dog bakery for Cruiser with the commission I'd earned on this case. I figured I could make a pretty comfortable living at sleuthing to supplement my writing income if I did it with any regularity. Just as long as it didn't get too dangerous. My escapades lately were about as dicey as I liked for life at Tahoe to get. If only he could talk, I'm sure my hound dog detective would heartily agree.

As though he had telepathically sensed me thinking about him, Cruiser turned to look at me and gave me one of those knowing little canine winks. Can dogs read your mind? Sometimes I'm certain they do. I only wish I could speak dog language as well as they do ours. If Buster could have talked, he'd have thanked me for returning him to Boney Crider at his high Sierra hermitage over in Lonely Glen. And Cruiser would have thanked me for reinstating him as alpha dog of the Mac-Bean pack.

As we sped past Fannette Island in the eye of Emerald Bay, the sun slid behind the great mountains towering in the west. A full August moon crested the eastern ridge of the Sierras, sentinels of the ages, bathing the island and its castle ruins in ghostly light.

The *Dixie Queen* was just navigating the entrance to the bay as we passed the inlet. We waved to the passengers who were aboard her for the dinner cruise. I couldn't help thinking about my momentous golden birthday voyage on her only a month earlier and all the incredible events that had occurred since then. I really knew how to have a midlife crisis! How could I have ever known that I would begin my fiftieth year by getting involved in a murder case and nearly ending up a victim myself? As for me, I preferred that all my future cruising be on dry land in my shiny red Cruiser.

At least I would never again have to turn fifty. It was a milestone I was glad to leave behind me. Now there was just my AARP membership card to face up to. It had arrived promptly in the mail the week after my birthday.

I slipped the card out of my wallet and stared at it long and hard before ripping it to bits. Smiling, I waved good-bye to the shredded remains of my senior citizen permit as they swept into the wake of the boat and drifted out of sight. Heck, I wasn't retired yet. And I didn't plan to be for a long, long time.

The passengers on the *Dixie Queen* returned our nautical salute. They waved and yelled at us, although I couldn't understand what they were saying. Cruiser wagged his tail with excitement and barked back at them as Skip laid on the horn of his new speedboat several times. The steamer whistle blasted back repeatedly as the paddle wheeler churned its way into the peaceful waters of Emerald Bay. The sonorous tones of the steamer's horn continued to reverberate in the bay long after the *Dixie Queen* had vanished from our sight.

Cruising homeward in the gathering darkness with Skip and my faithful hound, I heard it—the ringing of the familiar electronic Scottish melody on my cell phone carried across the waves. Then, as my Washoe ancestors surely had on such a peaceful summer evening as this, I also heard coming from somewhere out in the silent, uncharted depths of Lake Tahoe the primeval bellow that resonated in the night air. A series of infantile chirps and grunts answered the maternal supplication.

ABOUT THE AUTHOR

Sue Owens Wright is an author of both fiction and nonfiction about dogs. She is a fancier and rescuer of basset hounds, which are frequently featured in her books and essays. She is a seven-time nominee and two-time winner of the coveted Maxwell, awarded annually by the Dog Writers Association of America for the best writing about dogs. Sue's previous two books in the Beanie and Cruiser Mystery Series for dog lovers were nominated for a Maxwell Award. Her nonfiction books are *What's Your Dog's IQ?* and *150 Activities for Bored Dogs.* She also contributed chapters on dog care to *People's Guide to Pets.* She resides in California with her husband and two bassets.

For more information about the author, please visit www.sueowenswright.com.